Peckover and
the Bog Man

Peckover and the Bog Man

Michael Kenyon

St. Martin's Press
New York

PECKOVER AND THE BOG MAN. Copyright © 1994 by Michael Kenyon.
All rights reserved. Printed in the United States of America. No part
of this book may be used or reproduced in any manner whatsoever
without written permission except in the case of brief quotations
embodied in critical articles or reviews. For information, address
St. Martin's Press, 175 Fifth Avenue, New York, N.Y. 10010.

Library of Congress Cataloging-in-Publication Data

Kenyon, Michael.
    Peckover and the bog man : an Inspector Peckover mystery /
Michael Kenyon.
        p.   cm.
    "A Thomas Dunne book."
    ISBN 0-312-13582-3
    1. Peckover, Henry (Fictitious character)—Fiction.   I. Title.
PRPR6061.E675P45   1995
823'.914—dc20   95-21085
                                                         CIP

First published in Great Britain by Macmillan London Limited

First U.S. Edition: September 1995
10 9 8 7 6 5 4 3 2 1

For Vittorio

ONE

O Caledonia! stern and wild,
Meet nurse for a poetic child!
Sir Walter Scott, *The Lay of the Last Minstrel*

'Ladies and gentlemen, pray silence. Shall we stand?'

They had hardly sat down. Several of the thirty guests were still on their feet, shunting alongside the tables and peering down for their name on the place cards. Glass and silver glinted on white linen on tables pushed together into a T. Those at the foot of the T failed to hear the chairman and carried on talking.

'Please?' Andrew Dinwiddie, chairman, struck a spoon against his glass. He wore a kilt and a black jacket with lace at the cuffs. At his neck was more lace. 'May we have grace? The Reverend Dr Donald Wilson.'

A hush fell, punctuated by burbling from those at the bottom of the T, bumping of chairs, and the heaving of guests to their feet. The Reverend Wilson intoned,

' " . . . Some hae meat and canna eat—" '

'Tell me is this me?' demanded an elderly gentleman who wore a deaf-aid. He held a place card at arm's length. 'Ah'm blind as a molie without my specs!'

' "And some wad eat that want it—" '

'Ah dinna ken yer face but ye're a bonnie wee thing!' shouted the elderly deaf gentleman, thrusting the place card in front of the young woman to his left. 'Rabbie would hae had his arm aboot yer waist in a wink!'

1

'Ssh!' shushed the company.

' "But we hae meat and we can eat—" '

'Ye're welcome, Sassenach though ye may be frae the startled look on ye!' The elderly gentleman, flirty proxy for Robert Burns, put his arm round the young woman's waist. ' 'Tis Rabbie's nicht and a braw, daft nicht for the worrrld, the nicht.'

'Sssh! Angus, mon! Whisht!'

' "And sae the Lord be thankit!" '

'Ladies and gentlemen, be seated,' announced the chairman, mightily thankit that that was done with. He sat down fast.

On his right the guest of honour said, 'Splendid, splendid! You order these things most ceremoniously in Scotland, Mr Chairman.'

'We are not beginners, Sir Gilbert,' the chairman said. 'We have been celebrating Burns Night for a hundred and seventy years.'

'Jolly good. And the best is yet to be – the pipes, the haggis, and the surprise, the we-know-what, what?'

Patronizing ass, the chairman thought. Tomorrow Sir Gilbert Potter would be away back to Oxford, or London, his chair by the fire at the Royal Archaeological Society. There he would regale his cronies with tales of the quaint Scots celebrating their incomprehensible poet.

Still, tonight's Burns Night was a little different. For one thing they had imported an English cook. The chairman prayed that the cook – an adventuresome Escoffier type, he gathered – would be sparing with the cream sauces and garlic. The celebration needed to take off but not too far. He winced, hearing in his mind's ear Sir Gilbert regaling his professor chums: 'Blind drunk, those Scotties, sloshing their whisky down, warbling "Auld Lang Syne", eh, what?'

Another little difference, five guests from England, courtesy of Sir Gilbert. The Inverballoch Burns Club usually had a foreign guest or two for Burns Night – English, French, American – but five was unusual. Once they had hosted a trio of Germans, developers in search of a site for a theme park, a Scottish Disneyweld with hairy cattle, hairier Scotsmen in vests tossing cabers, and a Rumbledethumps Restaurant serving porridge, kippers, skirlie, roastit bubblyjock, rumbledethumps, and howtowdie with drappit eggs. Nothing had come of it. Last year the guest of honour had been Australia's vice consul in Edinburgh, a strapping lass and a Scotland freak who had responded to the the toast to the lassies. 'Oh, you Inverballochers, the best laid schemes o' mice and men gang aft agley!' she had irrelevantly enthused, tears in her eyes, Laphroaig in her bloodstream.

Inverballoch (population 600, sheep 85,000) in the peaty foothills of the South-Western Highlands, was an appropriate venue for the vice consul to have celebrated Burns Night. On a window in the sawdust bar of the Clachan Inn in Dewar Street was the name Mary, etched by Robert Burns with his diamond ring in September, 1787, on his three-week tour of the Highlands. Which particular Mary was vigorously debated. Highland Mary Campbell had died. Perhaps Mary Morison (O Mary, canst thou wreck his peace, Wha for thy sake wad gladly die?). Or the barmaid might have been Mary.

The Inverballoch Burns Club would have rented the historic Clachan for Burns Night except that it had space only for the landlord, his wife, and a dozen friends who were forced to eat their haggis standing. The club made do with the Ram Hotel.

The Ram was the only hotel for thirty miles around and had no Burns connection, having been built in 1972 to accommodate golfers and occasional tourists. Three AA stars, fourteen bedrooms, ample parking, and Aberauchter golf course. Its Claymore Dining-Room was reserved this evening, January 25, for the club. Hotel guests and itinerants, if any, had to make do with either a sandwich in the Rob Roy Bar, a haggis hand-out from the Clachan, noodles from the Chinese take-away on Argyll Street, or, best of all, they would drive the ninety minutes or so back to Glasgow or Edinburgh and remain there, or at any rate not return to Inverballoch. Why would anyone visit Inverballoch unless for golf, the megalithic Stones of Skelloch, which took five minutes, or, as from a few months ago, to dig for bits of broken pots? Never the liveliest acres in Scotland, once there had at least been warring clansmen, and more recently a mill, now defunct, that wove kilts and trews. Today, outside the village, were only black-faced sheep, golf, the Skelloch Stone Circle, and the Ram.

If the archaeologists lately arrived from England hoped to unearth buried treasure – Celtic silver, Roman gold – they were slyly not admitting it. The locals would shrug and tell each other, 'Och, treasure, dream on!'

The Ram lacked history but it pushed the boat out for Burns Night. Tartan shawls had been pinned to the walls of the Claymore Dining-Room, a piano manhandled into position, and Mrs Bell, kirk organist, had for the twenty-second year brought her Burns songbook.

Here came the first course, borne in by adolescents wearing plaid sashes.

Cock-a-leekie.

'Splendid, splendid!' gushed Sir Gilbert Potter, KCB, CBE, FBA, Wheeler Professor of Archaeology at Oxford University, translator of the Cush hieroglyph, and discoverer of the earthen Druid temple at Nether Hooey. He it was who had requested that supper be prepared by Miriam Peckover, chef from the Royal Archaeological Society, as a perk for her, a free holiday among the banks and braes.

'Hm,' hmmed the chairman, eyeing the soup slopped in front of him by a willing waiter.

His committee had said yes to the London chef. How could anyone ruin haggis? How could the committee have said no to a request from Sir Gilbert Potter? Might not his team dig up curiosities – indeed already had dug up one most odd item – that would put Inverballoch on the map, perhaps generate investment, and bring fame beyond a scratched Mary on a window in the Clachan, and hill and river scenery that caused visitors to gasp, though Inverballochers thought it dreary?

The elderly gentleman turned to the young woman on his left and introduced himself. 'Angus MacGregor.' Now that he was seated and soup was on its way his voice had subsided to less than sonic boom. 'And ye'll be?'

'Posy Cork.'

'Speak up!'

Posy raised her voice and enunciated like Eliza Doolittle. The trick was not to raise the voice to a level that would cause the rest of the company to fall silent.

'Cork.'

'Pork?'

'Cork! As in stopper or bung!'

'Bung?'

Posy's neighbour to her left squeezed her knee under the table. He was a beefy young man with a grip of iron. He had played rugby for Penarth. His hair was fair and his skin freckled, the sort of skin that would redden and blister in hot sun, not that he ran much risk of that in Inverballoch in January. He wore a dinner jacket and black tie. Everybody was dressed formally: black tie, kilts, lace, ladies in floor-sweeping silks and tartans.

Distantly at the foot of the T, as far beyond the salt as anyone could be put, a big man in his forties had squeezed himself into a dinner jacket he had plucked from an Oxfam hanger twenty years earlier and which at that time had more or less fit. A little counter to convention, a splash of colour in celebration of unconventional Rabbie – was he not in a modest way a poet himself? – his neckwear was not a black bow tie but a billowing cravat in a multi-coloured tartan unknown among Scotland's clans.

He had already met in the bar the bloke on his left, the vice chairman, in a chair at the bottom of the T and wanting to talk only about salmon fishing. Adjusting his cravat, he turned the other way, introduced himself, though not his job, which had an unnerving effect on some people, and was rewarded with a smile and a voice as soft and clear as a commercial for bottled water. She was a silver-haired patrician, thin as a stick, in a sky-blue evening gown. An elaborate brooch in the collarbone area clasped a silk swath of tartan which hung down her back and to the floor.

'Alice McSporran,' she said, watching for disbelief and the hiking up of eyebrows.

Up went the eyebrows. The amiably flushed face gave off a whiff of aftershave. His breath was delicately scented with whisky.

He said, 'It's a name – McSporran?'

'Not as uncommon as you may think. You're the policeman.'

'I'm on 'oliday. With the cook, my wife, though she's slaving over a hot stove. My first Burns Night. McSporran, eh? Marvellous! *Bon appétit!*'

Detective Chief Inspector Henry Peckover, Bard of the Yard, dipped a spoon into the khaki broth, shifted it around, and dredged up rice, chicken chunks, and soggy black objects that looked to be either prunes or truffles. He thought them unlikely to be truffles.

He wondered if he might not manage to wring an ode or two out of this jaunt to Caledonia. What rhymed with cock-a-leekie?

'No one would call the male sightly, not in the breeding season,' said Vice Chairman Dick Haig, solicitor, at the foot of the T. 'It's the snout. The lower jaw is bent up like a hook.'

Mr Haig was addressing a frowning woman directly across the

5

table from Peckover. The policeman hoped the corsage in her cleavage was securely pinned. If it were not there could be an almighty splash and cock-a-leekie everywhere.

A waitress whispered in Peckover's ear, 'Would it be the red, the white, or the malt, sir?' She wore a sash and her arms were filled with bottles.

'The red, thank you, and a dram of malt.'

Peckover had never before spoken the word dram. He resisted saying wee dram, utterly Scottish though it sounded, because a normal dram might be wee enough without requiring that it be wee, which might be invisible. Was a dram more, less, or the same as a tot, shot, snort, or finger?

Whisky was not his tipple but didn't he have to have some in readiness for the haggis? At the reception in the Rob Roy Bar he had tested three whiskies only because this was Burns Night. The gent with the deaf-aid and disrupting voice had told him that Rabbie, never mind his reputation as a drinker, could not drink whisky, and no alcohol to excess, because he had a sick stomach. Rabbie, a customs officer, had drunk a little claret and perhaps brandy, smuggled in by the barrelful on fishing smacks from France.

'The umbilical sack of the day-old salmon, or parr, measures seven-eighths of an inch,' Dick Haig told the woman with the corsage.

Escaper from Scotland Yard, three hundred miles from Scotland, Peckover resolved to stay sober if it were not too late. Unsober he could become the life and soul of the party, but the party was Rabbie's. He said 'Thank you' to the child who had filled one of his glasses to the brim with red and into another glass was doing likewise with a tan liquid from an oblong bottle probably ninety-eight proof.

'How reassuring to see the archaeologists dressed up and looking so feminine,' Mrs McSporran said. 'I'd been beginning to wonder.'

'Who?' Peckover said. 'Where? Sorry, I don't know anybody.'

'Posy Cork is the pretty thing in red. The man fondling her knee under the table, that's reassuring too. I've never seen him before but he's hardly her husband, unless they're on their honeymoon. His other side, the one in glasses he takes no notice of, she's Leah or Sarah somebody. She should find a proper hairdresser and try wearing contacts. They look awfully young to be archaeologists, don't you think?'

'Check their fingernails.'

'Oh?'

'Earth, bits of urns, slivers of Etruscan statuary.'

Peckover observed Posy Cork, many places away on the other side of the table. She looked fairly petite but sturdy. Nice pair of bristols under the red gown. That observation, he was aware, was sexist and unacceptable but policemen observed, so soddit. Clashing scarlet lipstick. Short, straightish hair sliced off in a fringe. The hefty, freckled fellow beside her had one hand dealing with his cock-a-leekie, the other out of sight. The Leah or Sarah somebody on the bloke's other side had tormented curly black hair and spectacles. The girls would be in their early twenties, the freckled gent a few years older.

Peckover brought out his own half-moon spectacles, though not to focus on the fingernails of the lady archaeologists. He studied the souvenir menu. A gruelling number of toasts, speeches, and songs were to follow the meal. They would be sitting here until dawn. The staff were scooping up the soup plates.

'Which one is the laird?' Peckover asked.

'Dougal?' Mrs McSporran inclined her head towards the top table. 'With the beard.'

Peckover had expected a laird to be a bristly ancient in a cloak, perhaps gnawing on a leg of mutton. Craning, he saw another youngster, early thirties anyway, and plumpish. The rust-coloured beard was closely barbered and cared for. The black velvet jacket, on the other hand, even at this distance, looked to be losing its nap, as if an heirloom from Stuart times.

Dougal Duncan was the eleventh laird of Dundrummy Castle and the one hundred and twenty thousand acres that embraced Dundrummy, Kildrooly, Benlochry, Inverballoch, Aberauchter, Spittal of Kegbeg, Garrymuck of Cud, Bridge of Grill, Kirkbuckie on Tay, and Bridespfeffer. Due to death duties and his late father's mismanagement of the estate, the laird was also broke. Dougal Duncan's debts were as deep and wide as his glens and braes.

He was hopeful though. 'Ah, indeed,' he answered Sir Gilbert Potter on one side, and, 'Oh, quite,' he replied to the chairman's wife on the other. He wished that both might shut up and leave him to his fantasies. These fantasies were of clawing his way out of debt, and when the fantasies ran riot, of making money.

Stranger things had happened. Posy Cork and her assistant were enthusiastic diggers, and their mentor, Sir Gilbert Potter, had clout. With work and luck, finds might be made that had commercial

7

possibilities beyond those of the peculiar artefact already dug up. His vast acreage – to be precise the heathery dig at Inverballoch that promised reasonably well – might qualify for a grant. Perhaps the National Trust would take it over. Or he would set up an on-site museum and restaurant that would bring in tourists with DMs, dollars, and yen. He would provide folk festivals with reels and strathspeys and a traditional storyteller to relate the legends of Inverballoch. Inverballoch had no legends except of buried treasure, and those were common as muck, so legends would have to be invented. An imaginative hack shouldn't be hard to find. He would put out feelers at the *Glasgow Herald*, surely a nest of inventive scribblers.

'Oh, agreed, agreed,' he responded to the chairman's wife.

First, of course, headline-grabbing artefacts would need to be found. Something to put in the museum. He had thought of burying artefacts at midnight with a shovel, planting Scottish treasures that the archaeologists would then dig up, as the police were said to plant drugs. Alas, he owned nothing worth planting. There was the family goblet, Celtic gold, but it was known. Everyone was advising him to sell it to help clear his debts. He could hardly pretend it had been freshly dug up.

At the distant foot of the T the vice chairman told Peckover, 'I caught a smolt eight inches long from the snout to the bifurcation. Threw it back, of course. A good eight inches.'

From behind the doors to the kitchen a murder was taking place to an accompaniment of audible death throes. First a shriek, next a moan, prolonged and pure.

TWO

It sometimes happens that the bladder bursts during cooking and spills out its contents. To avoid this, wrap the haggis in a napkin, as though it were a galantine, before putting it into boiling water.

Larousse Gastronomique

To the din of one beribboned bagpipe, into the dining-room in Indian file slow-marched five staff, stately as a funeral. Mrs McSporran brought her hands together in a clap, then another clap. All the members of the Inverballoch Burns Club clapped in unison with the pipes and the stepping procession. The archaeologists, the two-hundred-pound boyfriend, Peckover, and Sir Gilbert Potter joined in the clapping. At least there were no fifes and drums to wreak further havoc on the Ram's foundations and the brains of the seated company.

Leading the procession marched a self-conscious woman, the Ram's housekeeper. She might have been less self-conscious had she known what to do with her hands, but they were empty, unlike those of the rest of the procession. Unable to decide whether to swing her arms or hold them at her side, she did first one, then the other.

Second came the caterwauling, black-bearded piper, his ballooning cheeks crimson from blowing and booze. His naked knees were bony between the top of his socks and the hem of his kilt. The tasselled sporran hung and swung like a whiskery beastie shot dead in the heather, switching to left, to right, with each of the piper's stiff-legged strides.

After the piper, the chef. Peckover resisted calling out, 'Halloo, luv!' Miriam Peckover was grinning like a child who has perpetrated a mischief, which in a sense she had, having cooked the dinner's *pièce de résistance*. Her cheeks rosily glowed, she had put on lipstick, and she looked altogether smashing in her butcher's apron. She was embarrassed, delighted, and playing her part like a trouper. She bore theatrically high a silver salver on which sat three cannonballs.

Next, out of step, came an assistant cook with a platter that held a misshapen object cloaked in canvas, perhaps tarpaulin, anyway a sinister material concealing possibly – Peckover consulted the menu – bashed neeps and chappit tatties.

Last, a waiter with a bottle of what could only be usquebaugh, this being Burns Night in Scotland.

Hnnnng unnnng meeownnng nnnng, howled the bagpipe. The company clapped rhythmically and emitted Highland whoops, random and barbarous. The lament was of a relentless tunelessness, at least to Peckover's ear. He wondered if the piper had ever played a bagpipe before. Was there a chance he might leave off the wailing and break into something jolly like 'I Love a Lassie' or 'Stop Your Tickling, Jock'?

The procession having completed a circuit of the dining-room, the housekeeper led it to a muddled halt at the top table. She positioned with gestures her unrehearsed troupe. She motioned to the cook to set down the steaming cannonballs in front of the chairman, and to the assistant cook to do similarly with the cloaked object. She claimed the water of life from the waiter and placed it with the cannonballs and mystery item.

'Splendid, here's to the Scotties, what?' exclaimed Sir Gilbert Potter above the moaning of the pipes. Andrew Dinwiddie, beaming chairman, visited mute curses upon the head of the guest of honour, and for good measure on his doubtless equally unspeakable forebears.

The housekeeper shook her head at the piper. He skirled on oblivious, transported to a private world of mists and lochs. She had to pinch him to stop. The pipes painfully expired. She bowed to the chairman. 'Jolly good!' pronounced Sir Gilbert, applauding. Taking the assistant cook and waiter with her, the housekeeper scurried from stage centre, leaving Miriam and the piper standing at the top table.

Andrew Dinwiddie rose and said, 'Sir Gilbert. Our good and honourable friend, Dougal Duncan, who needs no introduction. Members of Inverballoch Burns Club, our welcome guests – among whom let me include from behind the scenes our chef,

10

Miriam Peckover – ladies and gentlemen.' He uttered a tiny, throat-clearing cough. The faces at the tables were silent, watching him, knowing what was to come. 'I give you our national poet's "Address to a Haggis". The darlingest man who ever trod the tender sod of Scotland or breathed its crystal air.'

Without further preamble, or the Address to prompt him, the chairman declaimed ringingly,

> ' "Fair fa' your honest, sonsie face,
> Great chieftain o' the puddin'-race!" '

Much more of the verse was to come, and seven more verses, but Andrew Dinwiddie chose this point to plunge into one of the cannonballs a serious dagger he seemed to have plucked out of thin air. Juice ejaculated.

> ' "Aboon them a' ye tak' your place,
> Painch, tripe, or thairm—" '

'Thairms are fiddle strings or small guts,' Mrs McSporran whispered to Peckover.

Peckover was obliged. He would have been surprised if more than one word in three was being grasped by the English contingent: Miriam, Sir Gilbert, Posy Cork, her hunk of a boyfriend, her assistant Leah or Sarah.

The chairman stabbed expertly.

> ' "Weel are ye wordy of a grace
> As lang's my arm." '

Sir Gilbert had assumed his listening posture, a contorted double-jointedness sideways in his chair, one hand scratching inside his jacket like Napoleon, the other fondling his scalp. The eccentric, unassailable academic. Having stopped listening, he chuckled or sighed when others chuckled or sighed. Now was his chance to rehearse in his mind the points of his speech, plus the ad libs. His scholarly ad-libbing would be over the heads of this company but he could not help that. What were those damn Burns quotes his secretary had handed him?

'Bravo!' he cried because suddenly everybody was exclaiming and applauding.

The Dinwiddie person had again stabbed the haggis. Juice had spurted and a splash had hit his, Sir Gilbert's, sleeve. The fellow was evidently not about to apologize either, if he had noticed.

> ' "Trenching your gushing entrails bright
> Like ony ditch—!" '

In his left hand Andrew Dinwiddie held a fork with which he pinioned the squelchy beast. He was not only stabbing but carving.

> ' "And then, O what a glorious sight,
> Warm-reekin', rich!" '

'Rich and medicinal, dinna forget!' Angus MacGregor shouted, and thumped the table with a hairy fist.

Mrs McSporran whispered, 'He means aphrodisiacal but he won't say the word with ladies present.'

'Is it?' whispered Peckover.

'Is what?'

'Haggis an aphrodisiac?'

'Yes, why not?'

She was not seducing him, he believed. By this stage she had learned that he was happily married to the cook and had two small children. But she was mildly flirting, he enjoyed the flirting, and she knew that he did. She was a widow with grandchildren. Her husband had been a brain surgeon at Glasgow Royal Infirmary.

> ' "Gie her a Haggis!" '

The chairman, fork and dagger aloft, trumpeted the words. End of the Address. The Claymore Dining-Room erupted in applause. The chairman poured whisky into three tumblers. The cook made beseeching gestures. He added water to her tumbler.

'Our chef has work awaiting her in the kitchen,' he announced.

Chairman and piper knocked back their potion to boisterous cheering. Miriam sipped, put down her glass, and to more applause, smiling foolishly, glancing at her husband *en route*, followed the piper from the dining room.

A waiter removed the platter of ravaged haggis to a side table where he attempted to reassemble the debris into less unsightly portions before returning it to the table for self-service. More haggis arrived on individual plates. Beside each crumbled, grey hillock of haggis shuddered orange and white dollops of bashed neeps and tatties.

'We'll take the high road and they'll take the low road, what?' Sir Gilbert said, peering in feigned ecstasy at his plate. He pushed the grey matter about with his fork.

Angus MacGregor shouted at his neighbour, 'Eat up, lassie! 'Tis only a sausage!'

Posy Cork dared a morsel. It was not going to kill her and the sooner she got on with it the sooner the gnarled old gentleman might leave her in peace. She chewed and swallowed.

In fact, not at all bad. Spicy, muttony, oddly familiar, though she had never before been even close to a haggis, not that she knew of. She speared a second lump. Mike had removed his hand from her person the better to eat. He was chewing well. If she failed to finish her plateful he would probably finish it for her. Mike ate everything in sight without comment, neither complimenting nor complaining. Whenever she told him he should cut back or he would become a fatso he did not sulk, tell her to mind her beeswax, he would strike a Greek discobolus pose, then a Mr Universe pose, and say, 'A pose for Posy.' If he were naked his pose would be lewd, like a satyr on an amphora.

Oh gosh, if she lighted on an amphora! Not whole and entire, that was too much to hope for, but a shard even! Decorated!

Sir Gilbert would take the credit. He would be totally in the dark until she enlightened him but he was her great white chief and that's how it was. He might or might not acknowledge her existence, braying over the port at his Oxford high table. 'Splendid little assistant, what's her name – Fork, Stork, Cake? Rosy Cake?'

Posy wondered about the chairman. Not the man sitting there in his dressy jacket and lace but the word. Surely by now these people in the boonies should know there were no chairmen any more. America, advanced beyond anywhere this side of the Atlantic, had only chairpersons and chairs.

'Mike, no,' she murmured.

Mike's hand had cleaned his plate and returned to her thigh.

'People are watching,' Posy said. 'Finish my haggis.'

Posy, America-struck, recently returned from a palpitatingly mind-expanding year at the University of Chicago, was not yet over her Chicago year and believed she might never be. A ten-week dig at an Amerindian site in Colorado, debate in the faculty lounge with spring water and sunflower seeds, rigorous standards for footnotes, and sexual advances from her supervisor which in retrospect she should perhaps have resisted, but oh well, *c'est la vie*, he'd had a superb intellect, and, face it, he could invite her back. She would have stayed for a second year but for this Scottish opportunity.

From bedtime digressions reading about the Antonine Wall – she'd had to be in Chicago to find the real stuff on Roman Britain! – she had spied a puzzlement, an outside chance, a hint that the Roman occupation had penetrated further north than every scholar claimed. She had pored over maps – the library had maps that made your eyes swim – and there was Inverballoch, which had that single reference in Lollius's *De Caledonia*! The Antonine Wall from the Firth of Clyde to the Firth of Forth was accepted as the furthest north the Romans occupied but Inverballoch was another fifty miles north! If all went well, Posy Cork, archaeologist, might unearth a major Roman settlement here, Inverballoch. And if here, why not still further north? Why not to the sea, the sea!

So home she had come, Croydon, kissed her parents, made telephone excuses to Mike, swarmed off to Scotland, and bearded the laird, Dougal Duncan, an enthusiast, though not especially for expanding the boundaries of knowledge.

Her mentor from Oxford days, Potter the Rotter, had grumbled, bumbled, then given her the nod, and a miserly grant, which he had intended to do from the start because here might be kudos for him, the fart.

Distantly, beyond the bread and salt, Alice McSporran said, 'D'you know, this is the most delicious haggis I ever tasted?'

'You're just saying that,' Peckover said.

'It's so juicy and different. Your wife really made it herself?'

Indeed she had, in the Royal Archaeological Society's kitchen with plenty left behind in London for her help to warm up for the archaeologists' lunch and supper.

Miriam's archaeologists would cope, accustomed to suspicious food as they were, stranded on excavations in Tabriz or the Mato Grosso, a hundred miles from a grocer's and extremely strange fare when they got there. Serving haggis to archaeologists was not like serving it to, say, the London Symphony Orchestra. Earlier in the week he had looked into one of the recipe books Miriam had surrounded herself with. They had titles like *Caledonian Cuis-*

ine and *Savours of Scotland* and were all open at Haggis, the ingredients of which were a sheep's stomach bag and pluck, onion, oatmeal, suet, salt, and pepper. The pluck was apparently the heart, liver, and lights, whatever lights might be. Miriam had instructed him that lights were lungs. She had said that making haggis looked straightforward but irksome – all the turning inside out, scalding, scraping, and overnight soaking of the stomach bag – and she would add thyme, garlic, double Cayenne pepper, and further to liven it up, perhaps a spoonful of asafoetida.

The noise level had risen in the Claymore Dining-Room. Peckover spread orange turnip on a gobbet of haggis. He chewed speculatively. Miriam's haggis reminded him of the lamb dishes at the Moti Mahal on Victoria Street, round the corner from Scotland Yard. He turned to Mrs McSporran, flattery up his sleeve.

'You're the 'aggis expert, Alice.' They were on first names already. She had started it by calling him Henry, doing as they liked being the prerogative of the elderly. 'Mean to say, 'ow often do you eat it?'

'Once a year,' said Alice McSporran.

There followed a choice of Arbroath smokie, smoked Moffat trout, pork Balmoral, or roastit Galloway beef. Then desserts: Cranachan, which was oatmeal, double cream, raspberries, and Drambuie, or Atholl Brose, which was the same but with honey instead of raspberries, and whisky in place of Drambuie. When the coffee arrived the chairman called on the vice chairman for grace.

Peckover thought they had had grace an hour or two ago and the meal was over, but the vice chairman had to be called on for something or there was no point having him. Nobody stood when Dick Haig rose to say this grace. His clear solicitor's tones were impressive. He had fine lungs from his days breathing the Highland air while standing casting in the gushy Tweed, his angler's hat squarely in place, legs apart in their thigh waders.

> ' "We thank Thee for these mercies, Lord,
> Sae far beyond our merits;
> Noo, waiter lads, clear aff the plates,
> An' fetch us in the spirits." '

Waiter lads and lassies padded round with the spirits. Peckover swallowed what remained in his tumbler and told his waitress lassie, 'Just a speck for the toasts.' The chairman proposed the toast to the Queen, and the national anthem was sung, Mrs Bell pounding the piano. Then was allowed a fifteen-minute break for all to ready themselves for the speeches, songs, and unveiling of the mystery object.

Peckover, sceptical cockney, heaved himself from his seat. He was already unimpressed by the mystery object. Sometimes, fortunately not often, he had to deal with mysteries to earn his salary. They seldom lived up to their promise.

THREE

I do like a little bit of butter to my bread.
                        A.A. Milne, *When We Were Very Young*

The ladies lined up outside the Ladies, their hems and trailing swaths of tartan picking up dust and tobacco ash from the carpet. The Rob Roy Bar was heavily locked. In the reception hall, Dick Haig stared at a fish in a glass case on the wall. He looked round for anyone he could explain the fish to.

Dougal Duncan said to Posy, 'So how's everything? Are we up to expectations?'

'It's great. Did you meet Mike?'

'Briefly, didn't we, in the bar?' The laird's black velvet jacket ought to have been donated to the Salvation Army, if they would accept it. Seen close to it was less black than a deep mottled grey and possibly not velvet. Badger perhaps. 'Hello, Mike. Not one of us, an archaeologist, are you?'

'Correct.'

'Not involved in our little dig?'

'I'm involved in Posy.'

Mike Trelawny, Ph.D., Cornishman, Junior Research Fellow in Primitive Religions, University College, London, author of *Grave Matters: Romano-British Burial Customs in South-west England* (Cambridge University Press), not a bestseller in spite of its quite racy title, and former centre-three-quarter with Penarth Rugby Football Club, circled a muscular arm round Posy's waist.

'Fortunate man,' said the laird.

'I'm aware of that.'

In the seat next to Posy's, Angus MacGregor was reading *Farmer and Stockbreeder* through a magnifying glass and smoking a stubby pipe. Either he had not heard the chairman's request for no smoking in the dining-room or he defied it as impudent. Mrs Bell thrashed the piano keys, impatient to be under way. People found the words in the souvenir menu. Burns, naturally. Some sang with inappropriate restraint, others giddily.

> ' "Robin was a rovin boy,
> Rantin, rovin, rantin, rovin,
> Robin was a rovin boy,
> Rantin, rovin, Robin!" '

Peckover sang. Three verses and the chorus. He had never heard the song before but the tune was predictable and if he went wrong he would sing louder, pretending he was singing the tricky baritone part.

> ' "Robin was a rovin boy . . ." '

Andrew Dinwiddie gave the toast to the Immortal Memory and spoke about Burns for half an hour. His words went down well with everyone except Sir Gilbert Potter. The quotation about a man being a man for a' that sounded dismayingly familiar to Sir Gilbert, as did those about things ganging aft agley and man's inhumanity to man making countless thousands mourn. Dammit, the Dinwiddie fellow couldn't stop quoting! When the blighter pleaded that some power the giftie gie us to see ourselves as others see us, Sir Gilbert gave up. The jackanapes had used up all his own quotes. Balls to you and to Burns too, sulked Sir Gilbert. If ever again he were invited to a Burns Dinner he would see to it he spoke first so he could get his quotes in.

Most of the audience in the Claymore Dining-Room would later agree that Sir Gilbert Potter, accustomed as he was to public speaking, spoke succinctly and challengingly, though he might perhaps have made a reference, any reference, to Robert Burns. He thanked all the right people, including the piper and the cook – 'Hear hear,' Peckover called out – before launching into his main points.

Archaeology, handmaiden of history, revealed much that history's written documents did not, he said. History dealt with literate societies. If we were to understand history's illiterate societies, not to mention aeons of prehistory, archaeological study was imperative. The savages who had once inhabited Scotland's Highlands – Lowlands too – had bequeathed nothing of the written word. Documentation inherited from ecclesiastics at the coming of Christianity addressed doctrine, law, and taxation, but told us little of how people lived, worked, played, if play they did, or fed and clothed themselves. This was the province of archaeology. A truism that none the less bore repeating was that knowledge of the past led to knowledge of ourselves and society in this last decade of the twentieth century. In Inverballoch no less than in every croft, village, and town from the border to the Western Isles, Scots would better understand themselves by understanding the aspirations and errors of their barbarian ancestors.

He had their attention, fairly glacial in many instances.

'Why, some of you may be wondering, am I here with you tonight?' Sir Gilbert asked riskily. 'I am here at the gracious invitation of your chairman, and the good offices of your laird, Sir Dougal Duncan, to say that the auguries for Roman remains in your own back yard are most promising. If we are correct in this supposition we shall put Inverballoch on the map.'

Sir Gilbert raised a hand as if to ward off a spontaneous outburst of gratitude and love – a wholly unnecessary gesture.

'It will not have escaped your notice that four months ago, with the generous permission of Sir Dougal, indeed, at his solicitation, we surveyed the area in an endeavour to discover whether Inverballoch might merit a concerted dig. We set up a modest operation, a preliminary excavation, following aerial photography, two miles west of your exemplary little town. Tonight I am able to tell you that our test trenches have revealed the remains of earthworks and possibly some kind of drainage channel or moat. The Romans, as you are aware, were consummate engineers. In addition we have turned up thirteen potsherds, five Roman coins, organic fragments which must await precise dating, but which we have reason to believe may date from the second century, under the governor Quintus Lollius Urbicus, and this item now on the table before us.'

'The first haggis,' said a giggling voice.

'Speak up!' called out Angus MacGregor.

'In short,' pursued Sir Gilbert, 'we have evidence enough to warrant continuing our excavations. Further, I would like to announce that I am hopeful that we will receive government funding. If I may say so, I am not without influence. As the adage goes, it's knowing who, not what, what? I would add only that the dig will be headed, under my guidance, by my talented pupil, Miss

19

Cork, in whom I assure you we may have every confidence.'

The guest of honour aimed a smirk in the direction of Posy, who coloured and stared down at a patch of haggis-stained tablecloth.

'With your permission, Mr Chairman, I will reveal the latest find from our Inverballoch dig.'

With a fine sense of theatre, slowly and suspensefully, as a magician unveiling his next miracle, Sir Gilbert started to lift the ratty coverlet from the excavated enigma. A woman gave a tiny squeal, though nothing was so far to be seen except lifting folds of repellent cloth. The company held its breath, leaned forward, and gazed.

Peckover whispered, 'What 'appened to the drumroll?'

Mrs McSporran said in his ear, 'It'll be the most dreadful anti-climax if it's not the head of Robert Burns.'

Unveiled, the item appeared to be a lidded tub or barrel, prob-ably of wood, and as slimy as its disintegrating wrapping, a segment of which had adhered to Sir Gilbert's fingers.

'Damn,' he said.

He looked about for something to wipe his fingers with. Andrew Dinwiddie handed him a napkin. A guest hazarded, 'A gallon of whisky?'

The tub looked the right size for a gallon of something. Sir Gilbert removed the lid. Some people stood up for a better view, the same who stand up at coronations and sports events, obliterat-ing the view for everyone else. Sir Gilbert tilted the tub for view-ing, whereupon several guests, before seeing anything, gasped. Others recoiled as if expecting rodents to rush out.

Whatever it was in the tub it was not a head, neither did it move, though unrefrigerated it might have. A film of sweat glistened on the grey, warming surface of what looked like builders' material, something essential to effective plastering. By the rim was a con-cavity where some of the substance had been scooped out.

'Butter,' said Sir Gilbert.

He was immensely pleased with himself. Andrew Dinwiddie held his hands prayerfully together, like Dürer's drawing of hands, and looked away in distaste. The laird had his hands clasped, cracking the knuckles, and fiendishly eyeing the tub of butter as if already hearing the chime of cash registers. Someone said, 'Pull the other,' and somebody else, 'I'll have marge.' Along the tables was grimacing and nervous laughter.

'We came upon it on Wednesday,' Sir Gilbert said. 'Miss Cork telephoned me in London and I instructed her to keep it refrigerated. In a moment we shall sample it – those of you with adventurous palates, what?'

A woman wearing a jewelled pin on her chest said, 'Excuse me, you're expecting us to eat prehistoric butter?'

'Madam,' observed Sir Gilbert, 'I, Miss Cork, and her helper, Miss, um' – he blinked at Posy's assistant, failing to recall her name – 'have already done so. We continue in excellent health. The flavour is salty, a little garlicky, but I have no hesitation in stating that for the gourmets among us it is a taste which may be acquired. I must, however, correct you on its age. This butter is not prehistoric. If I may be allowed an educated guess, I would say it has been buried no more than three hundred and fifty years. Four hundred at the outside.'

'That's all right then,' said the woman with the jewelled pin. 'I'll have half a pound.'

'Why?' somebody asked Sir Gilbert.

'Pardon?'

'Why bury it?'

'Ha!' exclaimed Sir Gilbert. 'Why bury butter? Excellent! The answer, with your permission, Mr Chairman—'

The guest of honour aimed his smirk at the chairman. The chairman was bent sideways, half under the table. Sir Gilbert, deducing that Andrew Dinwiddie was drunk, resolved never to return to Inverballoch, except in the event that the dig were a success, in which case his presence naturally would be required for television. He pressed on.

'This is by no means archaeology's first discovery of buried butter. We have found it in Scotland before, in Norway, Finland, Iceland, and several times in Ireland, where it may be seen in the Irish National Museum. But it is not a routine matter. At the right museum this example will fetch a thousand pounds. Even fifteen hundred. Butter was buried partly for safekeeping against the looting and pillaging of cut-throat clansmen whose internecine tribal warfare blots the pages of Scotland's sorry history. More importantly, in my view, the longer the butter in its firkin lay buried—'

'In its what?'

'—in this container – let us keep our questions until I have finished, I would so appreciate it – in a cold bog, the richer and more sumptuously delicious it became.'

21

'The bog, delicious?'

'The butter, madam!' Sir Gilbert was astonished at his forbearance. How civil he was! These Scots, when they were not impertinent rascals, were dolts. 'You will detect, when you taste the butter, no rancidity. The acidic, antiseptic properties of your otherwise worthless peat bogs preserve the butter from putrefaction. Mr Chairman, perhaps the staff will now serve our seventeenth-century butter – our *local* seventeenth-century butter – and the biscuits. Mr Chairman?'

Andrew Dinwiddie surfaced, stood, and gestured to a lone waiter at attention by the door to the kitchen.

He said, 'Aweel, gude gentles, Ah seem to hae misplaced my dirk.' No judge was ever more sober, though for whatever reason the chairman had switched from accentless English to brawny Burns Night Scots. 'Ah suspect it gaed awa' wi' the haggis dish tae the kitchen. Still an a', should any o' ye spy it Ah'd be muckle happy, belanging as it did tae my ain cut-throat clansman fader, and his cut-throat clansman fader afore him. Mrs Bell, gie us a chord! A sang, if ye please!'

FOUR

It was the owl that shriek'd.
Shakespeare, *Macbeth*

After a roistering 'Song of the Clyde' from everybody who knew
the words, and creative la-la-la-ing from those who knew only the
tune, such as Peckover, the soprano rendered 'My Ain Folk' until
not an eye was dry, and the tenor wailed soulfully about 'The
Northern Lights of Auld Aberdeen'. None of these songs had
words by Burns but by now nobody minded.

Dishes bearing scoops of seventeenth-century butter and a kind
of cakey bread circulated, as often as not stuck on the same spot
for the length of a speech before being peered at, sampled or
rejected, and passed on. Most of those who sampled took a portion
the size of a mouse-dropping. Angus MacGregor, who had
switched off his deaf-aid for the speech from the foreigner, Sir
Dig-Scratch-Scrabble, or whoever the nashgabbin' pock-puddin'
of a gomerel might be, helped himself to a spoonful, spread the
substance thickly, and ate with squelching sounds. Peckover and
Mrs McSporran chanced a smidgen each and watched each other
as they chewed, curious to see who would be the first to slide
unconscious to the floor.

The chairman struck his glass with a fork – *pnggg* – whereupon
Mrs Bell thumped chords. This was it. Peckover put on his spectacles. Everybody was suddenly standing, arms crossed and holding
their neighbours' hands.

' "Should auld acquaintance be forgot," ' carolled the company
in approximate unison.

Peckover was happy to notice Miriam returned to her cramped
slot at the top table, hair combed, free of her butcher's apron,
holding hands and singing. He was also pleased that the words

23

were in the menu, open on the table in front of him. He had not realized there were five verses. He wouldn't have liked to admit it but he hadn't known that Burns had written it either.

> ' "And surely ye'll be your pint-stowp,
> And surely I'll be mine—" '

What, wondered Peckover, singing and swinging his arms and his neighbours' arms, did it mean?

> ' "And we'll tak a cup o' kindness yet,
> For auld lang syne." '

Everybody at the top table except Sir Gilbert Potter, and indeed every Scot in the dining-room, sang with a serious joy. Mrs Bell at the ivories sang with rhythmic jolts of her head. Angus MacGregor, pumping his neighbour Posy's arm up and down, sang each verse at his own stately tempo. The lady with the corsage sang with her eyes closed. Sir Gilbert resigned himself to being upstaged, now and then allowing his jaw to move and his lips to pout in a simulation of singing. His pupil, Miss Cork, wan and leaden-lidded during the speeches, trilled a melodious alto, ignoring as best she could the tempo of Mr MacGregor on one side, and on the other her boyfriend's squeezing her hand to a pulp and vigorously hoisting and dropping her arm in the 'Auld Lang Syne' wave. Mike's disappointment was that two minutes after he and Posy would at last be solitary in their room, Burns Night over and good riddance, Posy would be asleep. He would let her be. She worked harder than he did. She was the brightest and best and there was always tomorrow, the day after tomorow, and *ad infinitum* for the rest of their lives.

Hoisting and plunging their crossed arms the Inverballoch Burns Night chorale crooned and boomed.

> ' "And we'll tak a right guid-willie waught,
> For auld lang syne!" '

After a kiss on the cheek for Alice McSporran, a handshake with the angler, goodnights elsewhere, the fumbling at the lock to their room, the dropping and hanging up of clothing, Peckover, in bed, said, 'What's a guid-willie waught?'

Miriam said, 'Go to sleep.'

24

'D'you bake it, wear it, water it?'

'Goodnight.'

Outside a wind rustled the trees. Miriam thought of the children, Sam and Mary, being spoiled rotten by their aunt, uncle, and granny. A toffee a minute and telly round the clock.

She said, 'Almost all the haggis went.'

Whoooo hooted an owl.

'Henry?'

Silence.

'You asleep?'

'Yes.'

'Did you try the mediaeval butter?'

'Not mediaeval. Seventeenth century.'

'All you know.'

Silence. Miriam listened for the owl to be eerie again for the tourists.

'Henry?'

'What?'

'You're composing, aren't you?'

'I'm decomposing.'

Peckover lay on his back, rhyming, his hands folded on his breast like a knight on a tomb.

> Is this the better butter, Potter?
> Or batter for a hotter fritter,
> Bitter as a satyr's trotter,
> Fatter than an otter's litter,
> Wetter than a hatter's blotter?
> Don't just mutter, splutter, twitter—
> Splatter it into the gutter!
> Counterfeiter Potter – rotter!

Never mix the grain with the grape, old son. He was old enough to have known that.

Miriam said, 'Be honest, what did you think of the haggis?'

Whoooo.

Inverballoch's witching time of night.

'Henry?'

Peckover was asleep.

The telephone rang. Since Peckover did not budge, Miriam groped and found the receiver.

'Henry. For you.'

She switched on the light. According to the clock on the television, verified by Henry's wristwatch on the bedside table, the time was 7.15 a.m.

Peckover said into the phone, 'I'll be right down,' and climbed out of bed.

'What?' Miriam said.

'That bloke, your friend, the archaeologist.'

'Potter? When was he my friend? We meet twice a year when he gets an idea for a menu.'

'He's why we're here.' Peckover buttoned his shirt. 'Since you ask – you did ask, didn't you? – your 'aggis is the best ever. Alice McSporran said so.'

'What about Potter?'

'Dead.' He zipped up his pants. 'Stabbed.'

'Oh my God!'

'Unless it's a Scots jape, a wheeze they play on English coppers. So we'll not excite ourselves.' He pulled on orange socks with concentric white circles. 'What's more, he's not dead.' He tied his shoelaces fast. 'Nobody's dead until the appropriate authority pronounces you clinically, legally, and irreversibly dead.' He plucked from the closet his holiday jacket – over-the-top charcoal-grey cashmere from a bankruptcy sale in Regent Street – and headed for the bathroom. 'Your 'ead can be in the left-luggage at Paddington and your severed limbs floating off Yarmouth pier, it doesn't mean you're dead.' After some moments of watery sounds from the bathroom he emerged with his teeth more or less scrubbed, his hair combed. 'To be dead you 'ave to have the right forms.' His watch said 7.24. 'She said, and I quote—'

'Who?'

'Mrs McSporran. Most delicious 'aggis she'd ever tasted. Juicy and different.'

He lifted the phone and dialled reception.

' 'Ullo? It was you just rang?'

'Aye,' said the voice.

'Why don't we meet at Sir Gilbert Potter's room? Which is it?'

'Waverley Suite. First floor.'

'You don't talk about this. Got it?'

'Aye.'

'So repeat what I said.'

'You what? Repeat—'

26

'Never mind. Waverley Suite. Right away.'

Peckover strode along the corridor, turned left, and peeked round the corner. Steps led down to reception. He descended the first two stairs, stooped, and saw by the desk a huddle of three women and two men. What he did not need was everyone aware that Scotland Yard was in place, ready and available. Gilbert Potter was nothing to do with him. If he were dead, if there had to be an investigation, Scotland's men in blue would look after it, not Scotland Yard. He would gather up Miriam and beat a retreat back to London. Plenty to do there, starting with rescuing Sam and Mary from an excess of love and sugar. The night manager evidently knew the Ram had a policeman guest but that would be the kind of information available to night managers. Everybody else didn't have to know. They probably did though.

One of the two men in reception wore a quilted car coat and a fur hat. One woman wore kitchen overalls, the others black-and-white waitressing uniform. They did not have an air of wheezers and japers. No tittering. If they cast their eyes towards the stairs where he stood stooped and balanced like a ballerina they would see his feet. Towards the stairs walked the second man, or youth, post-pubertal anyway. The night manager? He was not dressed for the outdoors. Peckover backed in search of the Waverley Suite. For a modest-sized hotel there were an awful lot of passages.

'This way,' summoned someone behind him.

'Quiet!' Peckover faced the youth not dressed for the outdoors. 'You want to wake up the hotel?'

Age: eighteen or nineteen. Build: undernourished. Expression: anxious. He wore a black jacket and tie as if in training for night manager at Claridge's. He would have benefited from a shave, though no more than a certain copper Peckover might have named.

'Name?'

'Gordon. I rang the real police first – ours, here. Inverballoch.'

'You did right. Lead on, Macduff.' Lead on or lay on? He was trying to be friendly at least until it was clear the lad was not Scotland's most wanted. 'Get going, then.'

The night manager led along a corridor with closed, numbered bedroom doors and round a corner. He halted.

'The Waverley Suite,' he said in a whisper. The door bore a plaque which stated Waverley Suite. 'It's our most luxurious. Split level. I locked it.'

Peckover nodded. The sprig was looking at him, awaiting a cue.

'You found the body?' cued Peckover.

Alarm spread across the night manager's face.

'That's to say,' Peckover said, 'perhaps we should open the door, Mr Gordon.'

'Smith.'

'Sorry?'

'Gordon Smith. I'm only here for the experience, like get a toehold. D'you know what they pay? I'll be movin' on, I can tell you.'

He put a key in the lock and turned it. Reaching for the handle he arrested his hand in mid-air, horrified. He stared up at Peckover.

'Fingerprints!' he said.

'You were 'ere before – what, twenty minutes ago? You went in?'

'I did not.'

'Make up your mind. Thought you said you did.'

'Not really in.'

'You saw in. You opened the door.'

'Aye.'

'You 'eld the 'andle and turned it.'

'Aye.'

'So what we've got is a nice set of night manager's prints. Don't worry, son, worse things have 'appened at sea.'

Whatever sight might lie in wait on the other side of the door, it could hardly be worse than sliced haggis and butter aged in the bog.

Peckover said, 'Be of good cheer, Mr. Smith. Open up.'

FIVE

The golf links lie so near the mill
That almost every day
The laboring children can look out
And see the men at play
Sarah N. Cleghorn, *The Golf Links Lie So Near the Mill*

Gordon Smith opened the door to the Waverley Suite for the second time that morning and stood nimbly aside. Peckover pushed the door wide. The Waverley Suite looked bigger than his and Miriam's room but with similar noncombustible furnishings and luridly patterned carpet. He would not have described it as a suite if suite implied connecting rooms where you could cook, play cards, and receive courtesans. This was a bedroom and the only other door led presumably to a bathroom. Split level referred to an area six inches higher than the rest of the room where probably plumbing and heating pipes had been boxed in. On this mezzanine had been set a table and two chairs.

Open-eyed on the carpet between the bed and the door to the corridor lay Sir Gilbert Potter with a knife in his neck. The hilt pointed to the ceiling, as did Sir Gilbert's toes. The white soles of his feet pointed at Peckover in the doorway. The knife handle was fancy, circled with studs of ivory, perhaps pearl, anyway white like the feet. The blade was not to be seen. It had gone through, or very adjacent to, the voicebox. Depending on the length of the blade, Sir Gilbert might well be skewered to the floor. He wore scratchy prison-issue-type pyjamas of alternating dark and light brown stripes.

Ample blood. (Who would have thought the old man to have had so much blood in him?) The Ram would need a new carpet for its Waverley Suite. A golden opportunity thrust on the management to improve on the present carpet.

29

Levity, Peckover usually found, was as good a defence as any against nausea.

He steered a diagonal path into the room, skirting Sir Gilbert. No signs of a struggle. No blood on the bed. The bedclothes were mangled but Sir Gilbert might have thrashed about in his sleep, or trying to sleep. No surprise after a Burns Night dinner. The television was off, the bedside light on. The door that he had surmised would open into a bathroom opened into a bathroom.

The bathroom was empty. Not even a wee, sleekit, cow'rin, tim'rous beastie, to borrow the line to a mouse that the chairman had quoted, nor any cow'rin, blood-spattered, human beast who had recently committed murder. Whoever had stabbed Britain's top archaeologist would have blood on him. Right now he would be washing it off, if he had not already done so. No blood in the sink or bath.

Touching nothing, watching where he stepped, Peckover returned to the bedroom. If Gilbert Potter had not been the top archaeologist he had been up there in the heights. He had chaired functions Miriam had cheffed for at the Royal Archaeological Society. He had proposed menus which she had considered on a par with an infants' school lunch. Her adaptations and inventions had made the society's dining-room the envy of the British Academy, House of Lords, Lambeth Palace, Guildhall, and every merchant bank in the Square Mile. He tucked aside the curtain over the window and looked out.

Through wall-to-wall glass, rosy-finger'd dawn was straining to do its stuff but had not quite got there yet. Nothing so far but a ribbon of zinc in the sky. Further north, not that you could get a lot further north – the top of Scandinavia, say, among the polar bears – you'd not even have the zinc, you'd have blackout round the clock, or so he understood. And 'orrible sun round the clock in summer.

Give the dawn another half-hour, perhaps he'd see the golf course, and the mill where kilts had been made, but no longer. Peckover wrapped his handkerchief round his fingers, jiggled window catches and levers, but failed to budge the window. Locked against suicidal golfers who had gone round in a hundred and fifty. Not that they would have had far to fall unless there was a pit. Try to end it all from the Waverley Suite and you would hurt your knees.

Why would the smiler with the knife try to enter or leave by the window when there was an adequate door?

He hadn't. He had knocked on the door and announced himself. Herself. 'Hello, it's me.' The person had been known to Sir Gilbert or he'd probably have either told the visitor to buzz off or picked up the phone and complained to the management. He had left his bed and opened the door. The visitor had pushed him back into the room and pierced him. Someone may have heard something, a yell from Sir Gilbert, if he'd had a chance to yell. If the Inverballoch constabulary deigned to show themselves and talk to everybody they might have a confession by lunchtime. The solution to messes like this was usually a confession, sooner rather than later.

Peckover doubted there would be a confession. This business looked too calculated. Anyway, it was none of his affair. He was three hundred miles off his patch, a foreigner, and the moment the local lads showed he would be out of it.

He had doubts about that too.

He turned from the window to tell the youth to phone again the Inverballoch police, suggest politely they get the lead out. No youth.

'Gordon, ah – Smith? Mr Gordon Smith?'

A black-sleeved arm arrived in the doorway, its hand waggling acknowledgment. Squeamish, Peckover reflected, today's youth, in spite of their daily dose of TV gore. He tracked back through the Waverley Suite, avoiding noticing Sir Gilbert. The youth stood at the corner of the corridor.

Peckover said, 'Sure you called the right number?'

'Here he is,' said the night manager, looking round the corner. 'So you'll not be wanting me any more.'

Peckover joined him. Someone in uniform was approaching along the corridor.

'I won't be but 'e will,' Peckover said. 'That your full complement? The Inverballoch constabulary?'

'He's a right bastard on parking.'

'Watch your language. And don't leave the 'otel.'

'I was off duty at seven! When do I sleep?'

'When 'e tells you.'

Sergeant Menzies – he pronounced it Mingies – held in one hand his peaked cap, perhaps the better to show off his abundant white hair. For some years computer records had quietly misread or misplaced the age of Sergeant Menzies. Born in Inverballoch on the day in 1931 when King George V, on an excursion from Balmoral, had bagged a record (for a king) 119 grouse and 34 brace of partridge, in an era when Harry Lauder and Will Fyffe were Scotland's stars of the music halls and wireless, he had forty years' experience as a policeman, mainly in the rawer stews of Glasgow. He had returned home to look after law and order in Inverballoch, and his mother, not that she had asked him to.

He looked with suspicion at the night manager and Peckover, then through the open door into the Waverley Suite.

'Holy Mother o' God!' he said, and crossed himself. 'Which of ye has the key?' He took the key from the night manager and locked the door. 'Gordon, ye'll wait here. I want no one attempting an entrance. I've roused Dr Lesley and am in touch wi' Glasgae CID.'

'D'you have another key?' Peckover asked the night manager.

'In the top drawer of the filing cabinet in reception.'

'Locked?'

'It doesn't lock. We have no pilferers here.'

'Remember, I don't exist. You're a witness, Gordon. You'll give evidence in court. Do as you're told, you could be in for an encomium from the judge.'

'An encomium?' the night manager said, terrified.

Sergeant Menzies said, 'Mr Peckover, sor, if ye'll come wi' me.'

The sergeant was not sure what he would do with the officer from Scotland Yard but Glasgow would decide. He had alerted Glasgow to the possibility of the death at the Ram of an English-man of the sort headlines are made of. Now he must let them know that Sir Gilbert Potter was indeed one with the choir invis-ible, presumed murdered, and their presence would be appreci-ated. He realized he had no evidence that the body was that of Sir Gilbert Potter, but no matter. He was violently dead whoever he was.

Peckover would have gone with the sergeant anyway. The bloke seemed to know what he was doing. His own shopping list was, one, nab the spare key to the Waverley Suite before anyone else did, such as the press, once they got wind of the goings-on at the Ram; two, a shave; three, Miriam; four, call the Factory, matter of courtesy, let them know a right kettle of Scotch salmon was on the simmer and too bad about his holiday but he'd be returning to London.

The Glasgow lot would be happy to be rid of him. Then again they might prefer him to hang on, if not as a copper with one or two successes on his record sheet, and of some modest notoriety, then as a suspect.

Gawd, what an unlikely situation! Eminent archaeologist slain at remote Highlands hotel and Scotland Yard in position before and during! Of course, the coincidence became less staggering if he took into account every crime that he had not been in position for. Five point three million criminal offences in Britain last year. Population say fifty million, that came to one crime per every ten citizens, babies and octogenarians included. By any law of averages he had been about due to be in position.

By another set of averages, Gilbert Potter might have been in position as one whose time had come. Poor patronizing buffer. He might have known his Piltdown Man from his Pompeii but he hadn't exactly had the common touch. To do him in, or at least to dunk him in treacle and roll him in oatmeal, must have crossed the mind of every self-respecting Scot who had sat listening to his prattling on about savages and barbarian forebears.

'Sergeant?' requested Peckover.

They had reached the stairs down to reception. A spooky hush seeped along the stairways and hallways of the Ram. True, it was Sunday and all honest folk were behind closed doors preparing for kirk.

'Andrew Dinwiddie,' Peckover said, 'our chairman, last night, he lost his dirk. The one he slashed up the haggis with.'

'Aye?'

'He asked for it back if anyone saw it.'

'Might ye be suggestin' that Mr Dinwiddie's dirk is the murder weapon?'

'No. He might 'ave got it back, all I know. Just thought you should have the picture.'

'We'll bear it in mind, sor. And ye'll bear in mind that Ah hae moral jurisdiction here.'

Peckover had never heard of moral jurisdiction but he was not about to challenge it. He was not up in Scottish law.

The huddle in reception had swollen to a dozen or so. Miriam Peckover in two jerseys. A man holding a rectangular briefcase, taking off his gloves with his teeth, who might be the pathologist. Posy Cork, eyes wide and mouth slightly open but no hangover. Beside her, uncombed – perhaps combed but here was hair in need of an assault beyond mere combing – Leah Howgego, assistant digger and sifter. No Mrs McSporran, laird, parson, chairman, angling vice chairman, Angus MacGregor, musical Mrs Bell, Posy's boyfriend, or anyone except breakfast staff, the doctor, if that was who he was, and two or three overnight guests. The man in the snow hat had vanished.

'If ye'll just hae the patience and stay put,' Sergeant Menzies told the assembly. To the man with the gloves and bag he said, 'Dr Lesley, I'll be wi' ye directly.'

Sergeant Menzies marched behind the reception desk and bumped into Peckover who was leaving with two keys initialled WS.

'Nae need at all for panic,' called out the sergeant.

Nobody was panicking. Everyone was dismayed and in need only of information. The sergeant entered an office behind the desk and closed the door. He knew his way around as a local bobby should. Peckover, pocketing the keys, trusted that the crime scene was now as secure as he could make it. He would give the keys to the sergeant when he felt a little more confident about him.

He was ready to return to London.

Too bad because he had been enjoying Scotland. The space, the washed air, people like Alice McSporran. He took Miriam's hand and led her outside to breathe and greet the day.

She said, 'It's warmer out than in.'

The sky had switched from deep zinc to pale platinum, a hue Peckover guessed it might remain. Beyond the parking area and the road, stony, nibbled fields with sheep reached away to a middle distance of conifers and a solitary derelict building that was the old kilt mill. The horizon was blurry mountains. Why, Peckover wondered, was the scene not peopled with artists, landscape painters? They could wear gloves, have a paraffin heater at their feet.

He said, 'You'll have to answer some questions. Who you are, why you're here, anything you saw or heard. Then you should go home.'

'What about you?'

'I'll know soon.'

After a second trip to the Waverley Suite, this time with the sergeant and the doctor, Peckover borrowed the telephone in the office behind the reception desk.

At his desk at Scotland Yard, Chief Superintendent Frank Veal, workaholic, said, 'Typical. You jaunt off to the land of oatcakes and next thing we hear you have a VIP with a knife in him.'

Peckover would not have bet on whether Frank Veal had just got in or hadn't been to bed yet.

He said, 'You're very *au courant*, mate.'

'Up to date too. Glasgow called. A Bob Geddes, superintendent, from his car. He's on his way. Know him?'

'No.'

'You're going to. He thinks he can use you.'

'Load of rubbish.'

'Exactly what I said. Well, crossed my mind. Nothing personal. What he thinks he can use is all the help he can get. He says this business smells.'

'Air's like Chablis up 'ere, mate. Smells of what?'

'Skeletons. Fifty years ago an archaeologist was poking about at wherever you are. Inverballoch? Hold on, I have it here. Sir Wilfred Cuff-Bingley. Nineteen forty-one. He disappeared. Never heard of again. Notorious case.'

'Before my time.'

'Before everybody's time. This Geddes sounds serious though. One archaeologist missing and fifty years on, same place, another one murdered. If there's a connection there could be local skeletons. I'm not sure he wants them disturbed.'

'I agree. Let sleeping skeletons lie.'

'But he'd like to identify them before putting them back in the cupboard.'

'He sounds confused.'

'Sounds to me he'd like to close the file, win himself a medal.'

'Can I come 'ome now?'

'No rush, Henry. Enjoy yourself. Learn golf. I'm sending you an assistant.'

'Ah.'

'What's "ah" mean?'

'Himself?'

'If he hustles he'll be with you for lunch. Feed him the leftover haggis. He looks too skinny to me, I wouldn't say pale exactly, but he needs building up. How's Miriam?'

'The star of Burns Night, Miriam was. She's off 'ome.'

'Love to the thistles and bluebells. Bye, Henry.'

SIX

O, young Lochinvar is come out of the west,
Through all the wide border his steed was the best.
Sir Walter Scott, Marmion

Detective Constable Jason Twitty, rhythmic son of Jamaican immigrant parents, caught the next departing air shuttle by a whisker.

When the call came he had been tapping out his report on an armed robbery at the post office on Fenchurch Street. Offered not a moment to costume himself appropriately for north of the border, he was dressed in his report-writing gear and carried only his boom box, Sunday newspapers, and an aged CID file handed to him on boarding for all the world as if he were an end of the millennium James Bond off to do battle with Son of Goldfinger and save the planet from nuclear meltdown. He wore his old-gold denim suit with a cerulean turtleneck jersey, a Tyrolean hat with a feather, and white jogging boots that had three-inch soles and tumescent ten-inch tongues. The joggers made him six feet nine inches tall. He was upset to have had no opportunity to dress Scottishly in chain mail or moleskin breeks or whatever was worn for stalking the stag.

All Twitty knew was that Our 'Enry was with his wife at somewhere called Inverballoch where an archaeologist named Potter had been murdered. Airborne, fortified by in-flight pineapple juice and peanuts, he learned from the file that another archaeologist had disappeared from Inverballoch, though back in mediaeval times, so what that had to do with the present trouble was obscure. The file on Cuff-Bingley, Sir Wilfred, still open after half a century, was mildewed and thin.

Glasgow's file might be fat. Sir Wilfred had been their case. Photos showed a pinched bloke in hornrim specs you'd sooner avoid. Beyond making its records and rogues' gallery available, Scotland Yard seemed not to have concerned itself.

The view from his flying bus of greenish England (snow over the Midlands) and hilly Scotland appealed more than the history of a gent gone missing quite a time ago. Maps of Inverballoch, photographs, a biography of Sir Wilfred, interviews with family and friends, unrevealing statements from long-gone Inverballochers. Presumably the statements were unrevealing or whatever had become of Sir Wilfred would have been revealed and the file closed and consigned to the vaults. The statements were blurry carbon copies with smudged erasings. How had anything ever got done in that Stone Age before the word processor and fax?

At Glasgow Airport DC Twitty dipped into the all-purpose shop for a bar of Cadbury's and something to read beyond the Sunday papers because who knew how drear and solitary Scotland's nights might be? Of course, it could be all over and he might be on his way back to London before the day was done, but best to be prepared. He risked paperbacks of Boswell's *The Journal of the Tour of the Hebrides* – where were the Hebrides and would he be near them? – and a Walter Scott, *Ivanhoe*, which looked lengthy but he had never read Walter Scott. He would add them to his expenses as essential background reading. As a gift for the Guv, the corkscrew with a timber handle? The lucky heather? The Dundee cake? He could not be positive how Our 'Enry would respond to a gift of any sort. He chose a tin whistle eight inches long: £1.99.

He rented a white Fiesta and bought the *AZ Great Britain Reversible Road Map*, nine square feet of map once he had unfolded it, Scotland taking up the reverse. He had not known there was so much of Scotland, though it looked fairly empty north of Glasgow. South of Glasgow wasn't exactly cluttered either. He asked the car rental girl in a pink blazer if she could pinpoint Inverballoch for him. She had shampooed hair cascading halfway down her back and skin like apricot yoghurt. Together they pored over the map, he on the customer side of the counter, she on the staff side, their heads almost touching. He inhaled shampoo. He hoped she would find Inverballoch fast before he fell in love with her. He doubted the Guv would react rapturously if he arrived for duty with one hand holding a tin whistle and the other the hand of his car rental girl.

She said, 'You the press, then?'

'Press, well,' murmured Twitty, non-committal.

'The murder, is it? I never heard of Inverballoch before today. It's somewhere here.' Her exquisite forefinger dabbed at white space not far from the sea. Nowhere was far from the sea. 'I'd say 'tis too wee to be shown.'

The darling fingertip had alighted around midway between a blue puddle – hey, Loch Lomond! – Ye'll tak' the high road and I'll tak' the low road – and another puddle – the country was awash with puddles – wowie, Loch Ness! He should take the A82 to Glencoe but at Bridge of Orchy bear right for Rannoch, then ask, his sweetheart instructed. Seventy miles, thereabouts.

Once out of Glasgow, Twitty gave the car its head. Seventy, eighty, eighty-five, into sheeting rain. He wouldn't be stopped by the police, there wouldn't be any, they'd all be in Inverballoch. Nobody else was on the road either.

The landscape grew rugged. After the downpour the sun came out. He drove by crusty humps of roadside snow that would not be there much longer if the sun kept this up. The desk sergeant, who knew everything, had told him, 'Whatever you take to wear in Scotland you'll be wrong.' He switched on his boombox on the front passenger seat and heard the last whining bars of something country-and-western about having to say goodbye for the sake of the children. 'The number of country-and-western clubs in Scotland is now one hundred and twenty-eight, yessiree, you better believe it!' cried the disc jockey from presumably Glasgow or Edinburgh. The voice dropped an octave and became husky. 'Next, Mona MacTavish and her hit single, "I'll dry the dishes if you dry your tears". Twang it for us, Mona!' Mona twanged and dried the dishes and promised her man she would not fail him again. Twitty didn't believe her.

Having done its duty, the sun retired, and rain fell. Twitty wondered if the white blobs on the dark hills were snow or sheep. A clump of raised stones on a distant heathery plateau reminded him of megaliths he had seen in the West Country. He had never heard of the Stones of Skelloch and if he had he would not have detoured to see them. Mr Peckover awaited. At twenty past one DC Twitty drew up outside the Ram Hotel.

He had company: fleets of police cars, anonymous cars, motorcycles, two television vans, and people coming and going through the glass entrance of a disappointing hotel. He had hoped for a skyscraper Hilton or Inter-Continental.

Twitty switched off the engine but allowed the boombox to pound on. Scottish Grand Ol' Opry had given place to Scottish rap. He felt a tremor of anticipation. He was in a foreign country. Not as foreign as Ecuador or Egypt but foreign all the same. Not England.

On the back seat lay his synthetic sable coat with the whiff of pauperdom from the Portobello Road, his hat, newspapers, and new books. He speculated on the chances of untapped pulchritude wasting away in the Ram. A receptionist named Fiona or Ishbael pining for a white Fiesta to pull up and decant into her arms an ethnic Romeo in denims of dusty yellow. He locked the car and walked springily into the hotel.

Twitty failed to find Peckover in the Rob Roy Bar. The bar was smoky and hopping with media, male and female, some of them fairly rowdy. He opened a door into an empty Claymore Dining-Room. The tables were in the form of a T and had been cleared, but the room needed vacuuming, the chairs neatening.

He opened a door that bore a plaque, Television Lounge, and above the plaque a paper with the scrawled order, No Admission, and an indecipherable signature. In the room, more smoke, rearranged furniture, and a degree of busyness. A dozen police, men and women, some uniformed, others in jeans and jerseys, talked with each other, into telephones, and sat staring at sheets of paper in battered typewriters. The murder room's technology did not resemble that of *Star Trek*'s Starship *Enterprise*. An engineer had taken up a strip of carpet and a floorboard and knelt frowning at a junction box. A bulletin board had been tacked to a wall, and beside it a map of the Western Highlands. There was a tea urn, saucers for ashtrays, banks of blank paper, and piled one on the other, a Bible, a dictionary, the AA *Illustrated Road Book of Scotland*, *Scottish Criminal Law*, *Road Traffic Law*, and for no reason that was clear to Twitty, *Kobbé's Complete Opera Book*, edited and revised by the Earl of Harewood.

The Guv sat at a table with a curly-haired man of thirty-five or so dressed in collar and tie and a three-piece suit of silvery corduroy. What at first sight looked to be a bullet-hole in his chin was on a second look a dimple.

Twitty had never seen the charcoal cashmere jacket the Guv was wearing, or for that matter the orange socks with white circles. He would have remembered if he had. The pair had each a pint glass of beer and were eating sausages and macaroni cheese.

39

'Greetings, sir,' Twitty said, and for the dimpled man he offered the briefest of bows, a downward tilt of the head that could be interpreted as deference if he were Scotland's chief commissioner, or insolence if he were a suspect. 'Smashing set of threads, Guv. Buckram, is it? Fustian? Must have set you back a bob or two. Bit tight under the arms, wouldn't you say?'

'Cheeky bugger.' Peckover surveyed Twitty's old-gold denim. 'Tell you one thing, it didn't come from your flea market. You look like a baked custard.' He took a swallow of beer. 'You're late. Been chattin' up the air 'ostesses? DC Twitty – Detective Superintendent Geddes, Glasgow CID. What's this then?'

Peckover took the tin whistle presented by Twitty.

'Sorry, sir, they didn't do gift-wrapping. It's a Scottish pibroch in miniature, twelfth century. A reconstruction, of course.'

'Bleedin' Irish, mate. Scots don't whistle, they pipe. Right, Mr Geddes?'

'I'm not an expert,' Geddes said.

Peckover held the instrument at arm's length and read the price-sticker. He handed it back to Twitty.

'I'm touched. Would you look after it for me? No offence but I 'ave two wee bairns' – after two pints of Bass he was happy to speak Scots – 'who already play drums, tambourine, ocarina, xylophone, football rattle, and music boxes guaranteed unbreakable and undrownable. Hot favourite, "The Farmer's in the Dell". Sit down. 'Ave you eaten? They do a decent banger. What genre of 'orrible rock music does your coiffure represent this time or aren't we supposed to notice?'

'Like it?' Twitty's haircut resembled a fright wig. 'It's a joint creation of mine and my stylist.'

'Sonny, why don't you not sit down but slope off?' Superintendent Geddes said, and he winked at Twitty. 'Why not be a reporter?'

'Excuse me?'

Twitty already quite liked the superintendent except for the 'Sonny'. He resolved to be on his guard. First impressions could be a disaster.

'Just a thought,' said Geddes. 'Undercover is what crossed my mind. One of the gentlemen of the press. Nobody here knows you, do they?'

'Wouldn't imagine so.'

'There are some might talk to the press who wouldn't talk to the police.'

'And vice-versa,' Peckover said.

He had been hoping Sir Gilbert Potter's killer might be in custody by teatime. He still hoped so. But the longer it took the longer it was going to take. The superintendent sounded as if he thought it might not be wrapped up by teatime.

'Don't take it seriously, sonny,' Geddes said. 'You don't look like a journalist either, unless you're with *Wham!*. Too late anyway.' His eyes were no longer on Twitty. 'Here come the assault troops.'

The door into the makeshift incident room had opened. Bearing down came a gangling young man in pebble lenses and an older woman holding a gin and tonic.

'Out,' Geddes told them. 'You saw the sign.'

'*Dundee Advertiser*,' the pebble lenses said. 'We've something for you, Super. Our library has cuttings of another archaeologist here but he vanished—'

'Out.'

'Only trying to co-operate.'

'Picklover,' the woman said. She eyed Peckover intently. 'Pluck-holder? Do I know you?'

'Mavis, enough,' Geddes said. 'Press conference, two-fifteen.'

'Puckrover? Passover?' Mavis Murray, *Glasgow Herald*, ignored Geddes. 'You're Jewish? That's fine with me. I knew Golda Meir. I knew Moshe Dayan. I could tell you about Moshe.' She took a substantial sip of gin and tonic. 'Bard of the Yard, yes? Can you confirm that your wife had a close relationship with the body, ah, Sir Gilbert, um – Sir Gilbey? Would that be the Gilbey's Gin people?'

'Mavis!' Geddes's voice had considerable edge. 'Why don't you get yourself a drink before the bar closes?'

Mavis looked in her glass and fell to reflecting.

'Pardon,' the myopic journalist said to Twitty. 'You'll be from Scotland Yard too?'

'I'm the *Echo*,' Twitty declared, and whipped a notebook out of an inside pocket. 'We'll get nothing from this lot, old boy. I've tried. See you at the press conference.'

He gave a little salute to the *Dundee Advertiser* and *Glasgow Herald* and loped from the murder room. On route to the bar for sausages, wondering what the outward and visible signs of a reporter from the *Echo* might be, he opened his notebook and read, Claudia 607–8533 Mon 7 Paul's WB Earlham St He recalled that Claudia danced with controlled frenzy, a sort of jungle dignity.

Whether he would make it to Paul's Wine Bar for 7 p.m. tomorrow was something else. Fat chance if this case dragged on like Sir Bluff-Clingley's, whatever his name was, missing since 1941. He reached the bar in time for a mouthful of lunch. Though the clock had still three minutes to go to two o'clock, the barman called, 'Time, gentlemen!' Twitty sympathized. With so many coppers on the loose, the barman would be eager to close on time.

A uniformed constable sang out, 'Hurry along! Outside, please!' Another policeman slung chairs together in a semblance of rows. Robust coppers cleared the bar of customers, Twitty included. Most of the customers then returned, several with cameras, announcing to the policeman at the door, '*Examiner*' and 'ITN News' and in some instances presenting a National Union of Journalists card as worthless evidence of probity.

'*Echo*,' Twitty said.

'What *Echo*?' the policeman wanted to know.

Twitty squared his back to whoever was behind him, obliterating the view, and flicked open his Metropolitan Police warrant card.

'So why didn't you—' began the policeman, but the old-gold beanpole with the swarming hair had shimmied through.

The chairs filled up. Twitty found an untenanted patch of distant wall and lounged against it, reporter-like. Beside him hung a framed photograph of a loch shrouded in mist.

'If we may begin?'

Geddes, business-minded above the hubbub. He sat with his bum and palms on the table, feet on the floor. Behind him, more or less in a line as in an identity parade, but sloppier, hands in pockets, stood several plainclothes policemen, a skeletal inspector in a drab suit, and a white-haired sergeant with folded, unsloppy arms.

'My name is Bob Geddes. I'm a superintendent with Glasgow CID and your source of police information in matters pertaining to the murder of Sir Gilbert Potter. What I have to say is on the record. You are free to quote.'

The press sighed. Two stood with a clatter and walked out. We're wasting our time, we're going to get nothing, thought every reporter with more than a year's experience.

Twitty observed a few of the press bring out a notebook, scraps of paper, but why didn't they all? They had total recall? Where was the Guv? Why was he not lined up with the support troops behind the superintendent?

The gaunt inspector in the brown suit, a Scot who made on the stock market twice his police salary, reached for the chair which had been intended for Geddes, and sat on it. Peckover arrived at the last moment and took up a discreet position by the door. He saw nothing to be won by announcing himself. His identity was known to the Mavis woman, probably to others, but best to be as anonymous as possible. He avoided noticing Twitty, propping up a wall. If their eyes met, the lad might wave.

Superintendent Geddes said, 'Sir Gilbert Potter was murdered between two o'clock and six this morning, Sunday, in his room here at the Ram. He had ended a Burns Night supper at which he was guest of honour, and, I understand, announced that a dig would take place at Inverballoch with the help of a government grant, if he could arrange it. You won't need me to tell you Sir Gilbert was one of Britain's leading archaeologists. The murder weapon was a knife that pierced his neck. He died almost instantaneously. The body has been conveyed to Glasgow for the post-mortem. The incident is a tragedy that has shocked the deceased's family, friends, and archaeologists world wide. We are following several lines of enquiry. An arrest will be made soon, depend on it.'

Geddes smiled through clenched teeth. I shouldn't have said that, he thought. Three months down the pike and the file still wide open it would come back to haunt him. Three months, if he had arrived nowhere, he would be off the case, put in charge of the car-clamp unit.

The faces watching him through a gauze of cigarette smoke were either blank or sceptical. They had blinked when he had invented the bit about the tragedy shocking the family, as well they might. He had no notion who the family were. But what should he have said? Sir Gilbert had been a pimple on the arse of civilized society? That is what he had gathered during his few hours at the Ram. The case might well become an unsolved stinker same as that of the other archaeologist, the one with the name nobody got right, Sir Cluffley Thing, of a hundred years ago. Bob Geddes, a passably contented family man, his forlorn ambition to tour the world on a cruise ship, had today come to hate archaeologists.

'Sir Gilbert's room is off limits until we have completed our routine procedures. That's it, gentlemen, ladies. Thank you for your attention.'

Superintendent Geddes summoned a smile and stood. End of

press conference. He was not so naïve as to imagine he would get away with it but nothing ventured, nothing gained.

After an unbelieving silence, childish bedlam broke loose, like Question Time in the House of Commons.

SEVEN

I have heard the mavis singing
His love song to the moon,
I have seen the dewdrop clinging
To the rose just newly born.
                    Charles Jeffreys, *Mary of Argyle*

Everybody shouted questions simultaneously. Someone was needed to cry 'Order!' and bang a gavel on a desk and on the heads of the questioners.

'Will you describe the knife?'

'Any lead on a motive?'

'Did Potter fight back?'

'Is it true Potter was having an affair with one of the guests?'

'What's the extent of local opposition to digging up Inverballoch?'

'Will Sergeant Menzies give us his version?'

Geddes resettled his rear on the edge of the table and raised and lowered his hands as if patting a dog. From this the press rightly inferred that he did not quite have the nerve to insist that the conference was over and to walk out.

'Who found the body?'

'Was robbery the motive?'

'Can you deny this is linked with Scottish nationalism?'

'Are you able to confirm it's an inside job by one of the staff?'

'Where in the neck and how many times?'

'Do you have a suspect?'

'Why have you called in Scotland Yard?'

Cheeky monkey, thought Peckover. Which of them asked that? His eyes sought the impudent hack without success.

'How many men do you have on the murder team?'

'What about women?'

Dammit! silently swore Peckover. The lad had to show off! He had raised his arm!

'What evidence was there at the scene?' demanded a Scots hack.

'How long before you make an arrest?'

'Do you expect the murderer to strike again?'

Twitty had dropped his arm, the brouhaha too much for him.

To the extent that Superintendent Geddes was able to separate one question from the next, they ranged from the half-baked to the too-close-for-comfort. With the tabloids he was doomed whatever he said. If he said nothing he was even more at risk. Murder Sleuth Geddes Maintains Silence on Dig Victim's Sex Life.

'We're in this together,' Geddes said, raising his voice. 'If you help me, I'll help you.'

He tried not to wince. This was straight out of the police manual, media relations. These reporters knew what he was about to say as well as he did. Unless they shut up nobody would hear what he was about to say but that was up to them.

'I understand your problem and you understand mine. My job is to bring a murderer to justice. Yours is to inform your readers and meet your deadlines.' Thank God today was Sunday. The Sunday press was the worst, publishing their sleaze in depth. Interviews, photographs. But they needed the big stories to break on Friday or Saturday so today they were absent. 'As you know, to make information public at this stage of our enquiries is to play into the hands of the perpetrator. He, she, or they, can only benefit by knowing what and how much we know. But in the interests of fair and accurate reporting' – Some hopes, thought Geddes – 'let me add the following.'

They had shut up.

'We have reason to believe that Sir Gilbert was surprised by probably a single intruder. We have no reason to suppose that the cause of Scottish nationalism is involved, though you may rest assured that we are neglecting no line of enquiry. The deceased was struck once through the front of the neck, through the voice-box, if you like.'

They liked it. They were scribbling, especially the younger ones. Mavis, he noticed, was burrowing in her handbag, probably for her cigarette lighter.

'The body was found by the night manager. He telephoned Sir Gilbert at seven o'clock with a wake-up call. Sir Gilbert's taxi to Glasgow Airport was ordered for seven thirty. After several unsuccessful attempts to rouse Sir Gilbert, the night manager visited his room, the Waverley Suite.'

They knew about the Waverley Suite and good luck to them. They knew from the register the names of all overnight guests and their room numbers. They had talked to every guest they had managed to run to earth. No way of stopping it.

'The taxi arrived on schedule and was later dismissed,' Geddes said.

An Arthur Walker, man of many hats: Inverballoch Limousines, landscaper, society photographer (weddings, babies), caddy, tourist guide. Walker had hung about in his snow hat, thrilled, then driven off to spread the news.

Worthless information. A television cameraman yawned.

'Our murder team is a full complement of investigators from Glasgow Central Crime Squad supplemented by units from the area with local knowledge.' Should he call on Sergeant Menzies to stand and be recognized? No, he should not. Someone among the press would pass a witty remark on his white hairs. 'Scotland Yard has not been called in. A Scotland Yard officer happens to have been a guest at the hotel, on holiday—

'Henry Peckover, yes?' a voice called out. 'His wife cooked the supper. Miriam, correct? She was an associate of Potter and now she's away out of it – gone.'

Peckover, glowering, identified the *Dundee Advertiser*. The impertinence, making free with Miriam's name, looking for puzzles where there were none.

'Mrs Peckover,' Geddes said, 'is chef to the Royal Archaeological Society, of which Sir Gilbert Potter was a distinguished member. We have her statement and she is on her way back to London to resume her catering duties. Thank you for your attention.'

Geddes stood up, turned, and nodded to his colleagues in the line-up. They nodded back and started forward and sideways with an air of efficiency, the press conference being over. The superintendent believed he had acquitted himself adequately. Peckover took a step towards the door. He would thank Geddes later for his dismissal of the Miriam question.

'Bob, a moment. This knife?'

A scribe was on his feet. Several were. As far as the Fourth Estate was concerned the conference still had some distance to go.

'Is it true,' the scribe wanted to know, 'it's the *sgian dubh*' – he pronounced it skeean doo – 'of Andrew Dinwiddie?'

'The what?' said another scribe.

'*Sgian dubh*, laddie,' a third said. 'The black knife, meaning hidden. In the stocking. The dirk he carved the haggis wi'. Hae ye no the Gaelic?'

'I'm not working on it either.'

'Mr Geddes, can you confirm it's Andrew Dinwiddie's knife?'

'No,' Geddes said.

'No it isn't or no you're not confirming it?'

'No comment.'

'Bob?' Mavis, hand aloft, without gin and tonic. 'Wilfred Cuff-Bingley, fifty years ago.' She was surprisingly coherent. 'We'd be safe in assuming you're following up the archaeology connection?'

Mavis Murray, legend, war correspondent, battle-scarred and bottle-scarred veteran of Mau-Mau, Cyprus, Aden, Suez, Vietnam, Beirut, the Falklands, and Northern Ireland. (She had been content in recent years, as was her editor, that she should skip the Gulf War, Bosnia, Somalia.) Latterly, one way and another, Mavis had become a liability. After discussion about her salary and what she would not be required to do (church fêtes, cat shows, farmers' ploughing contests, etc.), she had been returned to grass in the Glasgow office.

'We are pursuing every credible line of enquiry,' Geddes told her, rattled, and started for the door.

A time there had been when Mavis would no more have allowed the whippersnapper superintendent to get away with such an evasion than Israeli border guards could have stopped her conning, blustering, bribing, and wheedling her way into the war zone. Now she peeled the Cellophane off the next packet of cigarettes.

She said, 'Are you pursuing the Druids?'

'The what?' Geddes, a half-dozen paces from the door and escape, came to a stop.

'In a field the other side of the Stones of Skelloch. You didn't actually say this might not be an outside job.'

'No,' agreed Geddes. Did he mean yes? What was the question? 'We're paying it close attention.'

Geddes fled from the Rob Roy Bar pursued by cameras.

Peckover took the opportunity to shave. His room was very empty, the beds not yet made. Twin beds, separated by an unbudgeable bedside table made from probably iron and Highland granite, had been annoying but they had managed. Most traces of Miriam had gone, though she had forgotten her tights, hung up on the shower rail, and furled in the waste basket was her Friday's *Guardian* from Heathrow. On a Ram dinner plate on the dressing table lay Miriam's parting gift, a slice of cold haggis and a glob of butter, both grey. With the refreshment came a knife, fork, and a note, *Be a Man – Bon Appétit!*, with kisses.

Below, the murder room was lively with toing and froing, telephoning, punching of keyboards manual and electronic, and trips to the tea urn. Scotland Yard's operations and command centre the Ram's murder room was not, but it had progressed. A fax machine had arrived, also linked video monitors, computer screens, and printers with access to the police national computer at Hendon. An easel with a blackboard had been set up but nobody could find chalk. Constable Colquhoun, nineteen, was ordered to locate chalk and be back with it in five minutes or his guts would be stitched into garters and sold to the Saffron Kilts Pipe Band to keep their socks up. 'On the double, Colquhoun, ye stourie dundercluck!' To the bulletin board had been pinned Xeroxes of the pathologist's report, lists of names of those at the Burns Dinner, those who had stayed overnight at the Ram, all staff, seven residents of Inverballoch who had a police record, and photographs from many angles of Sir Gilbert Potter in his pyjamas, on his back, a dirk in his neck. Geddes, who had taken off his silvery cord jacket, was putting it on.

He told Peckover, 'I'm taking another shot at Dinwiddie. The knife's his.' He watched for Peckover's reaction. 'Too good to be true, that what you're thinking?'

'Something like that.'

'Dinwiddie announces that his dirk's missing, that it might have gone with the haggis back to the kitchen. All right, that's where it might have gone. A public announcement also lets everybody know that wherever the dirk is he doesn't have it. How do we know he didn't have it? He could have had it back down his stocking, deep down, out of sight. His father's and grandfather's dirk and he abandons it on the haggis plate as if it were Woolworth's?'

'Perhaps he wanted to show it off, give everyone a chance to fondle it.'

'He never wanted to before and he's carved the haggis the last five years.'

'Miriam looked for it in the kitchen and didn't find it.'

49

'That's what her statement says.'

Peckover frowned. He chose to interpret the remark as affirmation that Miriam had looked for the dirk and not found it. If Geddes was implying that Miriam's statement and the truth were different animals he would make allowances. Press conferences were notoriously a strain.

'If you want to check out Duncan, the laird, he's at the dig, or he was,' Geddes said.

'You asking me to?'

'Posy Cork's there, and the other one.' Geddes found a sheet of paper from among the assortment on the table. 'Leah Howgego. What kind of name is that? Uzbekistan?'

'Search me.' Twitty might know. Scholarship boy, classy schooling. Where was he and what was he up to?

Geddes said, 'The Cork woman's hinted she'd not say no to a police presence. She's nervous.'

''Ow about callous? Her mentor hardly cold in 'is body bag and she's off digging for pots. What's her hurry?'

'You could ask her.'

'I might. But no thanks to baby-sitting. Have one of your constables hold her 'and. Or can't you spare one?'

'Sit down a moment.' Geddes pointed to a chair. 'What you're thinking is I think you're dispensable.'

'Never crossed my mind.'

Peckover, standing, picked lint off his cashmere jacket. He felt like a ten-year-old about to be reprimanded.

'I want you in on this, Henry. If I get no joy out of Dinwiddie my next stop is the dig or wherever our fine laird has shunted himself off to. Seems he spends much of his time at the dig. So why don't you aim there, chat him up first, your way? Whatever your way may be it won't have a Scottish accent. Might catch him off balance. Up to you whether you tell him what you do for a living.'

'I could be another hotshot from the *Echo*. Fishing correspondent.'

'Facetiousness might enchant him, who's to know? You've not seen the file on Cuff-Bingley?'

'Never 'eard of him until today.'

'I'll have a copy run off for you. Read it, you'll know as much as anyone. Though it's possible we may have one or two oldies here with long memories.' Geddes lapsed into gloom. 'Unless we get a confession out of Dinwiddie I can see us having to ferret out octogenarians and listen to their remembrances of things past.' He brightened. 'Fact is, Henry, it's a rattling good yarn, should appeal to your poetic soul. Buried treasure, wartime, Clydeside in the blitz, Herr Hess landing his Messerschmitt at Eaglesham—'

'Where?'

'Other side of Glasgow. Amid all the confusion, the blackout, rationing – not that I was around – Vera Lynn singing "There'll be bluebirds over the white cliffs of Dover—" '

' "Tomorr-o-o-w, just you wait and se-e-e," ' Peckover sang richly.

Coppers at the tea urn turned their heads.

'So amid all the mess and disruption an archaeologist breezes in,' Geddes said. 'A celebrated sort like Potter with letters after his name, exempt from active service because he's no longer in the first flush. Arrives in Inverballoch, depopulated of most of its males and half the women because they're off out of it in uniform. One day he's prodding about in the bog, the next he's vanished for ever.'

'For ever's a long time. Some people choose to go missing.' Peckover pictured a pensioner with a cane, unsteady but resolute, doddering even now through the uncharted Highlands. 'How old is he if he's alive?'

'Hundred and twelve.'

'Long lived, these archaeologists. It's the fresh air. Who said, "An archaeologist is the best husband any woman can have. The older she gets, the more interested he is in her"?'

'Agatha Christie.'

'Blimey, 'ow did you know? Did you say buried treasure?'

'A legend. What's a yarn without buried treasure? Find Roman earthworks, you have evidence the Romans occupied as far north as Inverballoch. Who cares except historians? Find Celtic gold, everybody's wetting their knickers. Where there's one crock of gold there might be another. You'd have a gold rush.'

'Not finders keepers though, is it? Your treasure trove law the same as England's?'

'Far as I know. Gold and silver have to be turned over to the coroner. An inquest decides who's the rightful owner, and if the treasure was buried by someone who meant to return and recover it, but didn't, it belongs to the Crown. If the jury decides there was no intention to recover it, it's the finder's or the landowner's.'

'Like earthworks.'

'Earthworks, your Saxon ship at Sutton Hoo, stuff buried in graves.'

'Butter?'

'Don't be tricky, Henry.'

'Butter should be treasure trove. Somebody meant to recover it, God 'elp 'em. Gawd, there we were eating treasure trove. Should have gone to the Queen. Still, plenty left. She'll be thrilled, a barrel of suppurating, centuries-old butter arriving special delivery at Buckingham Palace.'

'Goes to the Crown, the nation – us taxpayers – not the Queen. All that Celtic gold and silver that's been turned up in a field wherever it was – near Norwich – that's treasure trove.'

'Snettisham. Not a silver salver's throw from 'Er Majesty's cottage at Sandringham. I've seen that hoard. Gold bracelets and stuff in the British Museum.'

'Didn't know you were keen on archaeology.'

'I took my children to see the mummies. They'd 'ad enough of the Zoo and the British Museum's free. I'm an expert on Snettisham. The Treasury paid the farmer and his pals with metal detectors the market value, hundreds of thousands of quid. Point being, buried treasure's worth finding if the government's going to compensate you, treasure trove or not. A legend, you said?'

'What exactly is your point?'

'A legend's an unverified popular story 'anded down from the past, right? Doesn't mean to say it didn't start off with an element of truth. Potter was an archaeologist. He might have had information he was keeping to himself.'

'My understanding is Posy Cork has more information than Potter did.'

'So she killed 'im before he could find out. Now she has the buried treasure to herself if she can discover it. 'Erself and Leah. And the boyfriend. She might 'ave to share with the laird, it's his land. Plenty for all though if it's anything like Snettisham.'

'Henry?'

'Here.'

'I never heard such a flight of fancy. Forget buried treasure.'

'You were the one mentioned it. Anyway, who can forget it? Buried treasure has allure. "Pieces of eight! Pieces of eight!" *Treasure Island*, Stevenson, one of yours.' Peckover sang, ' "Fifteen men on the dead man's chest." ' He had no notion why, especially under the circumstances, but he felt tuneful today. ' "Yo-ho-ho, and a bottle of rum!" '

Policemen looked towards him.

Geddes called to them, 'What're ye gawkin' at, ye smoutie blasties?'

Under stress the superintendent's Glasgow roots tended to resurface.

'No bad thing, Henry, if you got out and about a bit. Breathe the air. D'you have a car?'

Peckover shook his head. Geddes crossed the murder room to confer with a policewoman with an urchin cut who very few years ago would have been present only to keep the tea urn topped up. She was processing data from the police national computer and resented the interruption. Geddes summoned a detective constable in an army flak jacket. He returned to Peckover with car keys and a registration pencilled on a slip of paper.

'It's a blue Toyota round the back. You'll have the file in a couple of minutes.' He summoned from across the room the gaunt policeman in the brown suit. 'Ready, Alec?'

Inspector Alec Gillespie may not have been as rich as if he had discovered gold and silver buried by Celts twenty centuries ago but he was not hard up. He could have retired to the Bahamas. That would have meant giving up his inspector's salary so he did not think about it. Any source of income was money. One day he might even spend some but he could not imagine on what. He would have been happier studying the *Financial Times* than tagging along with Bob Geddes, but today there wasn't one, or a stock market. Sunday, dismalest day of the week.

Moments after Geddes and the inspector had left, Twitty glided in.

'Guv, you really ate that butter?'

'Which butter?'

'Last night. It's in the fridge in the kitchen. How are you feeling? It looks like something for infants to be creative with. What now?'

'I'm off to the dig. You could take a look at the Druids. Somebody mentioned Druids. No shenanigans with the girl Druids either. I know you. I'll have your report by six o'clock.'

'Dunno, Guv. They could be a real waste of time.'

'They could. It's called eliminating. When you've eliminated the impossible, like in this case Druids, whatever remains, however improbable, is what we're after.'

53

'Sherlock Holmes, *The Sign of Four*.'

'Don't come the scholarship boy with me, ye smoutie blastie.'

'Ye what?'

'Get going then.'

'Do I go as the *Echo*?'

'Go as what you like. Go as Sherlock Holmes. Try the gift shop, it's sure to 'ave a deerstalker. Just eliminate the Druids.'

'I could be a Druid. What do Druids wear?'

'Woad.'

'Woad's blue.'

'What's wrong with blue? Not your colour?'

'The shop might have a robe of some sort. I could be the Black Druid of Inverballoch. Guv?'

'What?'

'What's a smoutie blastie?'

'On yer way.'

EIGHT

Since there's no help, come let us kiss and part.
                                    Michael Drayton, *Sonnet*

Posy Cork and Mike Trelawny were having words, what might be described as a lovers' quarrel, or a marital tiff had they been married. Judging from the snap in their voices marriage seemed not the greatest idea.

'You have until summer to change your mind,' Mike said, 'but don't you see we should start planning now?'

'I can't imagine what makes you so sure I'm going to go with you to the States.'

'How can I turn down the offer? Besides, you like it over there, for pity's sake. It's not that fatso laird, is it?'

'Oh, please.'

'That tub of lard, the laird? I've watched him ogling you. You lapping it up because all this belongs to him, he's the laird, squire of all he surveys – heather and wet and sheep and local retards. Look, you'll get some sort of job at Princeton. I can help. Even if you can't line up a position teaching archaeology, you could teach freshman stuff, geography, a bit of history, but we have to start putting out feelers. I've told you, I can take care of us both on what Princeton's going to pay.'

'Wonderful. We'll have a bright new Buick and you'll man the barbecue with its tongs and skewers and basting brushes hanging just so.'

'Since when were you so hostile to money? It's not as if you've any future digging up pathetic Inverballoch.'

'You're so encouraging.'

'I'm being realistic. Your mentor who might have inveigled a grant is dead.'

'Can't you see it's because he's dead they're almost certain to give us something? He's dead straight after he announces he's going after government funding. They're morally bound to come up with a grant, like as a memorial.'

'Cloud cuckoo land. He's dead and the dig's finished. Those damn Druids, I wouldn't wonder. Don't think I'll be sending you cheques from the States so you can carry on shovelling out this stupid hole.'

'Stupid hole? What cheques? I wouldn't accept a penny from you! If I have to find money to keep this dig going I'll earn it honestly! I'll become a prostitute!'

Posy and Mike stood bickering on the rim of a functioning rectangular hole twenty metres long by ten wide. Half the hole was hardly a hole, only a skinny six inches of top sod having been dug out. But next came a shelf down to an empty chamber half a metre deep, and then a pit a metre deep that began to look like an actual excavation, or the start of an attempt at a swimming pool or a mass grave. Twine, easily tripped over, labelled and strung round pegs hammered into the ground at geometric intervals, sectioned into metre squares the area being dug, still to be dug, or sufficiently dug for now. In the metre-deep grave, on bejeaned knees and almost out of earshot of the bickerers, Leah Howgego scraped with a trowel. 'Mi Y'malel g'vurot Yisrael,' she crooned inappropriately, Hanukkah having come and gone.

Leah crooned to block out the bickering. Encountering something unexpected, possibly of interest, she put down the trowel, picked up a brush, and started brushing.

The only other human blot on the landscape was a heavily bundled figure like a yeti trudging up the moor towards the dig.

Peckover had parked the borrowed blue Toyota on a moorland road behind an estate car and a two-tone, mainly black Saab with rust. The road was less a road than a lumpy track off the main road, which had been a B if not a C road. He wondered if where the cars were parked might be a boreen or was a boreen exclusively Irish?

He trod by a stone footbridge over a gushy stream, the water foaming over polished boulders. The air was pure. The only problem was the temperature, around 55° Fahrenheit, and the clothes he wore. Overcoat, scarf, hat, gloves, and the usual underneath, including mountain-climber's thermal underwear. All this he had brought expressly for Scotland's January which he had assumed would be arctic. So as not to waste the winterwear, he wore it. From his car to the dig was only a hundred yards but already he was clammy.

Still, as one of the 95 per cent of male drivers who refuse to humble themselves by asking directions he was gratified to be arriving at what was clearly the dig. Ahead were a male and female whom he could not yet identify, though neither looked to be the laird. Just above ground level, in a hole, something stirred, perhaps a badger or a small stag, though without antlers. On the other side of the two people, the creature, and the dug-out patch of moor were a trestle table, items on the ground, and a prefabricated tin hut you could probably fold away into the back of an estate car. A loo, possibly, prematurely in place for the tribes of archaeologists who would descend if and when Sir Gilbert's grant was granted; or for the convenience of students who had helped begin the dig in the autumn then gone off to college. A further hundred yards distant were the scars of more spacious rectangles carved from the moor, some abandoned after partial excavation, others perhaps holding outlines of Roman earthworks.

Perspiring Peckover unwound his scarf, took off his hat, and advanced on the near rectangle, happy that here was where the action was. The action watched him.

'Afternoon,' he said, and returned his hat to his head so that he could raise it. From down in the dig, out of hibernation, the badger or baby stag lifted its head. It had curly black hair, specs, and held a brush.

Peckover bestowed a breezy smile on Posy and Mike. 'Ms Cork, correct?'

Posy nodded.

He said to Mike, 'Have we 'ad the pleasure?'

'Mike Trelawny. Pleasure's mine, old boy. Just leaving. I'll say goodbye.'

' 'Old on. Won't take a minute. I'm from the *Echo*.'

Posy said, 'You're from Scotland Yard. Peckover. The cook's husband.'

'Excellent! I like a lady who can take a joke.' So much for the *Echo*. Peckover was considerably relieved. 'Marvellous view from 'ere.'

Posy gave her nod.

'Nice digging weather,' Peckover said. 'Mean to say, it's not gelid.'

They waited for him to come to the point.

'And your, ah' – Peckover peered towards the distant end of the rectangle – 'co-worker?'

'Leah,' Posy said.

The woolly beast, kneeling, back towards the company, looked over its shoulder and blinked.

Peckover said, 'Truth is, Ms Cork, I was looking for the laird. Sir Dougal.'

'You missed him. He left fifteen minutes ago.'

'He was here.'

'He's always here,' Mike said incorrectly.

'Know where I might find 'im?'

'He probably went home,' Posy said. 'Dundrummy Castle. You go back to the road and continue on another ten, twelve miles.'

Sooner than return his hat to his damp head Peckover held it against his heart as if at a memorial service.

'I want to say 'ow sorry I am about – how do I call him? Your professor? Counsellor? Sir Gilbert. A savant and a gentleman. You must owe him a fair amount, I don't doubt. It won't be the same. A dreadful shock.'

'Yes,' Posy said.

'You're right not to mourn.'

'How do you mean?'

'There's some would mope, shut themselves off. Black arm-bands, wailing and gnashing. Work's the best therapy. You're young, if you'll permit me, but you've grasped that. This is what he'd 'ave wanted. No fuss. On with the digging.' Peckover's belief was that Gilbert Potter would have wanted nothing of the sort. He'd have wanted national mourning and a cortège to St Paul's with the Coldstream Guards playing 'Land of Hope and Glory'. 'The excavation's urgent, right?'

'I wouldn't say that. Anything we find has waited here for centuries.'

'But you're not taking today off.'

'If there's a cold spell, ice and snow, that's it. We'll have to close down till spring.'

'Buried treasure?'

'Sorry?'

'Pieces of eight?' Peckover's expression was gleeful. He beat time with his hat and chanted, 'Pieces of eight and we won't wait!'

Posy scowled. Mike looked puzzled. Distant Leah poked her head above the rampart. Peckover wondered if he had gone too far. If they believed him demented they might either run from the site or try to calm him, answering him as they would an infant.

He said, 'A local legend, so I'm told.'

'Local codswallop,' Posy said. 'My proposal to Sir Gilbert predicated the possibility of Roman remains. Not buried treasure or oil or a diamond mine or anything else.'

'Not butter?'

A wisp of a smile lit up Posy's face. She said, 'Serendipitous, that. Purest chance.' The smile gave way to impatience. 'The butter is finally of little interest. Butter, buried treasure, ship burials, graves, votive offerings, bog people – great, I'm not knocking it—'

'Bog people?' interrupted Peckover, but the query was swept away like a leaf in a wind.

'My proposition was and is solely that Roman occupation reached beyond the Antonine Wall if – the big if – I can turn up artefacts here, Inverballoch, a natural site for a camp on any route north from the western end of Hadrian's Wall. You've only to look at the map. And I've done it. You saw the sherds and coins at the Burns dinner. Sir Gilbert mentioned the earthworks. There was a settlement here. Of course, it would have been very small.'

'Of course,' agreed Peckover. 'What bog people?'

She was obsessed with her damn Wall. She had also switched from 'we' discovering artefacts to she herself alone. Alternatively she might be a scholar of sky-high IQ and relentless dedication, destined to become Dame Posy Cork in spite of currently looking gamine and Left Bank like that fifties actress, Jean Seberg.

He said, 'You mean bog people like, um' – he had to strive and search – 'Pete Moss? Where was he – it?'

'What you mean is Lindow Man in Cheshire ten years ago. The most famous is Tollund Man in Denmark. Denmark, Germany, Ireland, Scotland. They're, I don't say common, but they're a widespread phenomenon. Usually body parts, not the whole body. The peat preserves them. They keep turning up.'

'Like butter?'

'Quite different.'

'Finally of little interest, butter and bog people and buried treasure, compared with the Romans? That what you're saying?'

'It's relative, matter of preference.'

'You'd not be bored turning up a bog body?'

'I'd be thrilled.'

'You bet you would,' Mike told her. Hitherto simply standing there, he entered the exchange with vehemence. 'More thrilled than if you dig up a Roman camp complete with bath and temple except you're never going to admit it.'

'That's not true!' Posy said.

'Well it should be! You find a bog creature, your name's made. American universities will fall over each other. What do they care about the Antonine Wall?'

'They do! What do you care about history!'

'Posy, you're so innocent!'

'You're so impossible!'

Peckover hoped they were not about to start punching each other. As a diversionary measure he pointed across the dug rectangle to the trestle table and said, 'What 'ave we 'ere?' His impression was that Posy and Mike were admirably suited and would scrap happily for the rest of their lives. He was glad not to be young any more. Not that young anyway.

Leah Howgego had put down her brush and was kneeling upright, massaging the small of her back with both hands. Peckover realised that archaeology must be as hard on the back as picking strawberries. You needed a young back.

He headed round the rectangle towards the table, greeting Leah on his way.

'Rather you than me, miss. You're the sort keeps osteopaths in work.'

Leah stared up at him but said nothing. Deaf, Peckover assumed. He smiled at her anyway. He skirted a mound of peaty topsoil scraped from the dig in its early stages and a pile of poles and folded canvas presumably to protect the site from the elements. Near the table lay planks of wood, crates of sifted earth, sieves, brushes, a pick and shovel, cardboard boxes (Heinz Baked Beans), and on the table drawing boards, a pocket calculator, a vacuum flask, scrunched brown paper bags, and notes and diagrams in transparent rainproof covers, a stone on each to prevent it blowing away. The lovers were wrangling again, Mike going on about dollars and the exchange rate, Posy saying he should know, he thought of nothing else, Mike saying sorry but honestly that was enough, he was going, she could return with Leah, if she wasn't back at the hotel in a couple of hours he'd take it that that was that so he'd be off back to London. More in sorrow than in anger the ultimatum sounded to Peckover. He felt uncomfortable, an intruder. They should keep their voices down. Leah, crouched, was brushing again.

'What can you tell me about Druids?' Peckover called to Posy and Mike.

'Now you're talking!' Mike called back.

Mike and Posy's vexation with each other was none of his business but a change of subject, Peckover hoped, might distract them. They could stop quarrelling about themselves and quarrel about Druids.

He called out, 'Talking about what?'

'Potter,' Mike said. 'What else are you here for? Some of our latter-day Druids are weird enough to believe they're a reincarnation of the priests of prehistory.'

'They are? So?'

'So they were strong on human sacrifice. This lot might not have liked Potter poking about their holy places.'

'Inverballoch – holy?'

'You're the sleuth, old boy. There's the Skelloch Stone Circle.'

What the Skelloch Stone Circle might be, Peckover had not been informed, but his diversionary tactic was a success. Mike and Posy's next quarrel looked to be postponed. For one thing Mike was striding away down the hillside.

Peckover shouted, 'Mr Trelawny!' He waved his hat. 'Mike! One moment please!'

Mike hoisted an arm in acknowledgement but did not look round. Bentley motoring cap squarely on his head, he practically bounded, hurdling over heathery craters, chasséing past rocky outcrops.

Peckover walked past heaped canvas and hillocks of earth to where Posy stood. They watched Mike go.

'It'll be all right,' said Peckover, consoler.

'It will.'

Had they been less engrossed by Mike's exit, and noticed Leah in the dig's deep end, they would have observed that she kept looking round at them. She had turned greenish, victim perhaps of an occupational queasiness of archaeologists, all day on their knees, scraping and sifting, forever uncertain what, if anything, they might uncover.

Whatever Leah had uncovered she was now covering up. 'Oy, gottenyu!' she exclaimed in a whisper. She brushed soil back into place like a film running in reverse.

NINE

To have seen what I have seen, see what I see!
Shakespeare, *Hamlet*

Having reinterred what she had disinterred, Leah, for good
measure, placed a square of cardboard over the spot.

'These Druids, near some stone circle the other side of the
village, you know anything about them?' Peckover asked Posy.
'You and me would probably call them hippies, not that I've seen
this lot. Then again they might seriously think of themselves as
Druids. Is that possible? I was on Druid Duty once. Your field of
study, or adjacent, isn't it?'

'More Mike's. He'll know everything about Druids there is
to know.'

'He will?'

'No big deal. Mike would be the first to admit it. What's known
about Druids comes mostly from Caesar and would fill an eggcup.
I mean what's really known, not make-believe.'

'All their waving oak leaves about at Stonehenge is bogus?'

'We've no evidence Druids existed until long after Stonehenge
was built and none that there were sacrifices there or that Druids
were anywhere near the place. We're talking about before the
Roman occupation. Twilight time. The Romans wiped them out.
Suppressed them anyway.'

'Mr Trelawny sounded as if he thought that's what should be
done with today's bunch. Has he done research on twentieth-
century Druids?'

'I doubt it. What research? You'd have to ask him.'

Bit late. A hundred yards down the moor Mike Trelawny was
getting into the rust-rimmed Saab.

Peckover fanned himself with his hat. He prided himself on not

62

being a total ignoramus on the subject of Druids. Had he not been drafted to Stonehenge for the summer solstice rave-up eight, nine years ago? A gloating sergeant had kept saying, 'When do they start sacrificing each other?' Not to be middle class about it but some of those Stonehenge Druids had been pretty insanitary. He had failed to impress the Wiltshire police by identifying an acolyte of the Venerable Chief Druid as Eric Shorthouse, a nutter from Wembley, forever showing up in the North London cop shops to confess to crimes he had just read about in the *Standard*.

He said, 'If you ask me this business is spooky.'

She had not asked him but here was an opening for her and it would be nice if she contributed something before he went in search of the laird. It wouldn't need to be about Druids. She was giving him nothing perhaps because she had nothing to give. At the same time she didn't seem impatient to get him off the site.

'Druids, bog people, Gilbert Potter digging up more or less edible butter,' he said. 'I call that spookier than if the butter had turned to powder and was home to a rats' nest.'

'Potter dug up nothing. This is my proposal, my insight, my effort, my butter, my digging.'

'Exactly.'

Leah was currently doing the digging, not Posy, but he let that pass. Peckover and Posy Cork watched the boyfriend's Saab execute a U-turn through the heather and drive off along the track. A second car, matchbox-sized at this distance, was approaching across the moor. Peckover would have given a quid for binoculars. Mike's car, or the approaching one, or both, would need to steer off the track on to the moor or another story would be available to the media. Head-On Collision in Totally Empty and Uninhabited 1,000 Square Miles of Scottish Heather.

Why was Posy so edgy? Potter's murder? Uncertainty over the future of the dig? The quarrel with Mike? Peckover accepted that she might be nervous and short-tempered by temperament. She was ferociously proprietory about the dig being hers, as now he supposed it was. Whatever the row with the boyfriend had been about, it was hardly going to render her into a pool of calm.

She would be on edge if she were frightened for her life, which she would be if she believed her mentor's killer to be a deranged type out to stop the dig. After Sir Gilbert, Posy. After Posy, Leah. Bob Geddes's impression had been that Posy was apprehensive and probably wouldn't say no to a police presence at the dig.

Well, she had it, for the moment. So far she gave no indication she'd prefer him to push off.

He said, 'Any reason anyone should want to close the dig down?'

'Never. Why should there be?'

'That's what I'm asking. 'Ow about the Druid lot? Could you be upsetting them, digging up holy Inverballoch?'

'What's holy about Inverballoch?'

'The Stones of Skelloch?'

'I'm not excavating the Stones of Skelloch.'

They watched the two cars advance on each other a mile away in the glen. The cars slowed and passed each other without incident.

He said, 'The laird, you're digging up his land.' Now for an uncopperly question. 'What you know of him, might he go to the limit to keep his acres unsullied?'

'How do you mean?'

'Commit murder to keep them pristine, prehistoric.'

'Dougal's likely to profit from anything we find. You must at least have discovered he's short of cash.'

'Just groping, miss.' He was not sure the question had been answered but never mind. 'Could there be some archaeological reason, I dunno, like scholarship, advancement in the olive grove of academe, for someone to want to be rid of one of our leading archaeologists?'

'I've no idea what you're trying to say.'

'I'm not sure myself.' She'd be a tough professor if that was what one day she would be. He could hear her snapping at her misbegotten students. Explain yourself! Where's your evidence? Twaddle! 'Isn't there rivalry?'

'Plenty.'

'Sounds unlikely though, scholars doing each other in. Academe has to be just about the last bastion of civilized man. And woman,' he added hastily. 'Humankind.'

'All you know. The knives are sharper in academe than any-where. The stakes are small and the egos fat.'

She walked off to Leah in the pit. My bottomless ignorance is too much for her, Peckover concluded, and he grinned.

Still, if Posy had murdered Potter she had reason to be very much on edge. Because she was young, healthy, of the female gender, and easy to look at didn't mean she was incapable of going to the extreme. Charlotte Corday, Clytemnestra, Lucretia Borgia, Lizzie Borden, the woman, what was her name, Victorian times – Madeleine Smith – who had got away with poisoning her husband, if she had poisoned him, under Scottish law's not proven verdict. Peckover was uncertain whether this line-up of harpies had been young and beautiful, or come to that if they were harpies. Feminists would probably admire them. Point was that Posy Cork might be obsessed enough with her dig to kill sooner than see all the acclaim, promotion, articles in scholarly journals, stolen from her by Sir Gilbert. Assuming, of course, she would dig up something beyond butter and Roman pennies. Personally he did not find Roman penetration this far north riveting but he was not an archaeologist. He would have liked a look at her mental health records but unless she had been in trouble with the law or in therapy there wouldn't be any.

Of all the guests at the Ram, Posy Cork was the one Potter had known best and might most readily have opened his Waverley Suite door to. Mike would need to be asked if Posy had left their room during the night. And had she spent the rest of the night scrubbing her clothes in the bathroom?

Mike wouldn't know though. He'd have been sleeping the sleep of the Burns Night stewed.

The car drew up behind Peckover's Toyota. He started towards Posy on the rim of the deep end of the hole. She was looking down and telling Leah, 'No, you did right, keep it covered.' Leah, kneeling on cardboard, brushed with one hand, knuckled her back with the other. When Posy noticed Peckover on his way she intercepted him and said, 'If you want to catch the laird you shouldn't waste too much time. He was off to see someone so he'll not be home long.'

'See who?'

'I don't know. I think the library.'

'Inverballoch has a library?'

'He doesn't live in Inverballoch, he lives in Dundrummy. A travelling library.'

'I'll be on my way then. Keep what covered?'

'What?'

'You just told Leah to keep it covered.'

'The ground where we dig. Cardboard helps protect the ground and us. Housemaids get housemaid's knee, we get archaeologist's knee.'

'You should try knee pads. Foam rubber like coal miners wear.' He had no idea whether coal miners wore knee pads. 'And gardeners. You're expecting company?'

'No. Who?'

She followed the policeman's gaze to the two figures trudging towards the dig from the newly parked car.

'Your friends, not mine,' she said.

Peckover smiled a smile like thread. The two bundled bodies wending up the moor were not his friends more than hers. If she were innocent of stabbing Gilbert Potter, and afraid, the police were her best friends. Why did she suddenly want to be rid of him? Peckover worked to clear his head of the glaringly obvious reason for the woman's confusion and ill-humour. PMS. Miriam would have ground him to dust for considering it.

The arrivals up the moor drew closer, swaddled in fur, wool, headpieces, and dabbing at sweat. They were Scots who knew no better than foreigners what to expect from Scotland's weather.

Superintendent Geddes took off his hat and gloves and said, 'A fine view.'

Peckover made motioning gestures – Geddes to Posy, Posy to Alec Gillespie, Gillespie and Geddes to sunken Leah – introducing everyone in case they had forgotten whether they had met or not.

'This is the dig,' he said grandly. 'Where the butter came from.'

Geddes said, 'Impressive in its way.' He asked Posy, 'Any new finds today?'

'Not so far,' Posy lied, and eyed her muddy sneakers.

She had not herself seen what was new but Leah had.

'New thoughts? Old thoughts? Anything that might help us? Anything you saw or heard in the night?'

'Nothing.'

'Would it be fair to assume you knew Sir Gilbert probably better than anyone else at the dinner?'

'It's possible. I don't know who at the dinner knew him. I didn't know any of them – hardly any of them. Someone at the dinner killed him?'

'I didn't say that. I'm saying we look to you for help. How long had you known Sir Gilbert – professionally?'

'I certainly didn't know him any other way. Four years?'

'Where did you meet?'

'Oxford. I went to his lectures. I was on his team at the lake village dig at Maldon.'

'Maldon. Some traces, megaliths, press coverage, but no lake village. Am I right?'

'We hadn't the funds. It would have been an immense project and Sir Gilbert had so many other irons in the fire.'

Peckover wondered what they were talking about. Bob Geddes had evidently done some homework. Probably from Sir Gilbert's *Who's Who* entry on the computer. Alec Gillespie, looking about him, didn't appear to be listening.

Geddes said, 'Without Sir Gilbert you think you'll receive funds for Inverballoch?'

'Yes. I hope so. Why not?'

'You'll be able to carry on without him?'

Watch it, Peckover wanted to warn the superintendent. Touchy matter, this.

'Yes.'

'From your knowledge of Sir Gilbert are there those who didn't take to him?'

'You mean enemies?'

Peckover examined his hatband. He was curious to hear if Posy would say that she personally had been deeply fond of the old boy. His impression was that if Sir Gilbert had attempted more than a peek at her private and particular Inverballoch dig she would have poked her finger in his eye.

Geddes said, 'Anything you tell us will be treated in confidence.'

'No enemies I know of. Rivals, yes. They go with the territory.'

'What territory's that?'

'Scholarship.'

'Scholarship's hardly an endeavour that provokes murder.'

'It's just as well.'

'Do we know anything of his private life?'

'I didn't know he had one. He never married, far as I know. Any private life was probably his London clubs.'

Geddes caressed the dimple in his chin and said, 'Miss Cork, thank you. Anything at all that occurs to you, you'll let us know.'

'I will.'

'Don't let us impede your labours.'

Posy opened her mouth, thought twice, and closed it. Peckover approved. She had probably been on the verge of remarking that coppers were the last people she would allow to impede her labours. Something gracious.

The policemen sauntered past the piled canvas, out of earshot.

'Apologies, Henry,' Geddes said. 'You'll have been through all that already. Any discrepancies?'

'Hard to spot discrepancies when she's not telling us anything.'

'Because she doesn't know anything or because she won't say?'

'Hate to say this but so far I've no opinion on that. She's pretty possessive about this dig. If Potter had lived to dabble in it and interfere and claim credit he'd have had on his 'ands an enemy about on the level of a hag from hell.'

'As well for him he's been plucked to that kinder, gentler dig in the sky.' The superintendent's forefinger indecently assaulted the dimple, soothing away its troubles. 'No laird?'

'I missed 'im,' Peckover said. 'He may 'ave gone home, Laird Hall, then to some mobile library. My guess is she invented the library and she's had enough police presence because Leah Howgego is in the process of digging something up. More butter, I wouldn't wonder. That was Mike Trelawny passed you on the road. Miss Cork's close friend except they're 'aving a tiff. I've not asked what about or 'ow serious but if she's not with him at the Ram in a couple of hours he's off back to London, he says.'

'She doesn't appear to be rushing back to the Ram.'

They watched Posy taking her time with a tape measure and notebook in the dig's shallow end.

'Anything else?' Geddes said.

'Trelawny's an expert on Druids. Next to nothing's known about Druids so his expertise isn't going to win 'im any prizes. But they went in for 'uman sacrifice.'

'Is this a jest?' Inspector Gillespie enquired.

The question took Peckover and Geddes by surprise. Geddes had assumed Alec Gillespie to be off in his world of industrials, bonds, blue-chip stocks, treasuries, Eurodollar deposits, buyouts, rallies, issues, and options. Peckover's surprise was that Alec Gillespie's voice so suited his appearance, as sepulchral as the gaunt face and frame. Without make-up or rehearsal Gillespie could have played Mephistopheles.

Peckover said, 'No jest. I'm not your Druid expert but what we do know is they sacrificed each other. Terminally.'

'I'm not interested in what they did to each other,' Gillespie said. 'I'm asking do Druids warrant our attention?'

'Everything warrants our attention at this stage unless you know something I don't. Inverballoch has a stone circle. The Skelloch Stones. The dottier of our latter-day Druids, spiritual progeny of the priests of God knows 'ow many millennia ago, might consider it their duty to sacrifice anyone tinkering with their holy places.'

'Och, gammon. Trelawny said that?'

'He seemed to imply it.'

68

'Our expert witness seemed to imply it?' Alec the Crypt. Where had he parked his scythe? 'Might not a judge and jury have a wee difficulty with "seemed to imply"?'

'Trelawny was 'alfway down the mountain, mate. I'll pump 'im on the details next time I see 'im.'

'Mountain?'

'Hill then.' Peckover offered up a quick prayer that he be granted patience. 'Hump. Hummock. Hogback. Bonnie brae. Whatever you call this slope. Slopes, dunnit? Ascends. Up. Obliquely up in the sense of gaining altitude, not losing it, though it does that too, does both, depending where you 'appen to be, down or up. Where we are, looking down, it's upwardly sloping into, eventually, if it didn't level off 'ere, the stratosphere.'

'Stratosphere?'

'Seriously, you ever thought of seeking treatment? You've got galloping echolalia.'

'Echolalia?'

'Gor! Parrotomania!'

'Parrotomania?'

A little late, Peckover apprehended that Gillespie might be putting him on. The teasing and testing of Scotland Yard for the later regalement of intimates in the lounge bar. Och, wasna the puir Sassenach tatty-pow sae fashed he'd hae throttled ma thrapple had he kenned 'twas the clavers Ah'm bletherin'?

Peckover said genially, 'Up yours.'

'Aye, sir. Mutual.'

'Gentlemen,' Geddes pleaded

'Agreed,' Peckover said. 'Did you see Dinwiddie?'

'He's mystified, claims to be, but he must have left his dirk on the carving plate with the haggis and that's the last he saw of it. The waiter who removed the plate to tidy up the haggis confirms the dirk was there. He thought it was supposed to be there, a showpiece, and left it there. He returned the plate to the table so that anyone wanting extra haggis could help themselves and pass it on. You were all served individual plates with the food already on them, is that right?'

'Right.'

'This was the seating plan.' Geddes unfolded a sheet of paper. 'Was it? As best you remember?'

Peckover fished out his spectacles and found at the end of the T his name, H. Peckover, between Alice McSporran and Richard

Haig, vice chairman. Sir Gilbert, Dinwiddie, Dougal Duncan, Posy Cork, Mike Trelawny, and Leah Howgego seemed correctly seated. He knew none of the twenty or thirty other names. Named at the foot of the page were Miriam Peckover, the housekeeper, piper, and serving staff.

'What spot does the X mark?'

'Where the waiter put the haggis back on the table. Here's where the waitress cleared it from back to the kitchen before the dessert. Near you, in fact. It travelled a fair bit.'

Peckover tucked away his glasses. 'So we ask everyone if they 'ad a second helping from the plate and did they notice Dinwiddie's dirk on it?'

'We're asking. How about yourself?'

'I remember the plate because there was that savaged loaf of haggis.' Peckover bared his teeth and looked up at the sky, trying to recollect. 'I don't remember the dirk. I imagine I would 'ave if it had been there, all that mother-of-pearl or whatever it is. I'd have picked it up and fondled it for the sensation.'

'What sensation might that be?' enquired Gillespie the Tomb.

'Never found out, did I. Never 'eld it. I 'ad a sheath knife when I was a Boy Scout. Wouldn't cut anything but thrilling to hold. Yaaagh!' His fist holding an invisible sheath knife lunged through the air. '*Et tu, Brute!*'

'Your literary references do you credit,' intoned the Angel of Death.

Geddes said, 'Time to beard the laird. You coming, Henry?'

'Mightn't it give 'im a heart attack, three biggish cheeses descending? All we lack is your chief constable and the Lord 'Igh Executioner.'

'If the laird murdered Potter and the heart attack's mortal it'll be a handy saving of judge-and-jury time and taxpayers' money.'

Superintendent Geddes walked to the dug rectangle, Gillespie at his side. Peckover surveyed the mildew-green Glen of Inverballoch and wondered, not for the first time, when he would be home again with Miriam and the children. He caught up with his colleagues. When all was said he would be happy to see Potter's murderer brought to justice. If he could help, he would.

Posy was writing on a paper on a clipboard. Leah, kneeling, stood up when Geddes asked if she had helped herself to seconds of haggis and did she recall the chairman's dirk on the plate? She stood less out of respect, Peckover suspected, than because here

70

was an excuse to stand, stretch, and arch her back. No, she said, no seconds and no knife, though she hadn't really noticed. Had she enjoyed the haggis? asked Geddes to jog her memory. Leah, unjogged, said she had eaten some. Geddes tipped his hat. Dissatisfied, flanked by Inspector Gillespie and Scotland Yard, he set off down the moor.

Only when the policemen's cars began to drive away did Posy cast aside the cardboard in the dig's deep end. She and Leah knelt and delicately brushed away soil, exposing after some minutes the extremity of possibly a finger.

'I'm terrified,' Leah whispered, though for miles around there was no one to hear.

'Me too,' said Posy.

'We can't continue. Not without more preparation and a team.'

'You don't have to tell me. Look, we're not exhuming it. We only want an idea of how much there is. How it lies.'

Both women were perspiring, though hardly from physical effort. This was not pickaxe work. They brushed with the delicacy of picture restorers.

Four fingers and a thumb.

A hand.

A wrist.

They sat back on their heels and stared at each other.

'More?' Posy said.

'Yes,' said Leah.

'Try about there,' Posy said, pointing. 'For the feet. I'll try for the head, if there is one.'

TEN

Doun the brae frae auld Killiekrankie
Came the blue bonnets wi' Wee Willie Wankie.

H. Peckover, *Poems*

A creature in a cape fiddled with the fastening of the gate into
the field.

'Company,' said Ramona.

'I'm not blind,' said Dave, her common law husband and head
Druid.

'He's black. It is male, is it? Weird gear. Could he be one of us?'

'You flatter yourself. With a car like that? That's last year's
Fiesta.'

'Might be stolen.'

'Might. I want no aggro. We'll see if he's up for bridge. We'll
bring in Priscilla if she's not stoned.'

'Why not blackjack?'

'Behave, baby.'

'Dollar a point. We could win the Fiesta.'

'We offer him every civility and the way out.'

'Dave?'

'Yes?'

'Don't offer him food.'

'What food? Go play with your yo-yo, darling.'

The black male in the weird gear, an urban person unused to
farm gates, failed to manipulate the bent bar in the iron hoop that
would open the gate. He vaulted over the gate and dropped
balletically into the field. A dog the size of a moose charged
towards him.

'Grendel, heel!' somebody called.

Detective Constable Twitty would have agreed he might look a

72

little weird. He believed he would look still weirder after Grendel had finished with him, though not outstandingly so by comparison with the tatterdemalion dozen or so Druids. They sat about distantly and doing nothing much. None raced to his rescue. If they were London Druids they might be comatose from the Highlands air. Druids, dissenters, ravers, freakniks, second-generation flower people, New Age travellers, lager louts – whatever. He hadn't heard them speak yet, they might be German soccer hooligans camping out in readiness for a Germany–Scotland match. The Um-louts. He would offer the fancy to Our 'Enry for a poem.

His opera cloak's chief drawback had been its aroma of camphor and mushrooms, even more powerful than the reek of penury from the fake sable coat over which he dashingly wore it. He had splashed several ounces of his Aramis cologne onto the cloak, and now that he was in the winy outdoors the overall pong was diminished, he could live with it. Its effect on anybody who came close enough for a whiff, or on any charging animal, remained to be seen.

Twitty estimated that he had five seconds in which to do whatever had to be done to ward off being struck as if by a tank and gulped whole. Perhaps ten if the beast tripped. Grendel was its name? This was the way it ended?

He had felt himself lucky to have the cloak. Closed had been the Ram's gift shop, so he had driven to the village and homed in on the Annie Menzies Antiques Emporium, a terraced shop on Argyll Street adjacent to a door with a comforting sign, Police. The door to the police station had been locked and its window curtained as if closed for the season. Also closed had been the Annie Menzies Antiques Emporium and the other six or seven shops in downtown Inverballoch's business district. Except that as he had peered through the window, the door of the Antiques Emporium had creaked open and a frail, sylph-sized woman older than any of her antiques had shuffled out and plucked him in. First she had enthused about a stuffed six-inch lizard, a child relative of Nessie the Loch Ness Monster itself, she assured him. Next, the sword fought with by Robert the Bruce, no less, at a famous victory at Bannockburn. The sword was a strip of metal that looked to have fallen off an airplane. Then a clearly historic spade or shovel consisting of a rusted blade and four shattered inches of broken-off shaft or heft that should have been put out for the any-old-iron man and his cart a half century ago or whenever the Antiques Emporium had set up in the business of conning the tourists.

''Tis the spade of St Patrick himself!' she had whispered.

'Oh my!' he had whispered back.

'The holy saint of Ireland who shooed out the snakes and allowed priests to wed. Did ye ken that?'

'No.'

They were still whispering.

'Born in Kilpatrick, spitting distance from here, by Dumbarton, and swept off to Ireland by pirates. Going for a song it is, this lovely spade.'

'I could never afford it.'

'Two pounds.'

She's shameless, he had thought. Then he had spotted the shroud. At first sight he had taken the inky, smelly, threadbare, capacious garment to be a horse blanket. At second look it was possessed of what seemed intriguingly like a hood.

Annie Menzies – he had by now little doubt that the saleslady was the owner of the shop and had been for most of the twentieth century – had informed him that this was the opera cloak worn by Donizetti at the first night of *Lucia di Lammermoor*. How much? he had asked. Five pounds, Annie had said, quick as a fox. He had considered five pounds a snip for a historic opera cloak. She could not sell it to him though, she said. Today was the Sabbath. She would pin a Sold tag to it and he could collect it in the morning. He had suggested he wouldn't buy it, he would borrow it, and the five-pound note he was placing on the table was a donation to the Scottish Lifeboat Association. Annie had said, 'Och, ye're a cannie laddie, ye'll gang far,' and should she wrap it? He had left the Antiques Emporium with Donizetti's opera cloak bundled in the *Daily Record*. Incontestably the apparel for the Black Druid of Inverballoch.

'Grendel, heel!' cried again the voice from the Druid encampment.

Deaf Grendel, a blur, a mix of Dobermann, Norwegian elkhound, Aberdeen Angus, and jabberwock, sped like a train across the field and with a bound cannoned into the intruder, striking him with forepaws, foaming muzzle, and two hundred pounds of chest and abdomen. Only the gate against the Black Druid's back prevented man and dog going full length together.

'Grendel!' called the unavailing voice.

The beast vertically straddled Twitty. Its slobbery tongue raked his face from chin to temples.

'Gerroff, you brute!' Twitty gasped. 'Good Grendel! Grendel, walkies!'

With a judo hold dimly recalled from a Metropolitan Police probationers' course he wrestled Grendel to the grass. Grendel barked in his ear, a percussive sound like a howitzer. The hound's tongue, the texture of a grade twelve silicon-carbide sandpaper in spite of its coating of drool, lashed Twitty's nose and mouth with affection. Portions of Donizetti's cloak were taking a beating from paws and sputum. Man and dog rocked to left, to right, in lewd embrace. The monster's chops clashed and slavered, its tail thrashed the air. A brusque knee from Twitty into its ribs sent it circling and howling in rapture. This allowed the Black Druid an instant in which to rise and set totteringly off for the encampment, dodging Grendel's assaults and attempting nonchalance, no easy task with the creature springing up at him, barking in ecstasy, and spraying his face with mutton-flavoured dribble.

'Down!' Twitty swept Grendel's front feet from his shoulders and increased his pace.

Grendel lusted for his body, no question, unless it was the aromatic opera cloak. Here at any rate, in front of him, or they soon would be if he survived Grendel, sat two Druids, male and female, on collapsible beach chairs, not intervening. They watched his prancing approach like United Nations observers. They wore jeans and parkas. He looked more like a Druid than they did.

In the field beyond was the start of a promising scrapyard: two resprayed jalopies, a van with cardboard where rear windows once had been, and a lorry that was largely the cabin, having lost most of the posterior box that was the point of a lorry. A pair of legs protruded from beneath the cabin, whence rang out metallic hammerings. Also, two tents of the kind given to children for a birthday, and a campfire picturesquely smouldering. Nobody sat singing by the campfire, or cooking, or feeding it, so presumably it would soon go out. There were dogs less extrovert than Grendel, and similarly unconcerned children. Inevitable rock music thudded from somewhere. A man draped garments, possibly laundered, on the lower branches of the only tree in the field. Several other adults converged in no great haste on the Grendel hullabaloo. Figures in a Landscape. Perhaps the day's first excitement for them. The second if they had taken part in the murder at the Ram.

Grendel bounced high and would have licked the nose from the Black Druid's face had he not nimbly swerved. The frothing, peach-coloured tongue pasted saliva across Twitty's ear. When he halted in front of the pair on the beach chairs, the animal lay down across his jogging boots, tail thumping.

The Black Druid raised the palm of his hand and announced, 'Hail!'

From his chair the man stared through steel-rimmed spectacles. He lifted his hand and said, 'Hail.'

The woman glanced at her companion, looked at the visitor, raised her hand, and said, 'Hail.'

Twitty was delighted. He had got the greeting right.

'I am a brother seeking fellow brotherdom,' he declared. 'And sisterdom.'

Once, at dawn on a Saturday, in uniform, he had been assigned to patrol the fringes of a conventicle of Druids on Clapham Common. They had been Druids without the wherewithal to travel to Stonehenge or Camelot or wherever the Druids with transport had assembled. From what he had overheard, the speech of some of them had had an incantatory ring like the chorus in *Oedipus Rex*. A few had worn white robes and waved incense braziers and boughs snapped from oak trees. The majority had been in street clothes but these too had waved leafy branches. They had all circled peaceably about waving their oak branches and chanting, and the white-robed Venerable Chief Druid, aged about thirty-five, had raised his arms high and called out in a Harrods accent, 'Arise, O sun!', whereupon nothing happened, or not for another twenty minutes, his timing having been off.

The conversational matter of most of the Druids had been sex and football in a South London accent. Twitty knew which of the two forms of druidical accent he would choose now that he was himself a Druid. Here was his chance to throb sonorously. Every day of the week in Brixton he communicated in sarf Lunnun, dint 'e? Like wot the Guv spoke, Our 'Enry, except 'e wuz norf o' the river. Same difference.

Thank God for his scholarship-boy grounding in the vowels and articulation of Harrow!

'I too,' quoth the Black Druid in a rich tremolo, 'have summoned our gods at solstice-time. I too have borne the oak bough.'

'You're the press,' the woman said.

'Wrong,' said the man in the steel-rimmed glasses. 'He's the police. Hello. I'm Dave.'

'Ramona,' said Ramona.

Twitty retained his composure. They were guessing. They had never seen him before and he looked less like the police than he looked like a Druid, apart from being black, and for all he knew there might be black Druids. If there weren't there ought to be. Druids believed in peace, harmony, the equilibrium of man and nature, oak trees, and watching the sun come up. Druids weren't the Ku Klux Klan, though in their white dressing-gowns there was a resemblance. From his briefing on the Clapham Common Druids he recalled that a Most Ancient Order of Druids existed, two hundred years old and respectable. He raised his hand again, showing the palm like Sitting Bull.

'Dave and Ramona,' he intoned, 'I bring greetings from the south-east chapter of the Most Royal and Ancient Order of Druids.'

'That's nice,' said Ramona.

'Greetings to you from the Royal and Ancient golf club of St Andrews,' said Dave.

'I understand your scepticism and I sympathize.' Twitty did not sympathize in the least. He was becoming angry and his feet had begun to ache under the weight of Grendel. He felt like a petitioner in front of a king and queen on their thrones. 'As travelling people, trespassing, polluting, blighting the landscape, leaving behind a mess of garbage, your dogs savaging sheep, slaughtering poultry—'

'Now wait a minute.'

'—you may feel there are occasions when the police persecute you—'

'Yes, we do tend to feel that.'

'—with the result that you are suspicious of strangers, paranoid even to a point where in your fevered imaginings any visitor is the enemy until proven otherwise.'

'No one said you're the enemy,' Dave said. 'You're just not a Druid. You made it to the bar in the Ram in time for sausages and what was it – pineapple juice? We were down the other end of the bar. When it closed we cleared off. You presumably stayed for the press conference.'

'Doesn't make me not a Druid.'

'Oh, be a Druid. Be what you like.'

'All right, I'm not then. I thought I'd try to infiltrate for a story.'

Gladly, Twitty abandoned druidism. The role had been making him petulant like John Major.

He said, 'I'm with the *Post*.'

'With that mink coat and tatty burnous?' Dave said. 'Moroccan, is it? No offence but you look like Count Dracula meets Oscar Wilde. The press dress down, they're inconspicuous. My experience anyway. You, friend, are that rare species – statistically one in a hundred – an ethnic minority copper.'

'The *Post*,' Twitty growled. 'Willie Winkler, home news and features.' Never would he admit that steel-rimmed Dave was right and had been from the start. 'You lot may be worth half a page. Free spirits on the open road, but here's the angle, wherein lies freedom? You know the sort of thing.'

'Too well.'

Grendel's tail gave a thump. The ground shuddered.

'Willie Winkie, did ye say?' said one of a court trio who, deeply suspicious, had arrived behind the king and queen and stayed out of curiosity.

The Black Druid started to raise his palm having forgotten that he was the *Post*. He used the hand to pluck back the cowl, revealing a fizz of hair in a state of shock.

The courtiers were two weatherbeaten women and an unshaved tough, a Scot by the sound of him, unlike the king and queen. He may have been only semi-tough, or not tough at all, but he was shorn and beneath his sleeves probably tattooed. He was the one wanting to know about Willie Winkie and was surely, Twitty feared, about to recite.

' "Wee Willie Winkie runs through the toon",' recited the putative tough, ' "upstairs and doonstairs in his nicht-goon." Is it bananas ye're here for, Winkie?'

Ramona said, 'None of that.'

'Canna ye tak' a joke? What's this aboot then? If it's a polis reconnaisance afore they come in with their truncheons, Ah'm aff hame tae Dunfermline.'

Wherever Dunfermline might be it was where the king sat drinking the blude-red wine, Twitty unexpectedly recalled from some tragic ballad or other. A different king from this one in the glasses.

He said to the tough, 'What's your name?'

'Derek.'

Not too tough, not with the name Derek.

Derek said, 'Ah'd still like tae ken what's it a' aboot.'

'It's about the murder at the Ram,' King Dave said. 'So get your stories right.'

ELEVEN

Detection is, or ought to be, an exact science, and should be treated in the same cold and unemotional manner.
Sir Arthur Conan Doyle, *The Sign of Four*

Detective Constable Twitty brought out his notebook. Grendel, sensing tedium, rose from Twitty's feet and lay down across the feet of Dave and Ramona.

Twitty asked Dave, 'How long have you been whatever you describe yourself as? Druid, New Age knight of the road, nomad, vagabond, pagan, anarchist—?'

'All of those. Couple of years.'

'What did you do before?'

If anything, Twitty was tempted to add.

'Sessions musician.'

That stopped Twitty short. Top sessions musicians earned sixty, seventy pounds an hour. There were no bottom sessions musicians. Either you delivered or you didn't get hired. Same as performing with the Royal Philharmonic. He would have adored to have been a sessions musician if he had played a musical instrument. Sessions musicians were pros.

'What instrument?'

'Clarinet?'

Clarinet! His dad had a zillion Benny Goodman records that weren't bad, some of them.

'How long?'

'Twenty-five inches? I never measured it.'

'There's mony a lass has,' said Derek, grinning.

'Dave, ye cocky braggart,' the first female courtier said with a whooping laugh.

'Cocky and stuck-up!' said the second courtier, squealing with merriment. They were hardly able to keep their balance from the wit of it all.

Ramona said, 'Infantile.'

'Not Dave's,' said Derek.

The courtiers fell about with mirth. Ramona threw a beseeching look to heaven. Dave, who had started it, tried not to smile.

He said, 'Eight years.'

Twitty opened his notebook. Time to attempt a show of gravitas if it wasn't too late. He wrote down the figure eight.

'London?' he said.

'There's nowhere else for a sessions player.'

'You gave that up for this?'

Twitty guessed that the pop music world gave Dave up. Drugs, dissipation.

'Not drugs,' said mind-reader Dave, 'and nothing wrong with, as you call it, this.' He gestured at the horizon of mauve mountains. His other hand reached down and plucked at Grendel's ear. The tail thudded. 'The rock scene's a zoo. I was becoming a basket case.'

'A rich one.'

'There's money.'

'So why this?' Twitty gazed disapprovingly at the mountains, appropriate for sheep and tourists. 'You could retire to Bali.'

'Spare me.'

'Nice flat in Notting Hill then.'

'I don't have a penny.'

Twitty wrote in his notebook, *penny*. Gambling, he supposed.

Ramona said, 'He gave it away.'

'You did – he did?' A likely story. 'Who to?'

'What's it matter?' Ramona, answering for her man, sounded disgruntled. 'Oxfam got four thousand.'

Dave fondled Grendel's ear. He showed no interest in the matter. Twitty strove to quell feelings of guilt over this litter lout, chicken thief, tramp, druggie, sexual swankpot, and bandit who turned out to be a musical genius and a saint. Maybe. He sketched a smiley face except the smile was a scowl. The court jesters watched him in anticipation of he had no idea what.

He asked Ramona, 'And you, ma'am, in your former life?'

'For Druids all life is former life and all life is to come,' Ramona said. 'The soul is immortal and at death passes from one person to another.'

'What I had in mind was your former life before you took to the open road.' Like Toad of Toad Hall in his roadster going: 'O bliss! O poop-poop! O my! O my!'

Alternatively, not in the least like classy Toad. Twitty eyed the blotchily spray-painted bangers in the field.

'I sang,' Ramona said.

'Have I heard of you?'

Twitty modestly considered himself an expert on the rock scene. He'd have made a better critic than any of the current crop. If he had not opted for copperdom he might by now have been editor of the *New Musical Express*. He could not recall a Ramona anyone. Singers were out there in droves though. Nobody could have heard of them all. You didn't have to be able to sing to be a singer.

'No, you haven't,' she said.

She had glossy black hair, though it might have been dyed. Twitty wondered where she washed it now she was a Druid. He had seen streams but they would be freezing. Perhaps she slipped into the ladies between beers at the Ram.

She added, 'You might have heard the voice.'

'Sessions stuff?'

She named several TV commercials including one for British Airways that used to interrupt every programme that had begun to be interesting. Ramona had been the voice. Now that he listened more attentively her voice did have quite a meaty timbre. Asking for trouble, he sang, 'British Airways right on tra-a-ack—'

The courtiers joined in, then Ramona, arms aloft and waving, and for the wailing crescendo even Dave.

'—takes you there and brings you' – vibrant pause, and then, *molto affettuoso*, – 'ba-a-ack!'

Twitty thought it as well the Guv was not present. Henry liked to sing. Give him a singer and a clarinettist, he'd have had everyone singing until three in the morning.

He said to Dave, 'You mentioned a murder at the Ram. What murder?'

'Gilbert Potter. You have other murders?'

'You said, "Get your stories straight." A joke, I assume.'

'I'm afraid so.'

'Where did you hear about Potter?'

'On the radio. At the Ram. They were talking about nothing else in that Rob Roy Bar.'

'Where were you between midnight and morning today?'

'Thought you'd never ask. Here. Asleep.'

Remembering his notebook, Twitty wrote, *Asleep*.

'The rest of you?'

'Here, best I know. You'd have to ask them.'

'How many are you?'

'A dozen? I don't do numbers.'

'You're the leader though.'

'No leaders. I happened to be the first in your path when you came gambolling in.'

'May I see your driving licence?'

Twitty supposed he had blown it as far as the *Echo* went. The *Post* rather. He felt dull-witted. He had failed as both Druid and newshound because here was Dave digging out his wallet which he probably wouldn't have done for anybody except the police.

David Paul Webster, 139 Westbourne Terrace, etc.

Twitty wrote it down. This was police work, donkey work, getting it down. He would have liked to be not getting it down but to have been somewhere with these two, anywhere, talking music. Bean bags, candles, a decent CD playing, smoke if they smoked. Dave would ripple and mourn on his clarinet, Ramona's contralto would grieve and celebrate. Trouble with being a copper, you mustn't get too close. These two might be murderers. What did he know about them?

He asked Ramona for her licence, union card, some or any identification. She sighed and set off towards the vehicles.

He asked Dave, had he known Potter?

No.

Heard of him?

Possibly, not particularly, perhaps in the press.

Seen, heard, anything, anyone, out of the ordinary last night, today, and how long had they, he, and Ramona and the rest of them been camped here?

No, no, and six or seven weeks.

How long did they intend to stay?

Hadn't considered it. Did it matter? Not for ever.

The courtiers had sloped off. He, DC Twitty on duty, had to go after them.

Only one was able to produce identification, the plump miss with the cocky-and-stuck-up quip. He wrote down who the others said they were and the registration of their festering heaps. The Druid who had been hanging out laundry placed a hand on his,

83

Twitty's, coiffed head and said, 'Curly Locks, Curly Locks, wilt thou be mine?' Twitty swatted the hand away. They were strong on nursery rhymes, these Druids. He lifted the flap of a child's tent and discovered two women with the *Times* crossword and a dictionary. They were his age, thereabouts, and gorgeous but grimy. He would have invited either or both for a night on the town after they'd had a shower. Neither had any ID, or they said they hadn't. He wrote down who they claimed they were. One was from Bradford, the other was Welsh, from Llanrwst, which he couldn't spell. He lingered in the tent's opening in case they might need his help with the crossword. He would thrill them with solutions whereupon they would throw off their clothes in gratitude. The page in the notebook was filling up. That was good. He would numb the Guv with detail.

Should he note down the four filled trashbags? Here was environmental correctness. If you overlooked the vehicles, tents, laundry, people, and dogs, the camp was quite spruce. He peered through the rear window of the van at suitcases, one with its lid open to show jumbled clothes. Around it lay shoes, books, and perhaps somewhere a clarinet. Propped against the side of the van were a shovel and something technological that he was unsure about, a sort of disc on a stick, not unlike the mine detectors that soldiers walked forward with in newsreels.

An Aryan-type child aged six or seven, scabby-kneed, probably male, came towards him pointing a plastic rifle with a complex system of knobs and cogs. The child said, 'I've got a surge gun,' in an accent like the Queen's. 'And your name?' softly asked the Black Druid – with children he could be the Black Druid – awed and squatting, Biro poised. 'Pegasus,' answered the child with such flawless enunciation that he could only have said Pegasus. Elsewhere a commotion had erupted, mainly a maniacal barking. Twitty looked round. Grendel was galloping through the grass. Someone had opened the gate and was coming through.

Two people. A box-shaped woman and a gangling man, except that the man was retreating unchivalrously behind the gate. The woman, presumably blind and deaf, held her ground, the same ground into which she was about to be flattened and defiled by charging Grendel. She had a stick which she threw underarm with commendable vigour.

'Fetch!' she commanded.

Airborne Grendel twisted about, skidded into the woman's legs, scrambled up, and hurtled baying and foaming after the stick. The woman advanced on the camp, fearless. She had little to fear because Grendel, for all the raw energy and theatrics, could not find the stick yet had no intention of giving up, and made pouncing, snuffling sorties in the stick's general area. The gangling man in pebble glasses came through the gate with caution.

Twitty recognised the press. Mavis and the *Dundee Advertiser* who had tried to beard the Guv and Mr Geddes before the press conference. Was it the *Post* or the *Echo* he had told them he was with? Time to go before they accosted him and insisted on pooling information. He strode back to the king and queen and said, 'We'll be in touch.'

'No hurry,' said the queen.

'Right on,' said the king.

Twitty veered left to avoid oncoming Mavis, which left him aimed towards Grendel. Dave and Ramona's farewells had been pretty perfunctory, sending him on his way. No invitation to a clarinet gig. Grendel rootled about oblivious, perhaps on to the scent of something more enticing than a stick, like rabbit piddle or a Highland vole.

'Hello there!' hailed Mavis from the east.

Twitty quickened his step.

'Constable Twitty?' she called. 'Jason?'

Jason indeed! Trouble with oldies, they thought they could get away with anything, such as familiarity. She had won though, she was tracking over to him. He could hardly run away. She arrived puffing and genial.

'Anything new, Jason?'

'Superintendent Geddes may hold a further press conference at a time to be announced,' Twitty said pompously.

She was not that old. He judged she could be a young grand-mother but not a great grand-mother. She wore tweeds and red galoshes, as if expecting rain. The *Dundee Advertiser* was distant but homing in.

'Bob and your guv'nor are with the laird, if he's at home,' Mavis said.

Bob? The guv'nor? The cheek!

Twitty said, 'I know.'

He hadn't known but he wasn't about to thank her for the information. With nothing else in mind he thought he might seek them out. He had no idea who the laird was or where he lived but he was not about to show his ignorance by asking this beldam.

'Sir Dougal Duncan at Dundrummy Castle,' she said. 'He was drifting round the Ram after the press conference.'

'Exactly.' He was? 'Why?'

'Picking up what he could.' The beldam found a packet of cigarettes in her handbag. 'If the dig's at an end he stands to lose money, poor lamb. So go back to Inverballoch, the old kilt mill is down the road on the right, and take the B22 north. You'll pass close to the dig, up on a hill, but if you want to visit it you have to get off the road and leave the car. There's a boulder you could break your axle on where the track starts. Stay on the B22 for the castle. It's another fifteen minutes, about a quarter of a mile past an empty croft on the left. Don't expect Balmoral. Jason, that's a sensational cloak. I'll see you in the bar. Six o'clock.'

'Madam, I very much doubt it.'

'Seven then. Bob and your 'Enry will be there barring the unforeseen.'

'Miss, be informed that – aaargh!'

A mountain of fur and drool crashed to the ground between them. Grendel dropped at their feet the stick or a stick. The *Dundee Advertiser* was circumspectly on the retreat again.

Twitty tugged a jogging-booted foot from under Grendel's paw, observed the stick, and told Mavis, 'Your idea, you deal with it.'

'Druids in January? What's your opinion, Jason? Aren't Druids a summer phenomenon, on the whole?' She lit a cigarette. 'Don't you think it a little fishy?'

The failed Black Druid and *Echo* or *Post* put his rented car into reverse because parked against its front bumper was the big brown Honda of Mavis or the *Dundee Examiner*. He drove off as briskly as the cratered track allowed, resolved not after all to go hunting after the Guv, Mr Geddes, and Laird Drumgooley or whoever he was. The journalist woman's parting comment had further unsettled him. What was fishy about Druids in January? Why not Druids in January? The weather was not at all bad. No rain for two hours. If blizzards started up the Druids would presumably strike camp and go home, those who had homes. He would pen his report at the Ram and await the return of the Guv and Superintendent Geddes. He might make a start on Walter Scott. But he saw ahead a black-and-white signpost pointing off to the right, B22, so he followed it.

Deep into trackless wilderness, apart from this B22, drove Twitty. Was this that he was driving through, he wondered, a glen? To either side grazed sheep on mangy mountain slopes, though if you were in tourist mood, he would have conceded, the mountains might be breathtaking. The Fiesta purred onward, enjoying the outing, the only vehicle on the road. The lofty hill to his left, Brae Balloch – not that Twitty was aware it had a name – had a monument on top of it. The next hill, or the same hill but interrupted by a great dent, had, though a long way off, a look of something going on on it apart from sheep. A gash in the heather, a glint of metal. Looming in front of the rented Fiesta came a track that branched off the road, and a boulder.

Twitty braked and turned on to the track at 10 m.p.h., missing the boulder. If this was the reporter woman's jest at the expense of Scotland Yard he would not be pleased. The track obviously led nowhere. Neither had that been the only boulder. In places he had to slow to 5 m.p.h.

On the other hand, there ahead was parked a muddy estate car, and there up on the hill was the celebrated dig, or he guessed that was what it was. He discerned human life, possibly – something was moving – together with stuff not easily identifiable at this distance. A table, some piles of muck, an eyesore of a tin hut that might be the most vital item for miles if mixed archaeologists were up there digging for days, months at a stretch. Not a tree or bush anywhere, only bare grass and heather.

Twitty parked behind the estate car. He unfasted the Donizetti cape and dropped it on to the back seat. Away, Druidom! He unwound from the car, stretched, and inhaled the washed air once breathed by Burns, Annie Laurie, Andrew Carnegie ('The man who dies rich dies disgraced'), the American pirate John Paul Jones ('I have not yet begun to fight'), James Barrie ('Do you believe in fairies?'), and Burke and Hare, Edinburgh murderers of round about the 1820s. To burke was a dictionary word meaning to kill by strangling or suffocating so as to leave the body intact for medical dissection, he remembered from a law class. Delighted that he knew so much, DC Twitty filled again his lungs. With ballooning cheeks he exhaled. The human life on the hill, he noticed, was active, even animated, flapping about with a blanket.

'Quick, the pegs,' said Posy.
'Is it the press or the police?'

'What's the difference?'

Leah scampered with pegs and a mallet. Posy found herself wishing she were back in Chicago, so much calmer and more civilized than Inverballoch.

Barely half an hour since the two journalists had come probing, the woman in particular a nosy pain. Before them, the police, the more sinister for not being in blue but in everyday mufti. First the big Scotland Yard one with the cockney sparrow accent who came on like a favourite uncle. No doubt he'd have other methods of approach. Then the Scots pair, one of them dimpled, the other gaunt as a tree.

What was different about this latest visitor was that he was the first to climb the hill nimbly, like a goat.

His approach threw the young women into a minor panic as they pegged the canvas over the excavation's deep end. Whoever the new intruder was, he would be with them in two minutes rather than ten.

TWELVE

O me, why have they not buried me deep enough?
Alfred, Lord Tennyson, *Maud*

Given a choice he would not have chosen the mock sable, old-gold denim, and turtleneck for the workout up the hill, but after a day of sitting in an aeroplane, in a rented car, and standing about in the Ram, Twitty preferred an overdressed climb to no climb. The ground was tufty and hard, the sun a furry lemon. He arrived panting, exhilarated, and moist.

'Detective Constable Twitty' – gasp – 'enquiring into the murder of Sir Gilbert Potter,' Twitty announced, happy to be himself.

From somewhere in his cerebrum's memory drawer he recovered the name of Potter's student, leader of the dig.

'Posy Cork?' he asked the nearer of the two women who stood like sentries by the uncovered end of the trench.

'Leah Howgego.'

'I'm Posy Cork,' volunteered the other with a touch of impatience. 'Tribes of your colleagues have been here already.'

'A fresh eye, you never know, we can't afford to leave any stone unturned.' Twitty winced at his mindless drivel. 'Every little helps.'

'Mony a mickle maks a muckle,' Posy Cork said.

'Sorry?'

'Doesn't matter.'

Twitty frowned. Pert chit. Whatever what she had said meant, it hadn't sounded to brim with respect. He could hardly fault her because here he stood like a hollyhock with nothing to ask her that would not have been asked by the Guv and the Glasgow lot, and she probably knew it.

The best he could manage was, 'Packing it in for the day?'

'Some day. It's been nothing but interruptions.'

This too gave Twitty pause. Was he supposed to apologize?

He said, 'Today's different, wouldn't you agree?'

Posy Cork was silent on that. Leah Howgego seemed to be silent on everything. She was rubbing soil off her hands, working it well into the pores.

He said, 'So who exactly are these tribes who've been doing the interrupting?'

'The police, of course,' Posy said.

'Press?'

'Yes.'

'Anyone else?'

'No. Sir Dougal Duncan.'

No, Sir Dougal Duncan, suggested that Sir Dougal Duncan was either a nonentity or his presence so taken for granted that he was barely worth mentioning. Twitty had never heard of him before the reporter woman had named him an hour ago.

Yes he had. There was a Duncan in the file on the archaeologist who had gone missing in 1941. He could remember no inquiries he had started off on so woefully ignorant.

'Come here often, does he, Sir Dougal?'

'Why wouldn't he? It's his land. He's interested.'

'That's it, then? Nobody else?'

'No.'

Leah, cleaning her fingernails by nibbling them, glanced at Posy, a sideways flicker that was not lost on Twitty. Secrets? A difference of opinion? The tricky bit would be how to exploit it.

'You're certain?' he said, than which no follow-up could have been lamer.

'I should be. I've been here all day.'

Twitty took out his notebook and with it the tin whistle. He thrust the whistle back in the pocket and after fumblings found a Biro. He wrote, *Sir Dougal Duncan.* It was one of those names that worked equally well backwards. Sir Duncan Dougal. He knew of no law of nature which held that knights did not kill each other. Sir Dougal may have murdered Sir Gilbert. Somebody had. The thought that British taxpayers paid him to help bring villains to justice seldom struck Twitty but when it did he became uneasy.

He asked Leah, 'Perhaps you recall others?'

'Other what?'

'Visitors. Today.'

'Me?'

No, actually not you. The sheep on the mountain. The rippling breeze. How could you imagine I mean you?

He said, 'Some visitor or visitors other than the press, police, and laird?'

Like someone your Posy friend hadn't noticed because she's inattentive, digs with her eyes shut.

Another sub-standard question. How would the Guv have handled this? Leah now had soil on her cupid's bow. She was taking her time answering, eyes anxious behind the tortoiseshell. Perhaps anxiety was her permanent condition. Somewhere there would be for her a sensitive therapist who would soothe her brow and assure her she wasn't to blame, but he didn't see himself in the role. He preferred confidence in a woman. Not too much confidence, naturally.

'No,' Leah said.

Twitty had forgotten the question.

He said severely, 'All right then,' and wrote *No* in his notebook. The wind was brisk and his toes were feeling the chill.

'No Druids?' he said.

This time Leah and Posy looked at each other squarely and with utter blankness. Then at their visitor. Twitty waited. They had heard the question. If it baffled them, they were not alone

Posy said, 'The Druids are the only people who've not been here.'

'But you're aware of them.'

'I've seen them from the road if we're talking about the same people. The one from London asked about them. Peckover?' Posy too was now looking concerned. 'Are you, they, the Druids – um, do you? You know? I mean is there? Like anything?'

'Your meaning isn't crystal clear.'

'Sir Gilbert.'

'What about him?'

'The Stones of Skelloch! Sacred rites! Interfering archaeologists! Human sacrifice!'

'No need to get carried away, miss.'

Twitty cringed at this admonishment. He must have sounded fifty years old. Still, what Stones of Skelloch, sacred rites, human sacrifice? No one had mentioned any of this to him. Dave and Ramona hadn't. The Guv. Might the Stones be the dolmen-cromlech thing he had glimpsed on the moor on his drive into Inverballoch? He felt not fifty but twelve and inadequate.

He twiddled his Biro and said, 'Go on.'

'Go on what?' Posy's voice had risen a fifth from *do* to *so*. 'If the Druids are crazy and dangerous couldn't you have had someone here all day, just in case? Even yourself? All you all do is come and go asking dim questions. I suppose for the police the more murdering the better. See yourselves on telly. Bask in the glamour.'

Playing for time, accustomed to insults – in London did not the insults from the brothers and sisters fall like rain? – Twitty wrote in his notebook, *Hysterics*. He added, *Theatrics*? The time his notebook gained him helped not a jot. Human sacrifice? Dave and Ramona, gentle musicians and free spirits? On the other hand, he'd known odd stuff come to light in his six years of coppering.

Posy said, 'If they've killed one archaeologist, why would they stop at one? But what do you care?'

'Try to contain yourself, miss. Who'll not stop at one what?'

'The Druids! Killing archaeologists! Aren't Druids who we're talking about? You brought them up. You don't even listen.'

'Why would they want to kill archaeologists?'

'The stone circle, for pity's sake!' Posy looked to be close to stamping her foot. 'Look, we don't know if these megaliths were burial chambers – some were – or memorials, or altars and temples for human sacrifice – Mike says we still haven't a clue about Stonehenge—'

'Mike?'

'—but they took enormous effort to build. They were serious. Druids were judges, poets, astronomers, who believed the soul was immortal and they sacrificed people by shutting them in a wicker cage and setting it on fire. Some of our loonier current so-called Druids claim to be reincarnated from the Druids of two thousand years ago, they might even believe it, so what makes you think they'd be delighted to see Sir Gilbert and his team poking about among their holy places? Don't ask me, ask Mike. Mike Trelawny. He's already told it all to your Sergeant Peckover.'

'Chief Inspector,' corrected Twitty, and wrote down, *Mike Trelawny*.

He said, 'These ancient Druids who were poets and astronomers, were they musicians too?'

'You mean like Pan? Piping away while the sacrifice burned to a cinder?'

'Sir Gilbert wasn't shut in a wicker cage and set on fire, he was stabbed. In his hotel room.'

'So we heard.'

'Yes, well.' He had entirely lost the thread of what they were talking about. 'I'll just take a look around. Not a holy place, is it, this?'

He needed to move about. Neither he nor the women had shifted position since he had arrived and his toes knew it. The wind was blowing, the temperature dropping. The sun had retired without anybody noticing, like a government clerk after forty years' service. Poking about here wouldn't take long. He could see it all from where he stood.

He set off past the trench, circling his arms like propellors. On a trestle table he found drawing boards, sketches, stones, a vacuum flask, tape measure, pocket calculator. Near by, piles of earth, planks, more canvas, earth in boxes, and implements – sieves, brushes, brooms, trowels, a pick and shovel. Against a flimsy tin and tarpaulin contraption leaned a spade, a garden fork, and a pole with a disc on one end not unlike the one at the Druids' camp. Supposing the hut to be a loo, he lifted the flap and saw that it probably was. He would not have said no to slipping in for fifteen seconds but ladies were watching and he would have been embarrassed. Technically he should perhaps have had a search warrant, the dig being on private property, but the Guv and the Glasgow Rangers wouldn't have had one, and as the lady diggers were not making a fuss it was hardly for him to raise the matter. Anyway, he had seen everything, almost. He stamped back to the trench. He hoped Posy was not going to say, 'Satisfied?'

Neither woman had anything to say. They appeared to have nothing to do but wait for him to leave. He wished they would make up their minds whether they wanted police present at the dig or not. When he bent down to pull out a corner peg and lift the canvas he heard a squeak from Leah. He assumed it was Leah. He doubted Posy was a squeaker.

From across the trench Posy said, 'Stop! What're you doing? There's nothing to see. The canvas is to protect it against the weather.'

'Protect what?' He pulled another peg. 'Nothing to see, you said.'

Moving on, wasting his own and everybody's time, Twitty tugged out the next peg, and the next two. He raised the edge of the canvas shoulder high and flipped it to the other side of the trench. Leah tried to catch it. Posy took a step back. Twitty stooped and peered down.

The trench smelled faintly beefy, livery, like dog food. Chum, one of those, he couldn't be specific because he didn't have a dog, though his mum and dad had always had one, currently Betty, a vamp of lower-class ancestry from the Battersea Dogs' Home. The whiff from the trench could have been the natural pong of raw peat or it might have been something else.

Three feet down, embedded in the sombre earth, was the lumpy outline of what looked singularly like a body.

THIRTEEN

Gin a body meet a body.
Robert Burns, *Coming Through the Rye*

The excavation had not advanced far. Earth, both loose and impacted, coated most of whatever was down there. Photographs that counsel claimed to be of a human cadaver would have been laughed out of court. The tanglement of what might be limbs, torso, and head could also have been old newspapers and vegetables, artfully arranged.

One item that might have set the jury squabbling was conceivably a foot, upwardly jutting out of the earth, but rounded and toeless. The thing in the grave, the deemed corpse, lay untidily on its side, knees drawn up, if knees they were, and one arm (possibly an arm) twisted under an earthy, putative head. A semi-exposed hand, beside which lay a brush and a tablespoon, was a spray of aborted, blackened bananas in a scooped-out basin of peat. Not even bananas, more the little slimy veggies – Twitty failed to recall the name – that lurked in rice and sludge in ethnic restaurants south of the Thames if you weren't careful.

Okra. Right.

Twitty gazed down at the humpiness in the trench. He stamped his chilled feet. This, he sensed, might be a pivotal moment in his career. He would have liked to have exclaimed something apt and memorable. He stared down in silence.

So too the women on the other side of the trench. Whatever it was they looked at they were not forthcoming.

Yes they were. Posy anyway.

'It truly is, it's a bog man!' Posy exclaimed.

'Ah,' said Twitty.

He kept his eyes on the bog man in case it should move.

'He could be two, three thousand years old!' said Posy.

'Mr Peckover saw it?'

'He's perfect! He will be when he's fully excavated. Usually there's just an arm, a foot—'

'Excuse me. Mr Peckover, Superintendent Geddes – they're aware of this?'

'Oh, please! We just uncovered it.'

'You said there was nothing.'

Posy gestured, a dismissive, backhanded flick.

'Nothing to write home about, you probably meant,' Twitty said. 'Just a bog man.'

'And now you've seen it the rest of you will be here!' Posy cried. 'The press, cameras, trippers! I'll be nowhere again, nobody, lost in the crowd! Couldn't you have given me more time? I wanted to announce it!' She shut her mouth with a snap as if fearful of sounding demented, but only for a moment. 'Isn't that reasonable? This is a find that changes your life – it would if you were given proper credit! But what would you care!'

Twitty was glad the trench separated them. She might have hit him. This was Posy frustrated, unapologetic about having lied, unembarrassed by what sounded to be raw tooth-and-claw ambition. Leah pressed her fists against her cheeks. She had turned a pasty colour apart from the earth round her mouth.

Twitty said, 'I must ask you both to come with me.'

'Now?' Posy said. 'You're joking.'

'After we've put the canvas back.'

'I'm not leaving him like this.'

'Him?'

'No, all right, we don't know yet.'

'I said we'll put the canvas back. If it's been here two thousand years it's not going to get up and run away.'

'It's been here two thousand years because' – Posy shouted the 'because' – 'it's buried! If we leave it like this it'll turn to slop and dust!'

'So what do you propose?'

'Is that a serious question?'

Twitty thought it serious. He reserved the right to reject whatever Posy might propose. At the same time he had no wish to be held responsible for reducing a two-thousand-year-old bog person to slop and dust. The mention he would receive in archaeology histories would be grim. *What promised to be the foremost example*

of a bog dweller perfectly preserved in peat over many millennia
turned to slop and dust due to a police constable's refusal to allow
the team of Posy Cork and Leah Howgego to take care of it fast. The
constable was Jason Twitty, whose ignorance and officiousness, etc.

Ignorant, officious Twitty, destroyer of bog men, would have chosen at this point to contact his Guv for advice, but the rental car had no short-wave. He did not even have his beeper. By the time he found a telephone in this benighted tundra these females might have made off with the bog man. Why they would do that he could not guess. To hold on to it at all cost, so ensuring the kudos Posy seemed to think she would be denied once the hordes descended? He wouldn't have put it past her. She was a determined wench.

Footage from a film by whatsisname, the suspense fellow – Hitchcock – lodged in Twitty's head. Hitchcock hadn't actually made this film, nobody had, but he might have done had he thought of it. In this sequence, Jason Twitty, having left the females with the bog body, returns to the site bringing with him Our 'Enry and the cream of Glasgow's sleuths, and perhaps the laird bloke, because the laird would want to come along, this being his land and him being interested. They all bear flashlights. The Misses Cork and Howgego have left, hardly surprisingly. Why would they hang about, Sunday night in the dark and cold? Shown how by DC Twitty, his finest hour, the police unpeg and peel back the canvas, replaced as protection against the elements and Highland cattle. They beam their flashlights into an empty trench. No bog man. *The Bog Man Vanishes.*

Here the footage jumped and blurred. Hitchcock hadn't made up his mind. Either every flashlight would train on DC Twitty, lighting up his face in a Munch shriek, or cut to a grizzled Guv, thirty years on, entering a low pub in Deptford and telling the barman, 'Fancy, it's Jason Twitty, you who used to drink only pineapple juice. Too bad you 'ad to resign but what choice was there?'

Lacked plausibility because what would Our 'Enry be doing – retired, venerable, perhaps Poet Laureate – in a den of tarts and derelicts? Of course, he might have gone off the rails. He'd been more than once demoted in an up-and-down career that had alternated between obstreperousness – writing limericks about the assistant commissioner above the CID urinals, so legend had it – and coups. It was Hitchcock's problem.

'I am taking you both in for questioning,' Twitty said, and he meant it. 'You're saying that if I do, this bog man will not improve. I'm saying, what do you propose?'

'First we cover him over with soil to maintain conditions,' said Posy. 'Moisture, exposure, the sun, they'll be the death of him.' She paused, frowning, though briefly. 'We've removed only enough soil to determine how much of the body we have and how it lies. There's still time to cover him up. Next, a conservation team.'

'Sounds serious.' Probably expensive too.

'A wooden box with Styrofoam pellets,' Posy said. 'We cut out the whole block of peat and bring it to the nearest mortuary, probably Glasgow, because the temperature has got to stay – imperative – around four centigrade to prevent mould and bacteria once it's exposed to the atmosphere. Then let's hope to God we can get him to London or Oxford without any nonsense from coroners and the Home Office. Glasgow might do. We should be able to assemble a team from there, but there's always some insufferable functionary who refuses to release the body until there's proof the death was natural. Bog men's deaths were usually unnatural, those that have been found. Lindow Man was garrotted. Others were drowned or their throats were cut.' Posy's proposal gathered pace. 'We excavate him with brushes, toothpicks, our hands, and jets of water. Don't think you can even imagine the TLC the last stages of excavating him take, down to the skin, because you can't. We'll have a dentist's vacuum for excess moisture. Before turning him on his side and his back we cover him with Clingfilm and fibreglass bandages to keep him exactly in his position, to the millimetre. We have a constant supply of dry ice and wet paper towels in polythene bags from the fridge to pack round him. Every step has to be recorded. There'll be X-raying, CT, MRI, body scan. Ideally we'll videotape the whole procedure, but no hot lamps. The low temperature's vital. Highly filtered air conditioning, no heating of any kind, surgical suits and masks, and no one who isn't one of the team allowed near, breathing their hot breath. No news people, politicians, pundits, celebrities, local mayors, and that includes your lot, our men in blue.' Posy, panting somewhat, staring across the grave at Twitty, took a breath. 'Then he's freeze-dried, our beautiful bog man, and into the British Museum.' Her eyes were bright, her cheeks flushed. 'Inverballoch Man!'

Posy Cork's proposal ended on a vibrant C-major of triumph.

Twitty assumed it had ended. The only comment that came to him was Alleluia! He refrained from making it. In any case, Posy's ardour had already visibly diminished.

She said, 'But we've no conservation team and it could take a week.' Her posture had become slumped. 'And it's soon going to be dark.'

'I was wondering about that,' Twitty said.

'But at least we have to cover him up with earth.'

'Will it take you long?'

'Shouldn't. You can make yourself useful, Mr Um—'

'Detective Constable Twitty.'

'Are you to be trusted to be gentle if we show you how?'

An image visited Twitty of two toothsome archaeologists showing him how to be gentle on a bed, a rug perhaps, something pillowy.

'How what?' he said.

'How to cover him. I just said. With the earth, peat, we've taken off him.'

You dolt, Twitty waited for her to add. She was in frustration mode again.

He said, 'So we want him back to peatrifaction, as opposed to petrifaction, our bog man not being of stone, so as to avoid putrifaction.'

His wordplay left him smiling. Posy stared at him with hostility. The smile evaporated when he gave thought to the shovelling back of earth. It smacked of concealment of evidence.

'You weren't covering him with earth before. You were uncovering him.'

'We were doing what we could while we could before people like you came trampling in and before it's dark. We don't even know if it's male.'

'That's important?'

'It's all important!'

'Now you propose to bury him again though it's still light. You could carry on digging. What makes you change your mind?'

'You! The hordes descending! You – Constable Busybody!'

'Constable Buttinsky!' Leah declared through soily lips.

Having spoken, Leah put her fingers to her mouth, shocked.

'But you would have covered him or her with soil,' Twitty said.

'Yes,' said Posy.

'Not gone off with the bog man?'

'Not without a conservation team! Don't you listen?'

Leah had wedged a sizeable part of her fist in her mouth. Having said her say she was voiceless again.

Twitty spread his arms and mused aloud. 'Two thousand years! Perhaps three? It beggars the imagination. Who were these people? Are they the ones painted themselves with woad, or is woad a myth?'

'Who?'

Posy had hiked to his side of the trench to present him with a handbrush, the sort people skivvy with, sweeping up fluff and crumbs.

He said, 'I've always wondered, woad isn't only what they wore? It wasn't their entire wardrobe?'

He had not always wondered. He hadn't thought of it before. Now he was curious. He should have asked Dave and Ramona.

'This climate, practically up in the Arctic,' he droned on. 'They didn't survive simply by painting themselves blue, did they? They'd have been blue already, winter time in Scotland.'

Posy pushed lumps of earth off a trowel with her thumb. He guessed that he would not be trusted with a trowel. The brush he held would be what he would do least damage with. If the brush would help preserve a historic bog person, he would do it. He would brush as gently as Cinderella.

Then to Superintendent Geddes and the Guv with the two of them.

Leah had stepped into the trench, a delicate gazelle. She kneeled and began scooping soil with her hands. Back on to Inverballoch Man she scooped the soil that she had scooped aside.

'You should know, an archaeologist and all,' Twitty said.

'Know what?' said Posy, stepping with the trowel into the grave.

'Woad.'

'Don't ask me, I'm not a chemist.' Posy sank to her knees alongside scooping Leah. 'It's a blue dye from the leaves of the woad plant. I've never seen it, but the Cruciferae family. Until indigo arrived in the sixteenth century – from India, I'd guess – woad was the only blue dye in Europe. Caesar wrote about it. Woad isn't cultivated any more, not that I know of. The ancient Brits painted their bodies and dyed their clothes with it.' She looked up. 'The longer you just stand there the longer this is going to take. Use the brush or your hands. Look, like this.'

'What clothes did they wear?'

Clothes-conscious Twitty stepped into the trench with care. If he trod on the bog man he would be execrated, perhaps physically assaulted, by Posy. To say nothing of earning the contempt of generations of archaeologists yet unborn.

He said, 'I mean, hats? Jackets? Shoes? Leggings?'

'What're leggings? They'd have had something on their feet, like moccasins. They wore capes and robes made from skins and wool. They knew about weaving and they were hunters. They'd have had deerskins, rabbit skins, every kind of skin.'

'Why's this bog man wearing trousers? Looks like trousers. And lace-up shoes?'

FOURTEEN

I go barefoot, barefoot, barefoot.
Beatrix Potter, *The Adventures of Mrs Tiggywinkle*

When Posy leaned forward from the back seat and said, 'That's
Dundrummy Castle,' D.C Twitty, at the wheel of the white Fiesta,
was disappointed and disbelieving. Beyond woodland, on rising
ground, stood a big, boring house. On his own he would have
driven past seeking the true and only Dundrummy Castle.

'If you say so,' he said.

Also in the back, Leah Howgego, muddy with archaeology,
said nothing.

They had covered up the bog person, if that was what it was,
with peat to keep him or her warm, or cold, or moist, whichever
it was that was so essential, and next with sections of canvas
against the elements. Twitty had insisted on their company. They
would all be returning shortly to the dig so they could retrieve
their estate car then. If you're not both in irons, he had reflected.
The women had grumbled but capitulated. How could they have
not? Was he not after all a copper?

The road had started off empty and became more so, though
for a while it cut through an unpeopled golf course: acres of
kempt, undulous fairway with here a bunker, there a hazardous
clump of trees, and elsewhere glimpses of trim greens with a
beflagged stick in the middle, as if hopeful that someone, anyone,
might show up for a wintery round. Twitty had spotted a telephone
on a pole in the heart of gloaming, mountainous nothingness, and
next, near a clutter of stone cottages, an actual telephone booth.
He probably should have phoned ahead to the Guv at Dundrummy Castle but he hadn't felt like stopping.

Silence from the rear seat. They were an unamiable pair. Perhaps that was harsh. They were preoccupied with their bog man. Twitty trod on the accelerator. A touch of Le Mans should deter them from throttling him from behind. Car rental firms ought to keep a selection of those American police cars with steel mesh to hold the difficult ones at bay.

Probably a mistake not to have phoned. The Guv and the Glasgow lot might have left Dundrummy Castle by now, and the laird wouldn't be home either, he'd be off lairding, surveying his acres, shooting ptarmigan and poachers. There'd be only a bleak housekeeper, her hair tied in a bun, unless he was thinking again of Sunday afternoon Hitchcock on the tube. *Rebecca*? The laird's housekeeper might well be the one had murdered Sir Gilbert Potter. If she were old enough, say around seventy, she might have buried the one in the pit with the trousers and shoes, unless that or similar wear actually was what ancient Britons wore, and the thing in the pit really was a bog man.

Privately admitting that the protruding extremity out of the peat might not have been a foot, Twitty reasoned that if it were, it either had no toes – some kind of Scottish yeti? – or it was wearing shoes. He had asked Posy if bog people had worn shoes. He should have known better

Of course they had worn shoes, Posy had snapped. Did he imagine they went barefoot on stony ground and through ice and snow? Ashamed, inadequate, he had none the less persisted, unable to leave well alone. Didn't cavemen at least go barefoot? He had succeeded in not adding, from one of his favourites of infancy, 'I go barefoot, barefoot, barefoot.' Posy, with not too contemptuous a snarl, had said that 'caveman' was a meaningless term, a concept of cartoonists. If he had in mind the Stone Age, Neolithic Man, they wore shoes. The herdsman melted out of a glacier in the Tyrolean Alps a couple of years ago had lived between 3,500 and 3,000 BC, five millennia ago, and he'd had shoes. He had not had a penis because he had been vilely excavated and allowed to thaw but he'd had shoes. Size six. Sole and upper flap made of leather, and a net like a sock sewn to the sole and stuffed with grass, their equivalent of synthetic cushioning like latex and foam rubber. The net sock had laces, both sock and the laces woven from grass. The shoes had been much patched and repaired. They had probably been repaired every day because they were not custom-built bench-made hand-crafted shoes from Gribley & Smutch of Piccadilly, purveyors of footwear to the nobility since

1754, shoes that these days would set you back, what, how would she know how much, six hundred pounds, not that Gribley & Smutch would allow you across the threshhold unless they had cobbled for your father, grandfather, and so on unto generations back.

After which instruction, Twitty had not been about to ask if Neolithic Man had worn trousers.

'There, that's it – turn in there,' Posy said.

Steering castleward along a lumpy, uphill driveway besieged by trees, and tempted to imagine himself a duke driving to his ancestral pile, and wearing shoes from wherever she had said in Piccadilly, Twitty wondered why he felt suddenly, scratchily warm. Prickly heat? Onset of flu? The Met didn't accept flu. His sergeant didn't. 'Take an asprin and get out there, bring me back the villains,' the sarge would growl, head bowed over the crossword, fat fingers bent round a mug of tea. Or was the warmth pheromones? That was to say, somebody else's pheromones, those secreted chemical substances that influenced behaviour, or in his case his temperature.

Posy? Pheromones? No, no, no, no, no. He hoped he was not becoming amorous for Posy Cork. The prognostication to date was that any hopes he might build up would be dashed. Unusual, but he didn't seem to be her type.

The driveway deteriorated, appearing in places to have been lightly shelled. After a slow quarter of a mile, with glimpses now and then, through or over forest, of Dundrummy Castle, the Fiesta exited from fir trees into airiness where there might once have been lawns as cropped as golf greens, shrubbery as clipped as a sheep, rose gardens, and Scots gentry celebrating a birthday or wedding, summertime anyway, with whisky, tea, and oatcakes. Now this spaciousness was in need of gardeners. Summer's leftovers of grass reached halfway up a fountain whose cherubs might at one time have spouted water but were not currently doing so. On unweeded gravel outside the castle entrance were parked an assortment of vehicles – blue Toyota, a police Panda, decrepit Deux Chevaux with opaque windows that would flap in the wind, and a high-off-the-ground Jeep of the kind that looks to be leaning backwards, probably the laird's or his gillie's for patrolling the mountains. From one of the mighty chimneys, though from only one, curled smoke.

Twitty parked beside the Jeep, said to the ladies, 'Wait here, please,' and stepped from the car into weeds. He gazed in disapproval at Dundrummy Castle. He had not wished for, nor would have expected, a ghost piper slow-marching transparently along a battlement, bleating his lament. All the same.

If the Ram had disappointed, that had been his fault for having hoped for an Inter-Continental. The Ram was not to blame for being what it was. Dundrummy Castle disappointed because it wasn't a castle. He knew a castle when he saw one. This was a house.

True, a big house, a mansion, several centuries old, he guessed, and loaded with elephantine chimneys, but a house. No moat, keep, crenellated walls six feet thick, towers, turrets, and slits of windows through which arrows had once rained down on the invading McPhersons and McTavishes below. The chimneys made sense because you'd need a decent fire up here in Dundrummy. Twitty doubted that the place would have much in the way of central heating. Perhaps some system of hazardous ducts, and in the crypt flunkeys with bellows bent over hot coals. Heating a place like this would have cost a bomb. As he understood it, the current laird hadn't a penny.

The door was weighty, panelled, and fitted with a verdigris-encrusted knocker. He was reaching for the knocker when the door opened.

Not the housekeeper, not anyway the severe one with the bun who might have done in Sir Gilbert, and not the Guv or the Glasgow contingent either. A plumpish chap in his thirties and an Aran jersey. Smashing red beard if you liked red beards. Better trimmed than the grounds of Dundrummy Castle.

Behind him, a cavernous dim stone-flagged hall, antlers on a wall, a worn brocade armchair, probably for the dogs, and a rubbery whiff of galoshes and stalking jackets. In a gilt frame the size of a bed hung a portrait of presumably some rakehell ancestor, a leering bandit in lacy frills and a tricorn hat who lounged in what appeared to be a copse, one hand over his heart, the other resting on a pedestal or dog. Hard to tell through the interior gloom. Twitty cautioned himself to be alert for Dundrummy Castle dogs. Not that they could be more pesky than hotpants Grendel.

'Sir Dougal Duncan?'

'Still they come,' said the Aran jersey.

'Excuse me?'

'The bold *gendarmes*. The *carabinieri*.'

'Detective Constable Twitty. Sorry for interrupting, sir, but would Mr Peckover be with you? Or Mr Geddes?'

The Aran jersey was looking beyond Twitty towards the Fiesta.

'Is that Posy?' he said. 'And Leah?'

'You're acquainted?'

'Of course I'm acquainted. Why else would they be here?'

'I brought them.'

'Here in Scotland, fellow! Inverballoch! Digging! Bring 'em in!'

'I'd as soon not, sir – your lairdship – for the moment—'

'Well, you get on in, Constable. Warm yourself. We're in the den. To the left.'

Sir Dougal stepped past Twitty and headed for the Fiesta, one arm twirling aloft in a hailing gesture. Twitty could have brought him down with a flying tackle. If he hurried he wouldn't need to be so dramatic, he could probably halt him with a hand on his shoulder and discussion.

''Urry up, lad, and shut the door!' called Peckover from somewhere in the inner murk. 'It's brass-monkey weather in 'ere.'

Twitty squinted into the foggy hallway. The view reminded him of Paddington Station at three in the morning.

He called back, 'The laird has left!'

'Good!'

'But, sir, we don't want—'

'Shut that 'orrible door!'

Twitty pushed the door approximately shut without actually shutting it, not wanting to lock the *seigneur* out of his château. No knowing what trickery might be performed by locks on castle doors like this one. He was happy to have heard the Guv, present and moderately irate. His muse had probably flown off in mid-ode at the opening of the castle door.

Twitty sidled left into the hallway. He couldn't see much. From lugubrious wood panelling more framed ancestors ogled his uncertain passage across the flagstones. One ancestor looked fairly recent, *circa* perhaps 1850, a dignitary in black with a guilty look. If he, Jason Twitty, had been a magistrate, he'd have had that one transported to Australia. On a dusty table that would have accommodated a board meeting of president and ten directors stood a brass letterbox, presumably for show. Hard to imagine a postman dragging himself out here to gather the mail, though in the Highlands who could be sure?

No housekeeper, no dogs. Not so far. A mighty staircase. Teak, mahogany, one of those important woods. The staircase soared into fog. When you had climbed it as far as it would go, there at the summit you would open a creaking door into a garret and spy through the cobwebs Miss Haversham, or the Dougal Duncan family equivalent. The Hag of Dundrummy. Down the staircase would step, any moment now, the housekeeper and elkhounds.

'Find your Druids?' Peckover called, backlit and dim from a doorway.

Twitty trod towards the light, arm outstretched, hoping bats would not alight on it.

He said, 'I did. Thirteen of them. Others may have been off foraging. And the women, the archaeologists. They're outside.'

'Gawd! All of 'em?'

'The women,' Twitty said.

'Why?'

'Why what?'

'What're they doing 'ere?'

'I brought them. Guv, we may have a development. They've—'

'Shut up. Come in. Anything you have to say, Mr Geddes will want to hear.'

Light from lofty leaded windows left the den less Stygian than the hall, though not a lot less because of the smoke from a marble fireplace. This had to be the largest den Twitty had ever been invited into. He would have called it a banqueting hall, though without a table for banquets. The walls had a faded Regency stripe and the ceiling a moulded rose from which hung a chandelier, mole grey from smoke and the years. More portraits hung on the Regency stripes, also outsize paintings of sailing vessels, and a mammoth oil of nymphs and shepherds sporting starkers in a glade, probably the glade the leering ancestor had been on his way to when he had stopped by the pedestal to have his portrait painted. All Twitty could have said with confidence of the furniture was that there was not enough for the size of the room. The bare look. What there was – sofa, random chairs, side tables, a grandfather clock – looked to be a mix of old chintz with defective springs and possibly some choice antiques, though no Lovejoy he. Two rectangles of Regency stripes were vividly brighter than the surrounding stripes, as if a Sheraton tallboy or Louis Quinze escritoire had stood there but now been moved elsewhere, perhaps to auction rooms. The carpet was, or had been, a sumptuous Aladdin's carpet of a square footage double or triple that of his entire flat on Lavender Hill. Not that he would have bid tuppence for it, it being sumptuous only in spots. In front of the hearth it was charred and currently home to the feet of Superintendent Geddes and a doom-laden copper he believed he had noticed at the Ram.

Twitty took in all this over the next few minutes, not immediately, because Our 'Enry was telling him, 'Don't sit down and don't take off your coat. We're leaving. Actually you could put your coat on the fire, but little by little so we don't fetch up with a right old tassel.'

'What tassel?'

'Tassel – Windsor Castle. A conflagration, chum. Cockney rhyming slang. Where've you been?'

'Never heard that one.'

'I just made it up. Someone 'as to keep the language fresh.'

Twitty tried not to think about his possibilities of promotion to sergeant. He had passed the exams. Now it was a matter of luck, not treading on the wrong corns, like those of the Guv, and being brilliant. He wouldn't have gone so far as to say that seeing what Posy and Leah had not wanted him to see was brilliant, but these middling-high mucky-mucks in the laird's den had visited the dig and they hadn't seen it. The Guv was steering him towards the fireplace.

'You've met Superintendent Geddes. Inspector Gillespie – Jason Twitty. What development, lad?'

'The women, sir, the archaeologists. Outside. We've come from the dig. They're Miss Cork, that's Posy—'

'Get on with it,' Peckover said.

'They've dug up a body.'

Their reaction was in their eyes, eyebrows, and lips pouted, parted, pursed. Gobsmacked, Twitty thought. They could hardly have denied it.

They could have him back in uniform though. He had some theories but he would need to step gingerly with them. They could have had him on Hooligan Control, Saturday afternoon at the Chelsea game, dodging the bricks and unopened lager cans, skidding in horse droppings. They could have sent him to community relations as doorkeeper. Forget being upped to sergeant.

Meanwhile they had their flinty eyes on him, waiting for more.

FIFTEEN

All theory, dear friend, is grey.
                    Johann Wolfgang von Goethe, *Faust*

'Not actually dug up quite, yet, sir. Sirs. More, let's say, uncovered, partially, and we had to recover him. It. That's to say re-cover, not recover. Cover it over. Else slop and dust.'

This was only going to get worse. He had their attention, unfortunately. He transferred his notebook to under his chin so as to delve in the sable for tissue. The smoke prickled his nasal passages, bringing him to the brink of a sneeze. The Glasgow pair standing winterized in scarves and overcoats practically in the fire would be used to the smoke by now. They had been inhaling it since whenever they had arrived.

'See, sir' – Twitty joined them by the fire, trying to include each in the respectful but singular 'sir' – 'it's so minimally uncovered so far that it could be old cardboard, turnip tops, all you can tell. But it has sort of a human outline and Miss Cork says it's a bog man three thousand years old. There's what could be a foot. She's very thrilled, also terrified it could disintegrate, which is why we covered it over. Tomorrow, she and Miss, ah, Leah, will arrange for a recovery team, with your permission, naturally. Then we'll see.'

Geddes said, 'Sonny, are we talking about the same place? We've seen the Inverballoch dig. We weren't shown any bog man.'

'No sir. They didn't show it to me. It was at the end under the canvas.'

'I don't recall canvas.'

'Against the elements, sir. They may have brought it out after you left. Night, you know, evening, they don't go on digging in the dark. Actually it was nowhere near dark. Still isn't, except in here. But that's the impression they gave, they'd finished for the day, they were leaving.'

'This canvas was in place when you arrived?'

'Yes sir.'

'Then they removed it?'

'I removed it, sir.'

The stares became less flinty, more speculative.

'Nosy you,' Peckover murmured.

'Right, Guv – sir. This bog man's foot, if it is a foot, it may be wearing a shoe, and make no mistake' – Make no mistake, *gentlemen*, Twitty wanted to say, beginning to feel comfortable, gathering steam – 'bog persons, Druids, all those, they had shoes. The herdsman melted out of the Tyrol, a glacier, he'd had size six shoes. Five thousand years ago. Precisely so, it depends – if I may anticipate your next question' – he was a politician on a podium, his audience putty in his hands – 'on what we mean by shoes. Would leather with laces and a net sock woven from grass qualify? We'll know when the excavation gets further. It's a most delicate procedure, ah – gentlemen.'

There, he had said it! Effective too. Geddes, the Guv, and the gaunt one, Gillespie, eyed him as if he had become unhinged.

'But, obviously, if they're Harrods shoes,' Twitty hurried on, 'he's not a bog man.'

'Go on then, say it,' said Peckover.

'So he could be the bloke who went missing in the war, the one against Hitler, the archaeologist. Not Hitler the archaeologist. The one who went missing. Sorry, can't remember the name. Not Fortescue-Cholmondeley but of that ilk. Double-barrelled.'

'Sir Walton Clough-Burghley,' wearily advised Alec Gillespie, stirring a coal with his shoe.

'Chuff-Burney,' corrected Geddes without conviction.

'William Clapp-Berkhampton?' offered Peckover. 'It was half a century ago. Can we concentrate on Gilbert Potter?'

'Sorry, didn't want to muddy the waters, sir,' Twitty said.

'You've muddied them,' Geddes said.

He was fondling his dimple. Twitty could not make out if he was delighted or angry.

'The waters will clear, let's hope,' Geddes went on. 'You've done well. Finding out if the body is fifty years old, five hundred, or five thousand won't be a problem. What's too much to hope for, if the answer is fifty, is we get handed a confession as with Lindow Woman. Remember?'

'Not exactly, sir. You mean Lindow Man.'

'I mean Lindow Woman. From Lindow Moss in Cheshire. Thirty years ago a woman living there disappeared. Name escapes me.'

'Reyn-Bardt,' Peckover said.

'That's it, another of the double-barrelled, but not a toff, this one. Never seen again after she went missing. Probably done away with but no clues, nothing. Twenty years later the police – Macclesfield police it was – they're questioning two villains about something quite different, and these two say that in prison had been a character from Lindow Moss, Peter Reyn-Bardt, who claimed he'd done in his wife, cut her up, burned her, and buried the bits in the garden. The police interview him and dig up the garden. Nothing. Reyn-Bardt denies everything. This was ten or twelve years ago. Nineteen eighty-three? Three months later the peat company at Lindow Moss dig up a dinosaur's egg. With me so far, sonny?'

'Yes sir. A dinosaur's egg.'

'That's what the workers who found it told each other. They fell about laughing. When they hose the egg off it's a human skull and they stop laughing. What happens next is front page news. Nineteen eighty-three, you were a schoolboy, right?'

'Right.'

'Harrow?'

Twitty glanced at Peckover, informer, who had put down his hat and was jotting something in his notebook, probably a sonnet.

'Yes sir.'

'You had access to news of the outside world? Newspapers? You watched television?'

'*Fawlty Towers*, sir. Repeats.'

Frown lines furrowed the skin above the bridge of Superintendent Geddes's nose. He said, 'Confronted with the skull, found a hundred yards or so from where he'd lived, Peter Reyn-Bardt confessed. Something, was it, to do with his wife trying to blackmail him?'

'Aye,' intoned Gillespie.

'They never found the body,' Peckover said, making pencillings in his notebook.

'Found the skull,' Twitty said. 'The skull's enough.'

Geddes said, 'A couple of Oxford profs did their radiocarbon stuff on the skull. They dated it somewhere between, when – one hundred and five hundred AD? Late Roman, early Dark Ages.'

'Where'd we be,' Twitty wanted to know, 'without the higher technology? Lucky Reyn-Bardt.'

'How would you know?' said Geddes. 'You were wearing your straw hat and watching *Fawlty Towers*. Reyn-Bardt had confessed. He was tried, convicted, and put away.'

'But there was no body!' protested Twitty, aghast.

He remembered his age and that he must be cool. He assumed a loose posture and clicked his fingers.

'You're unhappy with the verdict?' asked Geddes. 'You fault the jury?'

'Never, sir. It's just that. I mean. What incredibly bad luck!'

'Bad luck?' said deathshead Gillespie. 'Sentimental claptrap. Gang awa', laddie, back to Lunnon and your fleshpots.'

'Quite, anyway, point being,' said Peckover, and he ground to a stop, searching for the point.

Peckover was on his constable's side, frowning down at his notebook and accepting that it had been only a matter of time before somebody would tell Scotland Yard to slope off back whence they had come. But he resented young Jason being the victim. A child, bright, lively company, sometimes, but in no position to answer back, same as royalty. Gillespie should pick on someone his own size. First chance he got he'd stick a finger in Gillespie's eye.

'Point being,' said Peckover, 'that we 'ave a bog body, according to Constable Twitty here, the competence, energy, and flashes of insight of whom I 'oleheartedly trust, not to mention that due to him alone we know we 'ave a bog body.'

Twitty blinked.

'A bog bloke or blokess as old as time, museum bound, destined for instant fame, and raw meat for the media, for five minutes,' Peckover said. 'Alternatively, we might 'ave Sir Chuff-Bumley, equally media fodder, and wouldn't it be nice to present Sir Chuff, what's left of 'im, to his murderer, if murdered he was, who would confess, as happened with Lindow Woman. Yes, it would be nice, but sod, frankly, Sir Chuff and bog bodies. We're looking for whoever murdered Gilbert Potter.'

On the blinding obviousness of this the policemen seemed to need to ruminate. Peckover studied his notebook. Twitty was not to know it but what the Guv had written was not a sonnet.

A crafty bog lady from Lindow
Would play Shenandoah on a dildo

When she'd done Shenandoah
She would do as encoah
Bach's *Mass*, on a nose harp, *con brio.*

Gillespie kicked a coal and growled, 'Anyone who murdered Sir Chuff would be seventy years old by now. He'd be eighty or ninety.'

'Like a few in Inverballoch, likely as not,' said Geddes.

'The local sergeant, Menzies, he's getting on,' said Gillespie.

'Loyal of you, Alec. Still, we'll take a discreet census.'

'Round up the usual sunset folk,' Gillespie said.

Peckover said, 'You miss my point.'

'I take your point,' Geddes said. 'You dismiss Chuff. You want to focus on Potter. Don't we all. But Potter and Chuff were both archaeologists. Fifty years apart, right, but can't there be a link? Inverballoch? Roman remains, bog bodies, buried treasure?'

Further ruminations.

Peckover put his notebook away and said breezily, 'That's it then, lad? A somebody in the bog at the dig? Nothing else?'

'Sir?' Some people! Wasn't a body in a bog enough to be going on with?

Geddes said, 'What about your Druids?'

'Yes sir.' Good, all right, since you ask. 'The ancient Druids were judges, poets, astronomers, who believed the soul was immortal and sacrificed people by shutting them in a wicker cage and setting it on fire.' Not every day was Twitty in a position to enlighten three senior police officers. He warmed to his lecture. 'If this crew I've seen believe they're reincarnated from the Druids of two thousand years ago – if they do they're not admitting it – they'd be unlikely to look kindly on anyone poking about in their holy places. That would include Sir Gilbert Potter. Perhaps Potter particularly, he being, having been, this dig's figurehead, so to speak. I'm not suggesting they sacrificed him. Still, may be worth bearing in mind. There's a holy place just south of Inverballoch. The Stones of Skelloch. Could be worth a look.'

The senior officers failed to come up with any immediate comment.

Geddes finally said, 'Potter wasn't poking about at these Stones of Skelloch, was he?'

'Don't know, sir. We'd have to find out.'

'Where d'you pick up all this?'

'Ear to the ground, sir.'

'Anything else on the Druids?'

'Druids past or Druids present, sir?'

'Ours in Inverballoch.'

'Musicians, sir.'

'Strolling minstrels, eh? They play for you?'

'They're retired. One oddity, though. They've got a kind of metal detector sort of instrument, you know, on a pole.'

Geddes said, 'That's a wee bit vague, sonny. You're sure this sort of instrument on a pole isn't, say, a musical instrument for weaving plaintive Druid airs?'

'Not a hundred per cent sure, no sir.'

'And you didn't ask,' Gillespie said.

'No.'

'You didn't consider it your job to ask or you didn't consider the instrument of interest?'

'I didn't make the connection until I saw another at the dig. Similar but not the same.' Twitty was sorry he had ever mentioned the thing on the pole. 'Dave and Ramona, the musical Druids, even if what they're doing is looking for buried treasure it's not an offence, is it? As long as they surrender anything they find?'

'If they surrender it,' Geddes said, 'and a coroner's jury decides that whoever buried it meant to come back for it, it goes to the Crown. That's purely for your information. The finder may or may not be compensated.'

'I know,' Twitty said. '*Animus revertendi*. It's an absurd ass of a law that goes back to Saxon times and was conceived by grasping monarchs who wanted every last scrap of loot for themselves. They didn't give a monkey's for preserving treasures for the nation. True, that was before archaeology showed us that old stuff is valuable simply by being old. Still, *animus revertendi* – common law, of course, not statute – is a pathetic travesty of even a retard's concept of justice. It's an insult to common sense, self-defeating, and one passing example among many why Britain is degenerating into a third-rate museum while – here's the irony – encouraging those with the metal detectors to surrender nothing but quietly flog our heritage to Texas beef barons and Japanese bankers.'

Momentary speechlessness in Dundrummy Castle. A puff of wind down the chimney sent fresh coal smoke gusting round the policemen's feet and up their nostrils.

'*Your* heritage?' enquired Inspector Gillespie. He had a hand in his trousers pocket, jiggling coins.

114

'Easy, Alec,' Superintendent Geddes said.

'North Korea, the last bastion of communism, so we're told,' Gillespie informed Twitty. He accelerated the jiggling. 'Ye'll be at hame there. Put on your swimmies and swim awa' to North Korea, ye preen-heidit gumphie.'

'Alec!'

Peckover to the rescue said, 'We were talking about metal detectors. One at the Druids' camp, another at the dig. Is that right, Constable?'

'Yes sir.'

'But you didn't grasp any special significance. You'd never heard of buried treasure here until Mr Geddes mentioned it a moment ago.'

'Actually, yes. It's a theory in the Cuff-Bingley file. Hey! That's who!'

'Who what?'

'The one who went missing. That's his name. One theory in the file is he may have been prowling about looking for a treasure trove. Apparently he wouldn't have been the first. More to the point, where did the Druids hear about it, because what else would their metal detector be for?'

'You just answered that,' Geddes said. 'The buried treasure is a legend, not a secret. Cuff-Bingley wasn't the first to look for it and he isn't going to be the last. See this?' He reached behind Peckover and picked up a battered greenish-gold goblet from among the photographs and bric-à-brac on the mantel. 'Celtic. Been in the Duncan family four hundred years. Worth a quid or two. The laird says if he had the time and money to dig up his acres and he found a hoard of Celtic treasure, his worries would be over. Except he doesn't believe there is buried treasure.'

'He says,' Gillespie said.

Twitty said, 'If that cup's so valuable he should have it in a bank vault.'

The superintendent returned the goblet to the mantel. 'That's where it stood for generations, there, middle of the shelf. His solicitor, Dick Haig, thought it risky so now he keeps it in a safe in the library. Brought it out to show it off to us.'

'Sir, excuse me?'

'What?'

'Where's the laird?'

'Outside, you said.'

'It's been five minutes.'

'Ten. You think he's run?'

'Couldn't say, sir.'

'It's too much to hope for. If he's run, that'll be the first real progress all day. Sit down.'

'I didn't want him alone with the women.' Twitty stayed standing. 'He barged off to them anyway. I could hardly restrain him – him a laird.'

'We'll make the jokes, sonny,' Geddes said genially.

'Not a joke, sir. It'll be too late but I'd be happy to see what he's up to. Not to mention the ladies. He might respond better to a senior officer.'

The senior officers exchanged looks.

'I mean, why isn't he here guarding his cup?' Twitty was fairly vehement. 'Personally, I've taken a fancy to it. I can think of six ways of nicking it and nobody would know. Not him anyway.'

Geddes said, 'So why wouldn't you want the laird talking with the women? Now Potter is dead Sir Dougal is practically their employer. He would be if he were paying them.'

'Sir.'

'Well?'

'Nothing.'

Peckover said, 'Don't sulk. You 'eard Mr Geddes. Sit. Answer the question.'

The closest item for sitting on was what looked to Twitty to be a milking-stool. The seat was padded and the stains presumably milk and dung. If it were a Celtic milking-stool it would fetch who knew how much? A quarter of a million? When he sat the milking-stool creaked and shifted sideways. So as not to collapse it and reduce its value to a fiver he had to sit leaning forward, his weight on his feet.

'This is only a theory,' Twitty said.

He thought he heard the hall door open. Or close. A door somewhere. At last the housekeeper with the dogs? Had nobody else heard? Might be Sir Dougal come to collect his coat, passport, and rations from the kitchen. If the super wanted the laird to have an opportunity to flit, that was up to him.

'It is not the least charm of a theory that it is refutable,' Geddes said.

'Absolutely, sir.'

Was the super quoting? The senior eggs stood in a row in the hearth, bums to the fire, which benefited them hardly at all.

Twitty said, 'The Cuff-Bingley file mentions how the laird got fed to the teeth over treasure-hunters rootling over his land. That's the dead laird, this one's father. Fergus? Our laird, Sir Dougal, whatever he might say about wanting this dig, what if he's inherited his father's horror of trespassers? He could have murdered Sir Gilbert to put a stop to it.'

'Good,' Geddes said. 'You're thinking. That had occurred to us.'

'And been dismissed,' Gillespie said.

'Absolutely,' Twitty agreed. 'Me too.' The milking-stool gave a lurch. He leaned further forward, putting more weight on his spongy white joggers. 'Alternatively – this will have occurred to you too – the laird may have murdered Sir Gilbert expressly to bring in the police. We go over his acres for clues, free of charge, with the highest technology there is, whatever's beyond Geiger counters – radar, sonic devices, magnetometers, robot dowsers – and if he's lucky we'll find the buried treasure for him and he'll be compensated for it.'

That plainly had not occurred to them.

'You on drugs?' enquired Gillespie.

'What clues are we looking for with your robot dowsers?' Geddes said.

'Archaeological clues? I don't know. More butter? He might have spied the Druids swarming about at night with shovels and their metal detector.' He was not sitting so much as squatting and it was demeaning. 'The laird would dream up something. He kills Sir Gilbert, hands us a box of red herrings, and hopes we'll dig and uncover his treasure trove.'

'Horsefeathers,' Gillespie said.

'If you think that's horsefeathers, try this, sir.' Twitty felt like Little Miss Muffet on her tuffet. 'The laird is in love with Posy. He kills Sir Gilbert so as to create a vacancy for a new director of the dig – himself. It's his land, he can do as he likes. He can sack Posy and stop the dig. Or he can marry her if she'll have him. What a team, right? Laird and lairdess of Dundrummy, happy ever after digging for Roman remains, treasure, and bog bodies.'

'He'd have to be as mad as you,' Gillespie said.

'He's certainly mad. Who wouldn't be mad to live in these benighted Highlands in a mausoleum like this?'

Peckover wanted to cheer.

Gillespie said, 'Watch your mouth, Constable.'

'Yes, watch it,' Peckover agreed, twisting round to peer at the fire, see how it was managing, and rid himself of his grin. He turned and said, 'We could equally suggest Posy is in love with the laird. She's also pathologically ambitious to control the dig and take for herself all rewards and prizes accruing therefrom. So she filches the dirk and disposes of Sir Gilbert, her mentor. Now she will seduce the laird. Sir Dougal and the Lady Posy, what a team, *et cetera*.'

Geddes said, 'Is no one going to propose that they might already be a team? Posy Cork palmed the dirk off the haggis plate. Later she slipped it to the laird, and he stuck it in Sir Gilbert.'

'Or vice versa,' said Gillespie.

'All I'm trying to say,' Twitty said, 'is that it doesn't seem the greatest idea allowing those two, at this point, to be alone together.'

'They're not alone, there's Leah Howgego,' said Gillespie. 'Clearly a conspiracy of three.'

Please, fade away, Twitty wanted to tell the sarcastic, corpse-eyed weevil of an inspector. Instead, coal fumes getting the better of him, unless it was flu, he whipped a tissue from a pocket of the nylon sable and sprang to his feet. The milking stool went skittering.

'Urrraaghssh!'

'Quiet!' Geddes said with surprising fierceness.

'Pardon. Sir. Honest.'

'Ssh!'

Through the hush sounded from somewhere, presumably outside, an engine's revving.

'I don't believe it,' Geddes said.

He was the first out of the den and into the gloom of the hall, Gillespie and Peckover at his heels. Twitty was last out, from politeness. He supposed he had misunderstood when the super had said that the laird doing a bunk would be the best progress all day. It still might be, almost as sure a sign of guilt as surprising somebody standing over a body with a bloody dirk in his hand. Either the super had been jesting or he had changed his mind.

Having revved, the engine-note was now dwindling, whether stalling in the cold or off and away. With evening closing in, the hall's murk had deepened. The policemen clumped across the flagstones, bumping into each other, exploring forward to where they believed the door ought to be. Gillespie cried out, 'Dammit, mon, that's my ankle!'

'Sorry, mate,' said Peckover.

Geddes yanked open the door to the outside.

Dusk encroached on Dundrummy Castle. The laird's Jeep was gone. Its engine sound could be heard, faint and becoming fainter.

The laird was gone too. So were Posy and Leah.

SIXTEEN

It is never difficult to distinguish between a Scotsman with a
grievance and a ray of sunshine.

P.G. Wodehouse, *Blandings Castle and Elsewhere*

Superintendent Geddes at the wheel led the pursuit down the
cratered driveway. Had the laird kidnapped the women or the
women the laird? Were the three of them in it together and what
was 'it'?

Unfamiliar with the driveway's twists and potholes, fearful for
the Panda's suspension, Bill Geddes made poor progress. The
laird's Jeep would be a mile ahead already.

Which way when he reached the road? The Jeep would be out
of sight.

Inspector Gillespie at his side issued orders into the shortwave
radio. His ankle throbbed from the Scotland Yard gamphrel's
deliberate hack. A hack plus a downward scrape. In a soccer
match the Sassenach sumph would have been sent off. Or he
should have been. The referees were mostly blind or bribed.

Chief Inspector Peckover switched on the headlights and followed in the borrowed blue Toyota.

Constable Twitty brought up the rear in the Fiesta. He reached
out to the boombox and pressed On. There might be weather,
news even, local news of a murdered archaeologist in Inverballoch,
and Scotland Yard assisting in enquiries.

What there was was Scottish country-and-western again. Did
Scottish radio have nothing else and hadn't he heard this one
already?

> 'The baby has colic, the rent's in arrears,
> I'll dry the dishes if you dry your tears.'

At the road Geddes swung south and pressed hard on the accelerator. South was Inverballoch and eventually Glasgow, where he would sooner have been than here. North he knew nothing about. Wilderness. No airports, only Kyleakin on Skye. Why would the laird go north? Why would anyone go north except tourists who knew no better?

He overtook a farm lorry, the only vehicle in either direction for the next four miles. Any sheep he met would have to take their chances. Ahead he saw two sorry hitchhikers. One stood in the road, waving and thumbing, the other sat on the verge, keening, resigned to a night in the Highland fastness.

'Sorry, laddies!' Geddes murmured, swerving past the thumber. He corrected himself. 'Lassies!' He swept helplessly by at seventy shouting 'Och, damn!' and flooring the brake.

Peckover, braking, came within a whisker of ramming the Panda's rear. Lagging Twitty, twiddling the boombox dial, arrived to find Geddes, Gillespie, and the Guv piling out of their cars, slamming the doors, and bearing down on two hitchhikers. Inspector Gillespie looked to be limping.

'What happened to you?' Geddes asked the hitchhikers.

'What does it look like?' Posy was close to distraught. Her cheeks were flushed with winter and passion. 'He left us here! He stopped and told us to get out!'

'The laird? Dougal Duncan?'

'No! Mab, the Queen of the Fairies!'

Gillespie said, 'Your attitude is unhelpful. Did he molest you?'

'Don't be absurd!'

'Absurd,' echoed Leah, on her feet. She looked thoughtful, as if wondering why there had been no molesting.

'Did he say where he was going?' Geddes asked.

'The dig, of course,' Posy said.

'He said that?'

'We were all going.'

'The three of you?'

'Yes, yes.'

'Why to the dig?'

'For Heaven's sake, to see the bog man. Are we just going to stand here?'

'You told him you'd found a bog man?'

'Is it supposed to be a secret? I'd have thought that now you know, everybody knows, or soon will.' She glared at Twitty, treacherous discloser of the news of Inverballoch Man. 'The bog man belongs to him, Dougal Duncan, unless and until the law says otherwise, doesn't it? I'm supposed to be working with him. Can you imagine me not telling him?'

'He invited you to accompany him to the dig?' Geddes said.

'We invited ourselves.'

'You didn't trust him?'

'I never said that.'

'He's discarded you by the roadside. Do you trust him now?'

'No. Yes. I don't know.'

'You said he wanted to see the bog man. Nothing more than see it?'

'What more?'

'That's what I'm asking. He's strapped for cash. Might it have crossed his mind that if he stole the bog man he could sell it for a very decent sum?'

'How do I know what crossed his mind? If he tries to steal it it'll be ruined.'

'Slop and dust,' Twitty said, nodding his head.

'Shut up,' said Peckover.

Whether reminded of Twitty's presence or having lost the thread of his questions, Geddes said, 'Miss Cork, the constable brought you to us at Dundrummy Castle. You realize that leaving like that without informing us is a serious matter?'

'Was I under arrest? I realize we're wasting time in pointless chitchat. Please, pity's sake, can't we get to the dig?'

Geddes said, 'It's in hand.'

And you, Miss, he came close to saying, are a handful. I've a mind to leave you here like the laird did. Ride home on a sheep, the both of you.

'Dinna fash y'sel',' Gillespie said. 'There'll be police at the dig before Sir Dougal reaches it.'

'He stopped and told you to get out,' Geddes said. 'Why?'

'He wouldn't say why. He said here was where we got out and he opened the door.'

Gillespie said, 'Ye're sure there was no molesting?'

'Oh, really!' Posy stamped her foot. Peckover was enchanted. She said, 'No, I'm not sure. Perhaps a modicum. How can a girl ever be sure? Yes, I expect there may have been a small molestation. It's rife, isn't it, molesting, today's most fashionable offence? Shall I write it down for you and sign it? Can we go now? Which car are we going in?'

'Which car?' Leah said.

Posy Cork glared at the policemen, lined up like a barber's shop quartet, and from the policemen to the cars. Matching individuals to cars, she clearly found all possibilities and permutations uninviting.

'In here, please,' Geddes said.

He walked to the Panda. For the second time in a brief while Posy and Leah had a door opened for them. The Panda drove off.

Peckover said, 'Seems obvious. The laird wanted our archaeologists away from the castle because he didn't want them telling us where he was off to. If they hadn't invited themselves he'd 'ave insisted.'

'But he doesn't want them with him at the dig so he jettisons them half-way.'

'So what's he up to? Why doesn't he want them with 'im at the dig?'

'Today's fashionable offence, Guv. He's molesting the bog man.'

'You're 'orrible. Off we go, then.'

Had a helicopter with a searchlight happened to have been flitting about the twilit sky above Inverballoch, its pilot, looking down, might have assumed that what was going on on one particular hillside was a funeral.

Seven mourners lined the edge of a shallow grave. An eighth mourner, or perhaps a gravedigger, who had been kneeling and squatting in the grave and shunting from one end to the other, got out and reported the contents intact.

No laird. No anyone other than those at the graveside. Together the mourners covered the grave with canvas. Six of them – four policemen and two archaeologists – straggled down the hill to their transport, leaving behind at the graveside uniformed Constables Colquhoun, nineteen, and Forsyth, twenty-two.

'Bog man duty,' Colquhoun said with a sigh. 'I had options too, I didn't have to be a copper. I ever tell you I trained for the kirk? Started anyway. Three months was enough.'

'Did ye learn exorcisms? Ah dinna trust this bog man.'

They watched in envy the cortège set off along the track to the main road, thence southward to the Ram, refreshments, a roof over their heads. Nothing was to be heard other than the dwindling drone of internal combustion engines and occasional bleatings of sheep, and nothing to be seen, once the car lights had gone from the dark and shaggy landscape.

The Ram was livelier than the landscape, though not by a lot. Television crews and many of the press had departed but others were hanging on in hope of a crumb from Superintendent Geddes.

According to the woman on reception, only one guest had checked out. Mr Trelawny had paid and left an hour ago, she said.

'Paid?' echoed Posy. She felt she should say something.

'Visa.'

'Any message?'

'Nae message.'

Posy looked at the clock on the wall. Mike had said that if she wasn't back at the hotel in a couple of hours he'd be off back to London. He had not waited about. Barely three hours had passed. There would be a message in their room.

If there wasn't, that might well be that. Posy determined not to think about it. Enough was going on without heartstrings stuff. For one the black policeman in the fur coat lurking behind her.

He either wanted her for further questions, his handcuffs primed, or he wanted her flesh. Probably both. She didn't have to tell him anything. Not without a lawyer.

She didn't know any lawyers. Her dad was always saying that every rounded family should include a lawyer, a doctor, and a clergyman. He would have to whistle for them. Her sister was a buyer for Selfridge's, her brother an architecture student.

More than a lawyer Posy wanted a bath. The fur coat behind her had started to lurk leftward. She watched it pad long-leggedly through the foyer, past the gift shop, and towards the room commandeered by John Law.

In the murder room hung a pall of tobacco smoke, as if in a café scene from a French film. The smoke gave the impression that the room was warmer and snugger than it was. While less frigid than the den at Dundrummy Castle, the heating was either faulty or controlled by a miser in the boiler room. Most of the police had kept on their jackets and their blue jerseys with leather at the shoulders and elbows. Becrumbed paper plates, derelict cups and mugs, languished on surfaces.

Sergeant Menzies, the sum of Inverballoch's constabulary, wore his peaked policeman's cap geometrically on his snowy poll. He surveyed the goings-on with folded arms and a frown. He had abandoned attempts to impress on these urban whippersnappers that here was his manor, and he, repository of local lore, might be more useful to the investigation than they were ready to acknowledge. The de'il take 'em. Mother of God, they were a sorry lot! Proddies, most of 'em, to judge by their blaspheming talk and capering, and they were damned, at least that. What did they know of the shadows of the heart, the frailties of humankind, including those of a few Inverballochers he might mention?

The murder room had advanced yet further in its bid to resemble the space control centre at Cape Canaveral. Yesterday, here had been the television room, tonight its least impressive example of modern technology was its TV, relegated to a corner, its picture on, sound off, awaiting the next news programme, because once in a while the media came up with something, not that the police would admit it. Among the fancier installations were an encrypted communications-control panel – sleek, slick, lava-coloured – and a two-way FM radio that encoded every word transmitted. Any villain, news reporter, or whiz schoolchild who tried twiddling into the radio's frequency would be rewarded with a buzz like a chain saw.

Alone near the silent TV, hands warming round a mug of tea, Peckover watched a genius in headphones, Sergeant Wilson, hunched over the radio as if in receipt of a may-day from the Celebes. Sergeant Wilson was co-ordinating the cars sent to all compass points in search of Sir Dougal Duncan, Laird of Dundrummy. A knot of rapt Glasgow fuzz, students of supertech, had gathered round him. They would melt back to their posts when Superintendent Geddes walked in, Peckover had little doubt. A hoyden in a white blouse with black epaulettes, immune to the chill, said, 'Have we missed the headlines?' She skirted Peckover and without a curtsy, without so much as a glance, turned high the volume on the TV.

' . . . unilateral action against Japan and Denmark trawling for Scotland's herring within the twenty-mile limit,' announced a comely lady-newscaster. News from Scotland, presumably.

Gilbert Potter's murder would be worth an item, perhaps the main item. Enough cameras had been swarming about. Perhaps the TV newsroom was saving him up as a treat, getting shut of the herring and all the dross before coming to a climax with Sir G.

'Evening, Guv. Nippy in here.'

'Put your coat on then. Second thoughts, better not. Fur like that, this lot will chalk you up as a poofter.'

'Takes one to know one. Anyway, I just took it off. Have to get going on my report, roll up my sleeves.'

'What's going into it you've not told us?'

'Nothing.'

'Who murdered Potter?'

'I could make a couple of guesses.'

'You already did. The laird or Posy Cork, either or both, with or without assistance from Leah Howgego. Skip the report, lad. Something tells me we'll be off again in five minutes.'

'Where?'

'Door-to-door. Not your routine doorstepping, mind. The middle classes. Upper-middle if we're not careful. We might get invited inside. Listen, if we're offered a dram, accept.'

'What's a dram?'

'Auld McNessie. Bumbeg. Glendroolie single malt, ninety years in the cask. Scotch whisky, lad. A cultural phenomenon. Brings in two billion quid per annum, I saw somewhere. Jobs for seventy-five thousand Scotties. If we're offered a snort, first they'll explain it. The limpid waters of the trout streams, the peat, the fat barley of the glens, the 'Ighland and Lowland nuances, the shadings between Speyside, Skye, and Islay, delicate and different as the taste of the kisses of the girls of our youth, the bouquet, the worm—'

'Guv? May I speak?'

The telly was droning on about a speech by the Minister for Scottish Affairs, a Tory, in which he had set forth reasons why Scotland should not have its own parliament.

'Scotch may be a cultural phenomenon, it's also foul,' Twitty said. 'Will there be pineapple juice?'

'Don't be funny. Look, after 'alf an hour explaining the glory of whisky they'll pour us a quarter-inch, if we're lucky. More likely an eighth. It's not my sauce either but when in Rome. To refuse it would be an insult. We're talking about Caledonia's water of life, its *uisge beatha*, inimitable, ambrosial, malt of the malt, *crème de la crème*, not your Brixton Star and Garter's sawdust-bar mix of fifty blends of panther piss.'

'I'm to throw up on an upper-class Scotsman's carpet?'

'You don't touch it, lad. You slip it to me.'

'Ah.'

'We can't waste a fine Auld Bonny Bumbeg. It's been a long day and it's not finished. Mr Geddes is going to urge us on an 'ouse-to-'ouse, I know it. All I'm saying, a bloke can get thirsty. If we're offered refreshment, you accept. Slide it my way. I'll make it up to you.'

'How?'

'Cheeky puppy. Here 'e is. Our chief. Watch your language.'

126

SEVENTEEN

Television has brought back murder into the home — where it belongs.

Alfred Hitchcock

Superintendent Geddes came into the murder room shadowed by Gillespie. The idlers round Sergeant Wilson, genius radio operator, melted away. Peckover sang *sotto voce*, 'Hail to the chief who in triumph adva-a-ances.'

He was not confident of the tune. He believed the words were Walter Scott but where had he heard it sung? Never in Britain. Perhaps those election circuses in America that came belting out of the box every four years. Bill Geddes did not look noticeably triumphant. After a word with Sergeant Wilson he looked even less so. What the sergeant was receiving was requests for directions from squad cars searching for the laird and lost on the braesides.

The TV was chattering about a punter in Ayr, a baker and family man who in the same week had won the million-pound national lottery and twice that sum by correctly guessing eleven one-all draws on his football coupon. The overnight multi-millionaire was lugubriously on camera in his parlour, flanked by a not bad-looking wife and random children. He told the interviewer that the money wad mak' nae difference, it wadna change his life at a', he was a simple man wi' simple tastes, all he asked was his health and the health o' the wife and bairns, turf for the fire, and a crust o' bread on the table. Money ne'er brought happiness. 'Then why do the pools and the lottery and risk winning a fortune and being miserable?' the interviewer asked, reasonably in Peckover's view. 'Ah ne'er expected Ah'd win,' answered the floury-fingered plutocrat, downcast.

Peckover would have liked to have sloped off to the bar for a pint. Twitty, given the green light, would have left for his boombox. Geddes would have chosen to be back in people, traffic-ridden Glasgow, noisome with petrol fumes and curry, or anywhere away from these eerie, unpredictable Highlands. Gillespie ached to closet himself with the financial pages. They would all have been happy to have jacked it in for the day.

Either the murder room had somehow missed any news item on the murder at the Ram, or the story had been dropped as too sensational for high-minded Scottish viewers.

Geddes consulted further with Sergeant Wilson and received only dusty answers. He advanced smiling on Scotland Yard, shuffling papers and plucking forth the seating plan of the Burns supper. He had improved it by circling some names in blue, others in red.

'All will become clear when we collar the laird, let's hope.' Geddes had chosen smiles and cheerfulness as the path to results, at least for now. 'Likely he's off to Glasgow to see his solicitor or rustle up an agent to help him exploit his bog man. Meanwhile we can't just twiddle our thumbs. We'll carve up these names between us. You choose, Henry, it's all one to me. I've had an hour with Dinwiddie and frankly I'm not excited. On the other hand, it's his dirk.' He found a list of names and addresses without a dinner table. 'I've had six of us interviewing the also-rans, they've been at it all day, but now they're off laird hunting. I'd say some of these names are not so much also-rans as non-starters, so we'll forget those.'

'Such as?'

'Such as – where is she? – here, Meg McKendrick. Left before the haggis circulated. A dizzy spell. Corroborated. Two of the waitresses are children – fourteen and fifteen – and I don't buy children, not in general.' Geddes presented the seating plan. 'What about for a start your dinner neighbours, Alice McSporran, lives somewhere called Glendour – Sergeant Menzies will know – and this one, the vice chairman, Dick Haig?'

'Fine with me.'

Actually not, not now he thought of it, thought Peckover. Not Dick Haig the fisherman, enthusing over tickling, the dimensions of smolt, and how to guddle carp.

He said, 'What if they're at evening service? Better throw in some more.'

'Here's one,' Twitty said, craning to read names. 'Angus Mac-Gregor, Four, Abercorn Place, Inverballoch.'

'Why?' said Peckover.

'Great name, Guv. You wouldn't mistake him for a Sicilian.'

'Angus MacGregor is deaf.'

'We'll speak up.'

'He's deaf and eighty. Might be ninety.'

'He'll be wise as an owl. He'll know every moment of Inverballoch's history, who's who, the human side, all the couplings and vendettas.'

'How d'you know he's not just come 'ome after fifty years in Australia?'

'Has he?'

'Might 'ave.'

'Is he vigorous?'

'You mean has 'e the strength to lift a dirk?'

'I mean what if half the village are his illegitimate children and grandchildren? I've read about isolated communities like Inverballoch. He'll know everyone and everything. I'm not saying intimately but he'll have his ear to the ground.'

'Ear trumpet.'

'Fact is, an oldie like Angus MacGregor—'

'Stop prattling,' Peckover said.

'Quiet, everyone!' called the policewoman with epaulettes, commanding as a film director. 'We're on!'

Everyone fell quiet and turned to the TV screen, filled by a female talking head plus torso, arms, and shiny studio table.

Unexcited by herring, irritated by the Croesus baker, scornful of a by-election in Forfar, and brusquely disposing of new measures to protect the osprey, the mature and desirable speakerine had suddenly come alive. She placed the flat of her hands on the desk and leaned forward. Her eyes pierced the eyes of her multitude of Scots viewers with an intensity that left them, the viewers, confident she gazed directly and personally at each of them individually, not at an autocue.

' . . . major development in the investigation into the murder at Inverballoch today of the archaeologist Sir Gilbert Potter. As we reported earlier, hotel staff found Sir Gilbert stabbed to death in his room at the Ram Hotel where he had been guest of honour at a Burns dinner given by the Inverballoch Burns Club.'

The murder room not having fallen quiet in time, and some still not having shut up, nobody heard if the speakerine had said there had been a major development in the investigation or if there had not been. If there had been, what was it?

'Heading the inquiry is Detective Superintendent William Geddes of Glasgow CID. He gave this exclusive account of the murder to our reporter at the scene, Sandy Farquharson.'

Exhalations of relief went up among the tea mugs and purring hard drives. A major development had not occurred, not that the media knew of. Or minor. An exclusive with any kind of development from the super for Sandy Farquharson, whoever he might be, was about as likely as a visit to the murder room by the Loch Ness Monster.

All the same, Bill Geddes, in Peckover's opinion, would need to decide soon when to release the fact of the laird's disappearance. The media were going to find out quickly enough so they might as well be told sooner rather than later. Release it now with a photograph and let the public muck in.

Geddes's account for Sandy Farquharson and viewers was exclusive to the extent that nobody else had wanted it, his remarks being ·a repeat of what he had said minutes earlier at the 2.15 press conference. Sandy turned out to be a woman, twentyish, her hair not sandy but chestnut, perhaps dyed. She was loud, eager, and touching, seemingly unaware how vulnerable she was to the scrutiny of thousands of thousands of Scots sitting with their TV suppers and poised to cry out abuse and ridicule at her least slip of the tongue, each gesture, her haircut. Peckover guessed that she was the daughter or mistress of a top Scottish TV controller. Her pals from university, still looking for jobs, would be suicidal at her success. Bill Geddes stood with his back to the blank front wall of the Ram, though nothing indicated that this was the Ram, staring glassily as if about to be shot.

' . . . mortal wound from a knife that pierced the neck,' Geddes was saying. 'Sir Gilbert died instantaneously. The incident has shocked his family, friends, and all who . . .'

Peckover listened for the promise that an arrest would be made soon. No such promise was forthcoming.

'We are pursuing several lines of enquiry,' said Geddes on camera. 'I have every confidence in my team.'

The Geddes of here and now, in the murder room, faced himself on the screen with his eyes shut.

'From Inverballoch this is Sandy Farquharson!' trilled Sandy. 'And now back to the studio!'

Cheers and jeers in the murder room. 'Weel done, Super!' 'Guid on ye, Mr Geddes, sir!'

Back in the studio, Speakerine said, 'For the latest update on the Inverballoch slaying, stay tuned. We shall return after these messages.'

On the screen a car in misty focus exceeded the speed limit o'er hill, o'er dale, to an accompaniment of *Die Walküre*.

'Great stuff, Super!' someone in the murder room called out. 'Next stop, Hollywood!' Whistlings, applause. A wag twittered, 'We'll keep it quiet about you and Sandy, Super! Trust us!'

A family at breakfast with cornflakes. Not rubbishy gold cornflakes but mud-coloured, fibrous, mineralized, multivitamin-supplemented cornflakes with iron, zinc, and beta-carotene.

'Och, gi' me porridge,' growled a detective sergeant.

Twitty watched to see if an elderly British Airways ad might appear, voice-over by Ramona, Queen of the Druids. It didn't. Madam Speakerine returned sternly, frowning at the murder room for its unseemly behaviour. Peckover believed it unusual for commercials to split a news item in two. A fresh wheeze to keep people from switching channels? Or did the news room really have something more?

'For the latest on the murder of Sir Gilbert Potter we're taking you to Dundrummy Castle, seat of the Duncans of Dundrummy, Kildrooly, Benlochry, Inverballoch, Aberauchter, Spittal of Kegbeg' – a tic had developed at the corner of Madam Speakerine's right eye – 'and environs' – she sensibly summed up, washing her hands of it – 'and home of the present laird, Sir Dougal Duncan. Over to our reporter at Dundrummy Castle, Gina Patel. Gina, are you there?'

'I'm here,' Gina sang out, as indeed she was, swaddled in goose-down ski jacket and woolly helmet with bobble, and floodlit in front of the stately pile's front door. 'Hello! Good evening! I'm standing outside this fab seventeenth-century castle, Dundrummy Castle, home of the eleventh laird, Sir Dougal Duncan. Sir Dougal was among those celebrating Burns Night at the Ram prior to the murder of Sir Gilbert Potter. Police officers heading the investigation have been here to talk to Sir Dougal and see if he could help advance their enquiries. We had been hoping to bring you the laird live. Unfortunately he has left. However, as you can see, we still have the castle. I mean we have the police. And here they are.'

The camera panned to two police cars parked in the weeds. Peckover thought that Gina was skating perilously on the thin ice of prejudicial comment, contempt of court, defamation, all those. If the laird was hard up and innocent he might make a penny or two from this.

Gina was Asian, gorgeous, and spoke flawlessly, if a little breathlessly, like an *ingénue* playing Hedvig in *The Wild Duck*. Why, Peckover wanted to know, hadn't one of the London channels snapped her up? Could it conceivably be that she preferred to live in Scotland? Also, were there no men on this channel? Gina's breath pumped like a horse's after a steepchase.

Reading from her notes, Gina said, 'The top-ranking police who were here are Superintendent Geddes and Inspector Gillespie, of Glasgow CID' – a cheer and a whistle in the murder room – 'and from Scotland Yard, Chief Inspector Peckover and Constable Twitty, who have been called in to assist in enquiries.'

Mutterings in the murder room. A muffled raspberry. Peckover scowled at loud-mouth Gina. Twitty, grinning, started to lift his fist in a salute to the Yard, caught his Guv's eye, and thought better of it.

'Also here were the two archaelogists working under Sir Gilbert's direction, Posy Cork and Leah Howgego. They left to visit the site where archaelogical excavations are under way. The police we see here now are replacements awaiting the return of the laird.' The camera panned again to the police cars in the weeds and back to floodlit Gina. 'They are, frankly, uncommunicative. At this moment in time no arrest would appear to be imminent but we can safely say that the investigation is on course. To borrow from the language of archaelogy, no stone is being left unturned. Of course, if that were literally the case the cost would be enormous – ha-ha-ha!' Gina's laugh puzzled the police in the murder room and viewers throughout Scotland. 'We have been unable to reach Sir Dougal on his car phone but can say that he is not at the dig or the Ram. I wish I could also say that he's expected back here at any moment and we'll be able to talk to him, but I honestly don't know. He may have car trouble. Be sure we will bring you up to date as and when. This is Gina Patel at spectacular Dundrummy Castle. And now, back to the studio.'

Back to the studio and on to the weather.

'Off,' ordered Geddes.

The boisterous filly with the epaulettes switched the volume off but left the picture on just in case. The weatherman was a man, frantically mouthing. His chart showed swirling stuff over the North Sea and volleys of jolting arrows. Either Armageddon was about to strike, unerringly aimed at Inverballoch, or nothing at all would happen.

Geddes said, 'Alec, check with Wilson and that machine of his. Suggest to him politely we want the laird. What's so difficult? How many places can he go? We want Dougal Duncan, not pleas for help from lost cars or the roaring of mating stags. Henry?'

'Bill?'

Peckover sympathized with the superintendent. This job was on Geddes's head, not the Yard's. Any kudos from a success, that would go to Geddes too, and that would be fine. Gillespie stalked to Sergeant Wilson, encoder at his radio, achieving nothing so far.

Geddes said, 'What was her name – Gina? – she had nothing to say. That's almost reassuring. She hasn't met our bog man and she doesn't know we've lost the laird.'

'Might be no bad thing to go public on the laird.'

'I'll look pretty ignorant, losing a laird. We'll give it another couple of hours. As for the thing in the bog, I'll be a lot happier once Posy Cork and her experts have got it out of here. Otherwise we're going to have a circus. Meanwhile, a quick pint in the Rob Roy, a handful of chlorophyll pills, and off to the house-to-house. All right?'

An electronic buzz erupted from across the murder room. The buzz, it had been generally understood, was intended to make eavesdropping impossible, not to put the kibosh on transmitting and receiving. Sergeant Wilson's fingers fiddled and stabbed, failing to eliminate the buzz. Startled coppers stopped what they were doing to watch.

'Ha!' announced Sergeant Menzies, eyes glittery with satisfaction. 'Didna I tell ye?'

Sergeant Menzies had not told anybody anything. Even now his observation was more to himself than for general consumption. What use trying to put sense into this pampered, illiterate generation of atheists?

Immoveable as a building, arms folded, Sergeant Menzies told the assembly, not loudly, in fact softly, 'Is the auld tried and true nae guid enough then, the fine wireless, the telegraph, the morse?' He dropped his voice to careful inaudibility. 'Ye're an unco midden o' fozy, fizzenless, lang-nebbit wally-draigles!' Sergeant Menzies was hushed but impassioned. 'There's nae a puir duniewassal amang the clairtie hirsel o' ye! Skytes, smaiks, sneckdrawers! Och, awa'! Back tae your byres, ye sackless, cheatry hallions!'

Bzzzzz went the advanced but difficult radio.

'Bring your coat, lad, I'll buy you a mango juice,' Peckover said.

The barber's shop quartet ganged awa' out of the murder room and through reception to the Rob Roy Bar.

'Jason!' sang out a voice from a barstool at the counter's distant end.

The policemen turned their heads.

Mavis.

Twitty smiled sicklily. He lifted a limp hand in greeting.

'Old friend, is she?' Peckover asked.

'You know who she is, Guv. She's the *Glasgow Herald* and the one with her in the goggles is the *Dundee Advertiser*.'

Peckover brought out his wallet. 'Papaya juice?' He caught the barman's eye.

The bar had a dozen customers and the makings of a smoky evening ahead. When Geddes asked, 'What's yours?' Peckover said he was getting them, so Geddes said he'd have a hawf and hawf. Gillespie said he would too. Peckover said that he had never heard of a hawf and hawf. Geddes said the barman would know, it was a dram and a half of bitter, a nip and a chaser.

'Guv, don't look but she's beckoning.'

'She fancies you.'

'She's old enough to be my mother!'

'Grandmother. Go tell 'er 'ello. Anything she's got to say, you listen. Mavis is a pro.'

'She was at the Druids' camp. She'd already been to the dig. She said we'd all meet here at six or seven.'

'She wasn't wrong, was she? If she knew the laird was missing she'd track 'im down quicker than most. You tell her nothing. She wants to milk you.'

'Do what?'

'Off you go. On parade. Your fig cordial will be waiting so keep it brief. You want a drop of something in it?'

'No.'

'That's what you think.'

Peckover turned away and tried out on the barman with a ram's head on his breast pocket a cockney 'Two 'arf and 'arfs 'ere, please.' Twitty, head erect, eyes half closed, set off to the counter's far end as if to the gallows.

When he returned the senior officers were finishing their booze. Awaiting him on the bar was a salmon-pink fruit juice with a cherry in it.

'So?' Peckover said.

'So I'll have something in it.'

'Such as?'

'How would I know? Rum?'

'Yo ho ho and a bottle of.' Peckover gestured to the barman. He asked Twitty, 'She wants to get to know you better?'

'She wants to know if we can confirm that the laird's done a bunk, and whose is the body in the bog?'

'Blimey. Told you. She's a pro.'

'She wants to know is it a bog man or is it Cuff-Bingley?'

'Tell Mr Geddes.'

'She said, what about the butter?'

'What about it?'

'That's what she said. Don't ask me.'

EIGHTEEN

'Speed bonnie boat like a bird on the wing,
Onward,' the sailors cry!
'Carry the lad that's born to be king,
Over the sea to Skye!'
                          Sir Harold Boulton, *Skye Boat Song*

Detective Chief Inspector Peckover pressed the bell.

He said, 'Knock knock.'

'Who's there?' Twitty said without enthusiasm. The Guv's knock knocks were usually a downer.

'Alice,' Peckover said.

'Alice who?'

'Alice fair in love and war.'

Peckover gave the bell another tap. 'Not one of my best. Forget it.'

'I already have.' Until the knock knock, Twitty had been feeling perky from his pink drink with rum. 'She's out, Guv. She'll be at mass. What's her denomination? She might be at a conventicle of presbyters.'

'Alice is a free-thinker. She's in and she has someone with 'er, more's the pity.'

Surely not a lover? Sunday evening in the Highlands? Even for free-thinkers, here were cultural restraints.

The house, Glendour, a mile south of Inverballoch village, was less grand than Dundrummy Castle, but it was substantial, and set in gardens or a mini-park whose dimensions Peckover, in the dark, could not begin to guess. To judge from the menacing silhouettes, rhododendrons did well here. He pressed the bell-button and kept his finger on it.

Inside, the house was extravagantly lit. The lad could be right,

136

though. She might be out, leaving lights on to deter burglars. Burglars in Inverballoch? Any local burglar with an ounce of ambition would have left long ago for Edinburgh or Glasgow.

Peckover trod along the front of the house, put his nose to a lit window, and saw only drawn curtains. Music within though, faint and dirge-like. Gawd, did Alice play the bagpipes?

Between the corner of the house and mountains of rhodies was a garage in which would be Alice's fine old Humber, bequeathed to her by her late husband, the brain surgeon. The car in the driveway was a Peugeot, not flashy, yet dashing in its way, and probably not a first car of choice for a widow in her seventies, albeit a merry one, as Peckover recalled. More a car for a middle-aged executive or a successful actor.

Or bagpipe tutor?

He returned to the doorstep and lifted his finger to the bell. Alice McSporran opened the door.

'Henry!'

She sounded delighted. Slim, erect, silver-haired, necklaced, robed in a blue gown and sensible shawl. Caesar's wife, above reproach, but more fun. He could not believe she had nicked a dirk off a haggis dish. Why would she? But then he hadn't been watching. Half the time he'd had to listen to fishing talk from his other neighbour.

'Apologies, ma'am—'

'Oh dear, this has every sign of an official visit. I should probably address you as Mr Peckover. Do come in. Inspector, is it? The cook's husband. Imagine, such a jolly evening, and to end like that.' She stepped aside. 'Constable Twitty? You were mentioned on the wireless too. So refreshing. Do you know we have not one Negro in Inverballoch or within thirty miles? It's as if the whole latter part of the twentieth century had passed us by.'

She closed the door behind them.

'Let me take your coats. Oh, Constable, yours is quite a feature! A perfect imitation. Young people are so much more conservationist than us wrinklies.'

Peckover and Twitty would sooner have kept their coats on but they let them go. The temperature in Glendour was less frigid than in Dundrummy Castle but not by a great deal. The hall floor was spacious parquet with shag mats you could trip over. Stuffed in a Victorian hallstand were brollies and walking-sticks: trophies of the departed brain surgeon, Peckover guessed. He and Twitty followed Alice McSporran through the hall and along a well-lit passage. No company so far, apart from their hostess, but lots of lights. Glendour might be cold but you could see. The music was doleful and growing louder. Still, it wasn't bagpipes, it was a choir. Mrs McSporran led regally into a drawing-cum-music-room. As well as armchairs there was a grand piano and against a wall a clutter of music stands and violin cases.

' . . . from henceforth,' boomed the choir. 'Blessed are the dead which die in the Lord from henceforth. Blessed are the dead which die . . .'

By a loudspeaker stood the room's sole occupant, a man holding an open score, and in the other hand a baton with which he ponderously carved the air. Arresting the baton in mid beat, he shouted above the singing, 'Why, hello!'

Dick Haig. Solicitor, angler, vice chairman of the Inverballoch Burns Club. Two birds with one stone, Peckover thought doubtfully. Better to have seen them one at a time. He still might have to.

He said, 'Good evening! Please, carry on!' But maybe turn the volume down to Faint. What with conducting and casting for salmon the bloke's arm must have been in fine muscular fettle. 'We don't wish to interrupt!'

'It is finished!' proclaimed Alice, as had Jesus according to St John.

' . . . blessed, blessed,' moaned fading voices.

Silence.

Dick Haig said, 'We have these musical soirées. Not too many of us this time of year. January. That was the Brahms *Requiem.*'

'I'm sure Mr Peckover recognised the *Requiem,*' said Alice. 'He sang most resonantly last night. This is Constable Twitty.'

Twitty bowed. He would have liked more music, though not a requiem.

'I'm afraid the topic is to be our murder at the Ram,' Alice said. She brightened. 'We usually close our soirées with a warming glass and I see no reason to make an exception tonight.' She wagged a finger at Peckover, her expression both severe and coy. 'No nonsense please about being on duty. Dick, be a dear. Perhaps the Talisker.'

Dick Haig set down his score and baton and jaunted from the room, clearly familiar with Glendour and its drinks cabinet.

Alice sat, made the policemen sit, and asked if the murder of Sir Gilbert Potter had been 'an outside job'. Peckover wondered if she were a five-a-week mystery fiction addict, first in line every Wednesday noon at the itinerant library van.

He said, 'We're looking into that.'

Alice said that positively no one at the Burns supper, or any resident of Inverballoch that she knew, and she was widely acquainted, was capable of murder. People who said we were all capable talked poppycock. She was aware of the dark recesses of the soul but none the less. Not in Inverballoch. Andrew Dinwiddie's dirk may have done the deed but Andrew could no more have killed than could an innocent baby, or for that matter, she herself. The mildest of men, Andrew. That slashing and gouging the haggis, all an act. Andrew was a thespian manqué, he should have gone on the boards. He was as gentle and innocent as Dick – as Mr Haig. Men, such innocents! She was not talking about the Druid campers, mind. She knew nothing about them but she had no objection as long as they cleaned up before they left. Sir Dougal now, she would hardly go so far as to describe him as innocent. The mill could tell some tales, though that was before.

'Before what? What mill?'

'You'll have to brush up on our local customs, Henry. The old textile mill by the river. Our trysting place for courting Inverballochers with nowhere else to go. I remember the minister would drive there in his rackety Talbot with two of the beadles and they'd storm into the mill to flush out the fornicators. They'd smite the doors with their sticks, and the fornicators, hip and thigh, and order them to the kirk. "Repent, O ye harlots, whoremongers, defilers, vipers, and sewers of filth and abominations!" It was quite a scene and all anyone was doing was cuddling.'

'Very colourful.' Peckover wondered if among the cuddlers had been Alice. 'You mentioned Sir Dougal. You said that was before?'

'Before the old laird passed away – that's Fergus, Dougal's father – Dougal may have frequented the mill. I'm not saying he did. No tittle-tattle. And, of course, Dougal always had a car. But Fergus wouldn't permit him bringing wenches to Dundrummy Castle. He was one of the old school, God fearing, strict to the point of, of—'

'Insanity?'

'Good gracious, no! Irascible, perhaps.'

'A little unbalanced?'

'Henry, you're not to put words in my mouth. Ah, Dick. I hope you found clean glasses.'

Gentle, innocent Dick, entering laden, said, 'I've seen cleaner. Mrs Menzies is past it. You should pay her to stay away. Buy a dishwasher.'

'Dick, you're ruthless.'

If the glasses had been clean before their encounter with Dick they would now be less so. He carried them upside-down in one hand, three fisherman's fingers deep in three of them, his thumb up the fourth. In the other hand, a bottle. He might have been more laden, Peckover supposed. He might have found a tray and added to it a soda siphon, nuts, cheese, Ryvita, a little smoked salmon. Evidently the *après-soirées* were kept pure and undefiled. He tried to catch Twitty's eye but the lad had bent foward to tie the laces of his jogging boots in an intricate four-loop clover-leaf bow known to few outside the Brixton youth scene and perhaps California.

Alice asked, 'Is the laird still missing?'

'Missing?' Peckover said. 'The laird?'

'It was on the news. Poor Gina Patel, waiting in the cold outside that perfectly dreadful castle.'

'He'll be at the mill.'

'Henry, you're too frivolous.'

'You hinted he has a reputation.'

'I hinted at no such thing. Dick, just a taste for me. Gina Patel thought he might have car trouble.'

'P'raps 'e's with Gina in his castle. Carried 'er up to the ottoman in the minstrels' gallery.'

'Henry!'

'Quite a Don Juan, the laird?'

'I don't know what gives you that idea.'

I didn't have it until you gave it me, Peckover could have replied. He accepted a glass of barley juice from Dick the Butler. Third of a glass. More a triple than a double. Hospitable, the Scots. This wouldn't have him bursting into song but it would warm his blood to a simmer. Twitty had received the same amount and was looking at him. Peckover looked the other way. Dick Haig's glass was similarly well supplied. Who was to be tonight's dissipated driver or was Dick sleeping over? Alice had a thimbleful, hardly worth dirtying the glass for, if it had been clean to begin with.

'Special, is it?' Peckover said, lifting his glass to the light. Good Scotch in Scotland was like a newborn baby anywhere. You had to be admiring. 'Tackle, did you say?' That wasn't its name. Began with a Ta though. 'Tally-ho?'

'Tally-ho,' Dick Haig said, and sniffed and sipped.

'Slainte,' said Alice.

Peckover tasted the silky, combustible fluid. He couldn't have said what it tasted of – Scotch, he supposed – but the texture was earth, air, fire, and water.

'Talisker is from the Isle of Skye, from its sole distillery, and is fabled, unique,' Dick Haig said. 'We have here a ten-year-old full-bodied single malt. Less full bodied than, for example, Lagavulin or Laphroaig from the Isle of Islay, though some consider that to its advantage. The nose is muscular and the finish memorable.'

Was he parodying a wine tasting? wondered Peckover. No, he was in earnest.

'Hold it on the tongue and against the palate,' Dick Haig said. 'Swill before swallow is the rule. Note the viscous, almost oily texture. Talisker dates back to eighteen thirty-one. Skye, of course, is where Bonnie Prince Charlie escaped to after Culloden.'

Peckover nodded agreement. If he stopped nodding he might nod off. Dick Haig was already as boring about whisky as he had been about fish. Peckover ceased nodding long enough to sip, swill, and swallow.

'Yes?' enquired Dick. 'I don't know if you find it, let's say, slightly smoky in flavour? Floral, perhaps?'

Peckover didn't know either. Was the bloke really asking his opinion?

'Most distinguished,' he said.

'Absolutely,' enthused Dick.

'Hrrrnksh!' uttered Twitty, trapping in his hand an explosive cough, nasal and watery. 'Excuse me.'

'Bless you,' said Alice.

Peckover refrained from looking. His assistant had evidently swilled and swallowed. He chanced a glance. The level in the constable's tumbler had fallen by half. The lad was dabbing his eyes.

Now he was leaning forward. 'Mrs McSporran, ma'am?' Twitty said. 'Just curious. The helpers, the Misses Cork and Howgego, they've not actually dug up anything today, far as you've heard? You're widely acquainted. Ear to the ground. Like dug up any-thing unexpected?'

'Butter!' pronounced Alice.

'More butter?'

'More than what? The tub we sampled last night. How much butter do you want?' She grimaced. 'You should have been at our Burns dinner, Constable. Next year you shall be. I'll see you receive an invitation. Rabbie would be the first to be thrilled. A true democrat, Rabbie, a man of the people, no matter their ethnicity.'

Dick Haig said to Peckover, 'You'll be with us in May, I hope?'

May? I bleedin' won't, Peckover assured himself. He would be back in London by midweek at worst, and staying there, the Potter case solved or not.

'I can think of nothing nicer,' he said.

'The season opens in March but they're still recovering from spawning. May is excellent, they're rising freely all day. Fine hatches of fly. By June they're ravenous for olives, gnats, and some mayfly. I'll show you the livelier stretches. We'll go together. Might land some five and six pounders, though if the water's low there'll be predations from the cormorants.'

'Tight lines, screaming reels,' Peckover said, wondering where he had heard the expression and what it meant. 'Salmon, eh?'

'Salmon?' echoed baffled Dick. 'Trout.'

Peckover took a genteel sip. He skipped the swill step. Too time-wasting. Twitty's query on progress at the dig was acceptable. Neither Alice nor Dick Haig appeared to be aware that the dig had uncovered a bog person.

Tomorrow, breakfast time, the nation would know, courtesy of Mavis and the *Glasgow Herald*. How Mavis knew would never be known. She would protect to the death her source, presumably a copper from the murder room.

Or Posy perhaps? As he understood it, Posy wanted Inverballoch Man kept dark and the hot breath of the media out of it until the body reached that controlled environment where whatever had to be done would be done to preserve it for the next three thousand years. But if Posy had had a hand in the murder of Potter she could be lying all along the line. The knives in academe evidently being twelve inches long and scalpel sharp, she might want to be shut of Potter for ever, and have the dig to herself.

The Druids as Mavis's source? Lurking near the dig with their metal detectors, the lure of treasure trove curdling their loins, and taking a peek under the canvas when nobody was around? There'd be some of them not above flogging bog man information in return for a cheque.

Peckover said, 'Mrs McSporran, thinking back to our supper, do you recall the dirk on the haggis plate, circulating?'

'I don't.'

'Mr Haig?'

Dick Haig gestured with his glass and shook his head. Peckover was not convinced that he had understood the question.

Twitty sat as still as a Quaker. His glass was empty.

Peckover put desultory questions to Alice McSporran and Dick Haig on what they had done, where been, after the dinner. How and when had they learned of Sir Gilbert's death? What did they know of the Ram's staff? Gordon Smith, for example, the young night manager. He probed further into the laird's satyriasis. A liaison perhaps with Miss Cork or Miss Howgego? To no effect. Alice insisted that the murder was an outside job.

His own glass appeared to be empty. He stood up.

'Most 'elpful. Anything at all occurs to you, don't 'esitate. We're at the Ram.'

'Ram,' Twitty emphasized loudly, and he sprang to his feet and to attention. 'You have certainly been. So obliged.' He bowed. 'Ma'am. Sir.'

'Too kind,' murmured Alice. 'Your coats. Let me see you to the door.'

Dick Haig said, 'Your best bet for salmon is September, early October. The beats are competitive but I should be able to book you something. I'll see to it tomorrow.'

Peckover could not cope with this. On route for the door he halted and donned an engaging smile. He believed the smile to be engaging. Next step would be to sound off-hand, only passingly curious, which wouldn't be difficult.

He said, 'So what's the hot word on Cuff-Bingley these days?'

As lines go, not a show-stopper, nothing to match, say, We'll tak a right guid-willie waught. But he seemed to have won their attention, Alice's anyway. Twitty was barely perceptibly bouncing in his pneumatic joggers, twitching his shoulders, and flicking his fingers. Within moments, from Quakerdom to deep rap.

Alice said, 'Henry, you've been delving into our dark secrets.'

'Nothing in Inverballoch is secret for long is what you said.'

'I said no such thing!'

'No? Thought you did. Someone did.'

143

'It's true anyway. My husband's theory was that Sir Wilfred was so in debt from expeditions here, there, everywhere – Mesopotamia, Peru, Inverballoch – that his creditors were after him with Rottweilers, so he sailed for the colonies. Were there Rottweilers then? I don't remember any. I do recall colonies.'

'You meet 'im, Sir Cuff?'

'Never. Robert and I were in Glasgow. Our house here was for weekends whenever Robert managed to escape from the Infirmary.'

After a proper pause for departed Robert, Peckover raised his eyebrows at Dick Haig. Same question. He restored the engaging smile. What with the eyebrows and the smile he looked like Pagliacci having to play the clown though his heart was breaking.

Dick said, 'Before my time. I wasn't born.'

'No theories? Something overheard from the older generation? Your parents?'

'Grayling, now there's a beautiful fish,' said Dick Haig. 'For grayling you'd best be here in October, November, which of course is when trout are in their worst condition. We'll need a light hand for grayling because they have a tender mouth and often break away.'

'A light 'and. Absolutely. We'll be on our way, then.'

Peckover, putting on his coat, was satisfied that the visit to Glendour had not been a total loss. One certainty was that nobody as batty as Dick Haig could have committed murder and got away with it for an entire day.

NINETEEN

Whisky is the life of man,
Whisky Johnny!
Whisky in an old tin can,
Whisky for my Johnny!

Anon.

Drizzle sprinkled through the cold. Glendour's door closed behind the policemen.

'Think you can drive, Guv?'

'Cheeky monkey.'

They scurried to the Toyota.

'Gimmee Bingley, gimmee Cuff, gimmee girls and all that stuff,' rapped Twitty. He loathed rap. He could not believe he was rapping. 'Bring on floozies, bring on fluff, if it's female, that's enough. If it ain't, man that's tough—'

'Shut up.'

Twitty stumbled against the side of the Toyota. He opened the rear door, closed it, and found his way into the front passenger seat. Peckover drove from Glendour and its rhododendrons into the night.

He sang *andante*, 'Pa pa pa pa pa pa paa—pa—ty tiddle iddle iddle iddle pom.'

'What's that, then?'

'The Trout. Schubert. You can 'ear the fish jumping about. Don't you know real music?'

'I've heard you doing your "Knees Up, Muvver Brown".'

'This is a piano quintet but there are words. I think there are. Dunno who gave it words. P'raps Schubert did. Franz. Died young of syphilis so be warned. It'd be nice to be able to sing it in German.'

145

It would be nice to sing it in English if it had English words. The wipers swished, the headlights flung out white cones that lit up wet hedges and a blank road.

Peckover sang, 'Plop plop plop plop plop plop – splash – tight lines and screa-he-heaming reels.' He felt cheerful and he knew why. 'What d'you make of Dick Haig?'

'Haig.' Twitty pulled his sable collar up around his ears. 'As a legal type, local pillar, all that, he might have shown at least a smidgen of interest in the first decent crime in Inverballoch in his lifetime and probably this century. A guilty party would button his lip tight or want to know how our enquiries were going. Haig asked nothing. He's on another planet. *Ergo*, forget him. Don't quote me.'

'Alice McSporran didn't ask anything either.'

'Asked if the laird was still missing. Loads of gossiping. Enjoyed herself. No stress, no sweat. Crosh off the lady dowager Alish too, say I.'

'You all right?'

'Course.'

'So be quiet. Go to sleep.'

Peckover needed to concentrate. A poem was gestating.

> We'll gang nae mair tae the loch, och,
> Wi' Jennie and Jamie and Joch, och;
> Jennie is game, Jamie the same,
> But Joch has a wen on his coch, och—
> Hey nonny the liver and lights!

Could be the start of a ballad pulsating with blude and virgins and shipwrecks off the Isle of Eigg, but to be authentic it would need a strong story and another thirty verses so he didn't think so.

'Let's 'ave some radio.'

'It's all Scottish country-and-western.'

'Short-wave isn't.'

The update from the murder room was that Superintendent Geddes and four cars had gone to the Stones of Skelloch. Person or persons, possibly Druids, believed sighted there by patrol car on main Glasgow road.

Laird still missing.

Firkin of seventeenth-century bog butter, last seen in kitchen fridge, Ram Hotel, also missing.

146

Peckover switched the radio off before anything else went missing.

Mavis Murray had known about the butter going missing before the police had. She'd known something. She'd have had spies in the kitchen.

'Which way are these Stones, then?'

'Way we've come, Guv. You'll have to turn round. Not far.'

High on a hill overlooking the Glasgow road Superintendent Geddes, Inspector Gillespie, and a dozen police with flashlights and hurricane lamps were preparing to leave the Stones of Skelloch. Whether the person or persons believed spotted from a patrol car had been Druids, tourists, bogles, spooks, or spirits that may be seen by one who has indulged in spirits, they had gone, leaving not a wrack behind, or lager can.

Peckover, muddy and damp, was surprised to find Posy Cork here. She had been heading for the Claymore Dining-Room when Geddes, hustling out of the Ram, had collided with her and invited her along. She was the closest he had available to an expert on stones and Druids.

Leah Howgego had evidently gone to bed, or at any rate to her room. Or so she had said.

'Any footprints, tyre tracks will have to wait till daylight,' Geddes said. 'I'm not hopeful after our trampling about.'

'But someone was 'ere?'

'Who's to say?'

Bill Geddes had not expected Stonehenge but the Skelloch Stones were a let down, especially by artificial light. He remembered visiting on Orkney a far more impressive stone circle. That circle had only four upright stones but the loftiest had been seventeen feet high. These dozen, mossy Skelloch stones were so eroded that only one reached a length of five feet and that lay flat. They were so higgeldy-piggeldy that there was no discerning a circle. The best he could have said for them was that they were old and they were free from graffiti. He guessed that guide books gave them a sentence, scholarly books perhaps half a page.

Peckover lifted his hat to Posy Cork. 'Sorry, I missed all this. Since I'm 'ere, what am I looking at?'

'Probably the fourth millennium.' Posy sounded reasonably civil, for Posy. She had already said her piece to Geddes but she enjoyed the role of pundit. 'That was the peak of megalithic architecture.

We're standing on the tumulus. Underneath was a tomb but it collapsed inward centuries ago. You'd have to be here when it's light. Skelloch, I'm told, is Gaelic for a screech. There's a legend, or was, that the stones screech at the full moon, and another that they screech on the death of the head of a family.'

'Any family?'

'Presumably an Inverballoch family. I've no idea. I'm not into fairy stories.'

Peckover picked up a lantern and put the muddy toe of his shoe on the stone that lay flat. Two standing stones, what was left of them, flanked it.

He said, 'This the sacrificial altar?'

'You mean the dawn sacrifice, the sun rising, Druids chanting, dogs howling, and the victim beheaded? Boys' adventure story stuff and really extraordinarily puerile. You can believe it if you want to.'

'You don't?'

'I'm not saying there wasn't human sacrifice. There was. This stone is almost certainly the recumbent stone. They're not common but some circles have them to the south as a sighting point. If you stand at the centre of the circle the recumbent stone is directly beneath the highest point of the lunar path.'

'I see,' fibbed Peckover.

Astronomy was not among his stronger subjects. He thought he wouldn't ask for elucidation. Twitty wasn't asking either. He had returned to his Quaker mode, unless he had switched to Trappist monk.

'Thank you.' Peckover tipped his hat.

Posy sought out Superintendent Geddes for a ride back to the Ram. The drizzle had become steady rain, the drift of police down the hill to their cars was under way. Peckover took off his hat and shook rain from it. Not too many sheep hereabouts. Possibly some rabbits, chafing for the intruders to leave, and whether Posy Cork liked it or not, perhaps the shades of legions of Druids.

'Off we go, lad.'

'Where?'

'Angus MacGregor. You chose 'im, remember? You liked 'is name.'

Peckover nosed the Toyota along a street lined with stone cottages. Street lights, lighted windows, a Clydesdale Bank, a bloke in yellow trawlerman's oilskins on a bike. Pretty dreary. The rain didn't help. If he found Argyll Street he might get his bearings. He told Twitty to watch for Abercorn Place.

'You just passed it,' Twitty said.

'Thanks a lot.'

'Knock knock.'

Twitty pretended not to hear.

''Urry up. You'll like this one.'

'Who's there?'

'Angus.'

'Angus who?'

'Angustura bitters and gin make a pink gin. You don't 'ear much about pink gin these days.'

Four, Abercorn Place, was one of a half-dozen bungalows *circa* 1955. Lights were on inside. Peckover again lifted the knocker and let it drop with a thud.

Twitty said, 'That what this one's going to give us? Pink gin?'

'You'd best 'old back.'

'Nonshense.'

Angus MacGregor in a dung-coloured dressing-gown with a tasselled cord opened the door, peered, and said, 'Who're ye? Will it be the polis?'

'You're expecting the police?'

'Aye, Ah'm no mistaken. Ye'll be the queer fellow from Scotland Yard. And a blackie, is it? Come in then, if ye must. Wipe your feet.'

Peckover had known worse welcomes. At least at last a house that was warm. Angus MacGregor must have been boiling. Under the dressing-gown he had on a wool shirt, jersey, and presumably underwear, probably also wool. Between the bottoms of striped pyjama trousers and fleecy slippers could be glimpsed wool socks of that thickness and density that never wears out. The slippers looked spanking new, probably a Christmas present from a great-grandchild. Peckover was impressed that Angus MacGregor should be wearing them. Men beyond a certain age seldom used new items. They stored them. The British Isles creaked beneath the weight of stored, unused apparel given to elderly gentlemen at Christmas and on their birthday.

'If ye've a mind to stay, tak' aff your coats,' said the gnarled old oak tree. He closed the door. 'Nae obligation. Depairt anytime.

Ye'll hae a dram. If it's wasted on ye, it's wasted. Sae be it.'

'Thank you, sir,' Peckover began, 'but we might forgo the dram because . . .'

He gave up because the old boy was walking away. Angus MacGregor either couldn't hear or wasn't listening. That was all right because the last dram had left Peckover thirsty. He was not about to be churlish towards whatever hospitality might be going.

The men from the Yard followed Angus MacGregor into a scalding sitting-room.

'I didn't know you were queer,' whispered Twitty

'That's enough from you,' Peckover whispered.

'He said you were.'

'Queer in this part of the world means mildly eccentric in an engaging way. Appealing and solid. It's 'Ighland usage derived from the Gaelic.'

He pointed Twitty to a chair and seated himself in another, an arrangement of metal tubes and elk hide spawned in Helsinki or Stockholm and once upon a time *de rigueur* among subscribers to *House and Garden*. The room looked to have been furnished several decades earlier and lived in with reasonable care. A dog should have been in attendance, sniffing the visitors and chewing the furniture, but it was presumably shut in the kitchen. The heat came from radiators tuned to conflagration pitch. Tobacco smoke old and new infused every crevice and pore. Atmosphere-wise the room was brother to a snug at the Carlton, White's, any gentlemen's club in Piccadilly or whatever the Edinburgh equivalent – the Auld Alliance, the Balliol, the Bannockburn. The most comfortable chair, clearly Angus's, or the dog's, had been acquired from such a club, being of cracked, split leather, shiny, and smelly. It was low slung and scooped from the pressure of countless overweight bums. Any woman sitting in it would have had skirt trouble, finding her knees higher than her head. On a table beside the chair were four pipes, a packet of St Bruno, and ash and dead matches in an ashtray with the diameter of a frisbee. On another table lay books, newspapers, and a magnifying glass. The walls were white. The ceiling, also white at the last paint job, was arsenic yellow shading to bronze in the area above the chair and pipe smoke.

Angus fumbled a hearing-aid into his ear and padded from the room in his Christmas slippers. Twitty stood up and tacked towards the books.

''Urry up, lad. So what's he reading?'

Twitty read aloud from the spines, '*Diary and Correspondence of Samuel Pepys. The Normans in Scotland*, R. L. G. Ritchie. *Mustang Man*, Louis L'Amour. *Ride the Dark Trail*, Louis L'Amour. He's on a cowboy kick, Guv.'

'Siddown.'

'We're not finished. *Showdown at Yellow Butte*, Louis L'Amour. *The Shadow Riders*—'

'Pssst!'

Twitty retreated to his chair as Angus MacGregor came in with a bottle and glasses.

'Mr MacGregor, sir,' Peckover said loudly. 'About Sir Gilbert Potter. Wretched business.' He raised his arm in an attempt to attract the old man's attention. 'Might I ask, d'you recall at all the murder weapon, the dirk, on the haggis dish, the plate of haggis that went round the table? Last night?' No reaction from Angus MacGregor, lining up the glasses. 'The Burns dinner?' Hell's bells. 'The chairman's dirk? Andrew Dinwiddie?'

Angus poured whisky.

'Sir!' shouted Peckover.

'Nae need for that, Ah'm no deef.' Angus MacGregor presented tumblers half filled with pumpkin-coloured venom. ''Tis The Macallan. Your health.' He lowered himself into his clubman's chair. 'What did ye say?'

Peckover launched into his litany of questions. Dirk, Druids, stone circles, buried treasure, butter, the textile mill, Sir Dougal Duncan, Posy and Leah, Ram staff, and would Mr MacGregor give an account of what he did, where he went, after 'Auld Lang Syne'?

The answers, mainly monosyllabic and negative, failed to add to the policemen's store of knowledge on the murder of Gilbert Potter.

Did Mr MacGregor have an opinion on why anyone would murder Sir Gilbert?

'Aye, I have,' said Angus. 'He was a flatulent, gumptious gawpit. He's nae loss.'

He thumbed St Bruno into his pipe.

Peckover said, 'If every flatulent what-you-said had to be despatched to 'is maker we'd have a much diminished population.'

'That one was worse. Bletherin' on aboot cut-throat clansmen and barbarian ancestors.' Angus glowered, then twinkled. He lit and applied a match. 'There's irony in that cut-throat clansmen,

wouldn't ye agree? A self-fulfilling prophecy if ever I heard one.'
A rasping like a death rattle sounded deep in Angus MacGregor's
throat. The rattling emerged from his mouth along with smoke.
He was laughing. 'Sup up. I'm nae offering one for the road. Ye've
had enough and it's lost on ye. 'Tis The Macallan o' Speyside. A
bonnier whusky ne'er graced God's earth.'

Peckover could not blame Angus MacGregor for wanting them
on their way. The old fellow heard well enough, watchful and
supine in his chair, and at frequent intervals setting fire to the
soggy compost that inhabited his pipe. But he showed little interest
in Potter's demise beyond being in favour of it. He had not known
Sir Dougal was missing and did not give the impression he would
lose sleep over the matter. His chief concern was keeping his pipe
going. Of the laird's reputation as a ladies' man, he said, 'Ye've
been with Alice. She's a great one for the clatter. She's gibble-
gabbled tae ye aboot courtin' couples at the mill. It's lost oppor-
tunities o' her youth she's regretting.'

'What was lost? She had a long, happy marriage to a brain
surgeon.'

'Lang, aye. But second best if ye'd once had a mind tae be Lady
Duncan o' Dundrummy, paying your respects at Balmoral, and
motoring off tae garden parties at Buckingham Palace.'

'That would be the late laird, Fergus, the father? Not Dougal.'

'Ye're quick. There's the making o' a detective in ye. Ask me
nae mair. Ah ken nothing.'

Peckover suspected he kenned more than he was saying. On the
other hand he had never heard of a Posy Cork. The lassie beside
him at the supper, he insisted, had been a Posy Byng or Bung.

'A corker,' Twitty said.

Peckover shot Twitty a look. Twitty sat tapping his feet, an
inane smile on his face. His glass was empty.

'Our other archaeologist, Sir Wilfred Cuff-Bingley, long ago,'
Peckover said, and he stood. 'You'll 'ave an opinion on him?'

'Ah hae nae opinion. Ah wasna here.'

'Where were you?'

'North Africa, Italy, France. It'll be in your file. Ye maun be
awa' tae your hamework, mon. Ah'll bid ye guid nicht.'

Angus heaved himself out of his chair. Trailing clouds of St
Bruno, he headed from the room, the policemen at his slippered
heels. Peckover supposed it might have been worse. They had
been spared a dissertation on The Macallan.

'My 'omework says you're of a generation that could have ideas about a lost archaeologist.'

'Canna ye no let sleepin' archaeologists lie? What's it tae anyone what became o' the puir mannie, fifty years after? Dinna be rattlin' skeletons best left in peace. The fella's dead and buried.'

'Aye – I mean, probably. But where, why, and how?'

'Try Tasmania.'

'Misleading the police is a serious matter.'

'Ah'm no apologizing. Off wi' ye tae Tasmania!' Auld Angus opened the front door on to a wild night and thrust his head out. ''Tis nothing, a touch o' moor grime. Ye'll likely survive unless ye hae a weak chest.'

'Mr MacGregor, sir.' Peckover removed Angus's scraggy hand from the doorhandle and closed the door. 'Two archaeologists in Inverballoch, one of them vanished, the other stabbed through the neck. Not enough to be an epidemic, but to learn about either might be to throw light on the other. True, it might not. Gilbert Potter may not 'ave been a favourite of yours but just the same. Why are you hostile to seeing justice done?'

Angus MacGregor took his pipe from his mouth and thrust his lower lip damply forward. He appeared to be pondering. His hedgerow eyebrows twitched. He adjusted the button in his ear, stuck the fumey pipe back between hazel-brown teeth, sucked, and removed it.

'Twa points, for your information. First, afore ye gang tae Tasmania' – he emitted rasping sounds that were a chuckle – 'ye maun hie tae Speyside. Frae the blank look on your faces, that's Inverness east to Banff and MacDuff. Seek out Craigellachie. There's a bridge wi' four stone turrets across the river. Will ye remember this or am Ah wastin' my breath?'

Peckover took out notebook and pencil. He feared he was entering a Gaelic twilight of sprites and boggarts. At Craigellachie, Angus MacGregor would be about to tell him, he would meet a bristly hag wearing an enchanted tam o' shanter. She would recite a rune with the refrain, *Sing hey for Cuff-Bingley, och aye*, and lead him to the Cave of the Magic Wart. And so forth.

Angus said, 'Thomas Telford designed the bridge. Ye've heard o' Thomas Telford?'

'Possibly.'

'Designed Cadelonian Canal,' Twitty said. 'Scotchman. Deshigned lots shtuff. Menai Shtrait Shushprension Bridge.'

153

'Aye, weel, a mile or twa up the road frae the bridge at Craigella-chie is The Macallan distillery. Since ye havna asked, Ah'm tellin' ye The Macallan ye seemed tae hae nae trouble drinkin' doun is a single malt aged eighteen years i' the cask. Anyone but a puir untutored Sassenach wad hae noted the sherry flavour. The balance and the finish—'

'What was your second point?' Peckover asked.

'Ye say Dougal Duncan is missing? If ye're curious about the Duncans o' Dundrummy, talk tae Annie. That's Annie Menzies. She has the Antiques Emporium by the polis station.'

TWENTY

If you can say
'It's a braw bricht moonlicht nicht,'
Ye're a' richt, ye ken.
R.F. Morrison, *Just a Wee Deoch-an-Doris*

The Annie Menzies Antiques Emporium and the adjacent police station were closed and in darkness. All Argyll Street looked to be closed.

While Peckover rang the bell to the shop, Twitty said carefully, 'Donatello, the opera singer. She sold me his cloak. Old friendsh.'

'What're you talking about?'

'We've met her son, Sergeant Menzies, he of the snowy hair.'

Twitty did not care what he was talking about so long as it distracted Our 'Enry from his next knock knock.

'Op-er-aaa, O mama mia-a-a!' Twitty warbled in a light tenor to the accompaniment of Peckover's jangling of the bell.

'Donatello wasn't an opera singer, mate, 'e was a sculptor. Wasn't 'e? David, right?'

'David Donatello.'

'David the bronze – Gawd! 'Olding a sword and wearing an 'at.'

'Cost a fiver, that cloak. Belonged to Donny somebody. Great saleslady if she's still alive.'

'Why wouldn't she be?'

'Getting on, Annie Menzies is. Older than Angus MacGregor. Rose-red Annie half as old as time.'

'It's not Menzies, it's *Mingies*. Rhymes with Thingies. Wait in the car.'

'Don't be like that, Guv. You'll need me. Annie's pet, I am. One of her cash-paying cushtomers. Can't be many. This her?'

The policemen peered through the window. A light had gone

155

on in the back of the shop illuminating bric-a-brac and a stick of a woman making a shuffling advance between piled cast-off clothing, tables loaded with mismatched china, and wrecked furniture.

They eventually heard a key in the door and a creak as the door began to open. Peckover raised his hat in readiness for the presenting of compliments. Annie Menzies in a long knitted dress blinked upward at the two hulks on her doorstep. On her head she wore a woolly cap perhaps picked off the top of a clothes-heap on her journey through the shop.

'Closed,' said Annie. ''Tis Sunday.'

'Evenin', madam,' said Peckover, hat raised. ''Ave I the pleasure of addressing Mrs Annie Menzies?' Damn. After all that he had pronounced it as it looked and ought to be pronounced. ''Enry Peckover, Scotland Yard. This is Constable—'

'The opera cloak!' Annie pointed a chicken-bone finger at Twitty. 'No refunds. No merchandise returnable except at the discretion of the management. That's me. Sale of Goods Act, nineteen sixty-one.' She smiled slyly. 'I made that up. I couldna say when or what it was. Come in. I've heard tell o' ye. Would either o' ye be wanting ashtrays? I have a plethora. Half price. 'Tis the January sale.'

She locked the door behind the policemen, shuffled back through the shop, and led the way into a snug kitchen smelling of baking cake and tropically hot from a coal-burning Aga. Stoveside rocking-chair, TV, radio, and a capacious cat basket containing a mottled cat that lifted its head to appraise the visitors.

'Sit ye doun. Not in the rocking-chair.'

Annie Menzies continued through the kitchen and out by a far door.

Peckover chose the armchair facing the rocking-chair. Perhaps this chair was the son's, Jamie, Inverballoch's law enforcer. The kettle by the stove looked promising, or it would if Annie were to fill it and apply heat. On a shelf among the jars of jam, packets of toffees, cocoa, oatmeal, and fig newtons, he spotted a can of Darjeeling. Just the ticket. In twenty-four hours he had imbibed more Scotch whisky than in all last year and it was still only January.

Twitty sat at the scrubbed table, drumming his fingers on it and observing, a little glassily, on the wall to his left, a water-colour of a haloed, panchromatic Mary with the Infant Jesus. The colours were vivid, as if chosen by the Infant. Fat, floury edibles cooled on a wire oven-rack at the table's corner, within reaching distance, but he was not tempted. He no longer believed he might be coming down with flu, but if he were, the potions *du pays* that raged through his system would kill every germ dead in its tracks.

Annie Menzies shuffled back bearing a bottle. Routine Black & White, a blend, perceived Peckover. A Scotch he had actually heard of. Two-handedly she poured out a half tumbler for each of her guests and presented the result. Twitty mumbled, rose to his feet in gratitude, reseated himself, and set the glass down distantly by the baked goods.

Annie Menzies at the sink poured for herself a teacup of water. She sat in the rocking-chair.

'I know why ye're here. 'Tis in furtherance of your enquiries into the matter at the Ram. My son is the police in Inverballoch.'

'A fine policeman,' Peckover said.

'He was at the scene in a jiffy.'

'He was.' A jiffy in Inverballoch-time evidently lasted about forty minutes. 'A brief question or two, madam. Sir Gilbert Potter—'

'I know nothing of that. I never set eyes on the dead mannie and I wasna at the Burns Night. I don't get out a lot these days. Except Sundays, of course. Father Ross will tell you I never miss mass.'

'Exactly. And you know Inverballoch. You know its folk.' She was not so old as to have been at school with Posy Cork's bog man but she couldn't have been that many generations away either. 'You'll have memories.'

'Will I tell you my story?'

'Please.'

What was he saying? Dare he ask her to keep it short?

Annie Menzies said, 'My husband left me in nineteen thirty-one when I was carrying Jamie. He was not the father. That was his excuse for going, the sorry wee cuckold, but he'd have gone anyway, and good riddance. He was no an honest man. He should never have married, not to a woman. These days he would marry a man. They do that in some places, in churches themselves even, did ye know? Not in a Catholic church. Mother o' God, we're not to that yet. In the heathen churches with the women bishops. I'd say it's mostly in America, but take heed, the day is coming, though I'll no be here to see it, thanks be to God. Will ye no be writing this down? 'Tis my statement.'

'Constable, take this down.'

'I'm familiar with police procedure,' Annie said. 'I've typed statements. I've seen all sorts, this being a police station and Jamie the law, y'understand?'

'Sergeant Jamie Menzies, your son, with the grand head of hair,' Peckover said. 'Got that, lad? Perhaps, madam, you'd be so good as to begin at the beginning.'

'I have. That is the beginning. I'm nigh the end. He emigrated to Vancouver, my husband. If he were alive he'd be a hundred and two and my husband yet. Folk didn't divorce in those days. You had to be Henry the Eighth to divorce. Not that I hadn't grounds for an annulment. One thing I'll grant him. Me and Jamie needed his name as father on the birth certificate and he made no fuss. So the bairn was and remains Jamie Menzies, and the laird and I we saw each other another ten happy years.'

She took a sip of water, shut her eyes, and gently rocked.

Was that it? The end? Peckover kept quiet, trusting that Twitty would do the same. What laird? Was Annie seeing the laird the same as knowing him in a biblical manner, as when Judah, or Jeroboam, went in unto Adah, daughter of Jonah, or Moab, and he knew her and she did conceive and bare a son named Omar, or, as the case might be, Jamie Menzies? Annie had closed down with what promised to be interesting, unless every word was make-believe. Angus MacGregor had struck him as mischievous enough to steer him to Scotland's best-loved tale-spinner.

Perhaps he should prompt her. Without prompting she might lose her train of thought. Not to be grim about it but she might expire. She was no sprig.

Twitty, who by now should have fallen asleep, pre-empted him.

'The laird you saw for another ten happy years' – DC Twitty speaking, consulting his notebook – 'would thish be our current lairsh' father?'

Pen in hand, he addressed Annie Menzies loudly in case she was hard of hearing like The MacGregor, or had that been the name of a whisky? Why was the Guv glaring at him? Twitty eyed the tumbler and its contents beside the scone-type items. He looked about for a potted plant in need of a dram. In vain. The Guv was too far away to be of help unless he hauled himself up and collected the tumbler, and anyway he had on his displeased look. Mr and Mrs Twitty's boy was going to have to stiffen the upper lip and swallow the stuff down. He would too. Was he not an Englishman?

The old lady had opened her eyes. They were fixed on Peckover's orange socks with white circles. Her grip on her teacup was shaky.

She said, 'This current laird's father?'

'For the shtatemen'.'

'Of course this laird's father, ye ninny. What other laird would we be talking about?'

'Thash all right then.' Twitty searched his memory and his notebook. 'Sir Fergus?'

'Fergus,' breathed Annie, and closed her eyes.

'Sir Fergsh whom you were happy with another ten years is, was, father of your son, the Sergeant Menzies,' Twitty read aloud. He added something and crossed out something else. 'Husband emigrated to Vancouver.'

'I heard nothing from him. Never a word. Nor from anyone. No death certificate. He could walk through that door any minute.'

Twitty wrote down what Annie Menzies was saying, close enough, gaps to be filled in later. He used a homemade shorthand which on good days he was able to read back and on bad days not.

Peckover said, 'To whom else, ma'am, 'ave you pitched this – er, informed of – this history to?'

'No one.'

'Ever?'

'Aye, ever.'

'Your son, Jamie, Sergeant Menzies, he must know.'

'He does not.'

The cat had assessed the visitors as unthreatening and useless, and returned to sleep.

'But you're telling us,' Peckover said.

'Unless we count Father Bridie.'

'The confessional?'

'Father Bridie absolved me on the spot. A lovely man. He died the week after, a victim of a long illness.'

'Taking the secret of you and the laird and your son to the grave.'

'Then we had Father Gunn who had only half his wits about him. I told that one nothing. The one telling was sufficient.'

'Until now.'

No answer. Not, to be exact about it, that there had been a question. She may not have heard. She may have been lost in memories of the ten happy years with Fergus Duncan.

Peckover said, 'It's a long time to keep that sort of secret, place as cosy as Inverballoch. Fergus never told his son, Dougal, he had an 'alf-brother in the police?'

'He did not.'

'You never mentioned to your son that he had an 'alf-brother at Dundrummy Castle?'

'I did not. I'm not saying there weren't one or two had suspicions.'

'Alice McSporran?'

'Ha! Wouldn't she have liked to have known – the witch!' Annie cackled with glee. 'Did she ply ye with the Talisker? She waters it.'

'I don't think tonight. Dick Haig gave his approval.'

'Dick Haig is as bad. Sunday, soirée night. Alice thinks I visit for the wages, dusting about and washing the teacups. It's to remind myself I won Fergus and she did not. And to feed her low suspicions that he was mine, as he was.' She cackled again. 'Aren't I the spiteful one, may God forgive me.'

'There must have been twenty years between Fergus and Alice.'

'What of it? There's plenty would grab the chance to be mistress of Dundrummy Castle. Did Alice say she told Fergus she would wait for him at the mill and he never went? From the empty face on ye she did not. But she wouldn't, would she. 'Twas a humiliation for her, the daft girlie. So she's sent you to investigate me?'

'No.'

'Angus MacGregor, then. He's another had his suspicions. He set his cap at me. He wanted me for his scarlet woman. He was too young and I couldna abide the pipe smoke.'

Annie coughed, though the kitchen was a smoke-free zone apart from seepage of anthracite fumes through the top of the stove.

Peckover said, 'Still, there's Dougal. An heir was born. Someone succeeded in becoming mistress of Dundrummy Castle.'

'A Lowlander, Rowena Blake. Much good it did her. After Dougal came into the world she died of pneumonia because Dundrummy Castle is damp as a sponge. Nineteen sixty-three. Fergus was gathered on July the eighth, Nineteen seventy-five. He was seventy-one and my ain true love. And I was his.'

She paused. Perhaps this time she had finished. She had fallen into a reverie. Peckover saw with alarm that Twitty's glass was empty, not for the first time tonight. The lad was writing gamely, catching up with Annie's last little monologue.

Annie said, 'We shall meet again shortly.'

'Where?' Twitty said, writing, not looking up.

160

Peckover glowered. 'So after the death of the laird's wife you and he didn't – um – resume seeing each other?'

'Fergus wanted to but 'twas too late and too difficult. There was the bairn and tutors and all sorts at the castle. The bank wouldn't listen. Such lovely furniture he had to sell. Carpets. And of course he'd changed since the commotion and the war.'

'How changed?'

'None of your business, young man.'

I knew it, Peckover thought, triumphant. Laird Fergus had become irascible and unbearable. Probably fornicating at the castle, the mill, and round Loch Lomond and back again with Alice McSporran.

'Commotion and the war' was an odd turn of phrase. War was commotion, but commotion wasn't necessarily war, so was she talking about two separate commotions? These 'Ighlands biddies and geezers weren't always easy to compranny.

Peckover wondered if any of this had anything at all to do with the murder of Gilbert Potter. The commotion and war was going back a bit. Unless Dougal Duncan turned up and explained his vanishing act, and the rest of his involvement, his father having had a love child with Annie Menzies led nowhere, not that Peckover could see, though the child becoming the village bobby was comical, and if the bobby fetched up clapping handcuffs on the laird, his half-brother, there might be the makings of a ripe old farce. Meanwhile, probing the love life of nonagenarian Annie made him uncomfortable.

He should probably soldier on. She had sprung one surprise, there might be more. Keeping names and dates and epochs straight wasn't easy. He hoped the lad was getting them down. He took a swallow of Black & White to sharpen his mind.

Twitty sat with Biro poised and his upper body slanting at twenty degrees from the vertical.

Peckover said, 'There'll be quite an age difference between the 'alf-brothers, your Jamie and the laird.'

'Thirty-one years.'

'And during your ten 'appy years when Jamie was growing up, and ending, I gather, with the war, your 'usband was off in Vancouver for ever, and the laird, Fergus, 'e was a single man. No earlier wife at that time?'

''Twould have been adultery!' Annie said, outraged.

'The globlet,' Twitty said.

'Lad,' warned Peckover.

'Shold the lovely furniture, carpesh. Fergsh did. Why not golbet? Ma'am. Celtic. In family four hundred yearsh.'

'Yes, well, most grateful, Mrs Menzies—'

'You've sheen inshide castle in the happy yearsh? Damp as sponge. You were there?'

'I was of course. Mony a time.'

'So you'll have seen the gobelt?'

'I have not. What gobelt?'

'Cup. Whysh nobody sell it?' Twitty was reaching crookedly across the table, forefinger testing for springiness the nearest of the floury buns on the baking rack. 'End of problem. Shounds sentimental, hanging on to—'

'Constable!' Peckover said.

'I dinna ken what ye're bletherin' about.' Annie Menzies watched Twitty's finger. 'They're buttery rowies, though some call them Aberdeen butteries. Ye maun tak a sampling wi' ye for your supper.'

Whether or not this was an invitation for Scotland Yard to leave, Peckover seized the chance. He stood up. Any dawdling, the lad would be incapable of standing up and they'd both be in the mire.

Annie Menzies had not been at the Ram for Burns Night. She was hardly going to have revelations about the chairman's dirk, and anyway, Bill Geddes was looking after that. Little point asking about the Druids. Her memory was long but didn't reach back to Celtic Britain, and he doubted she would be on intimate terms with Inverballoch's current Druids. Still.

''Ave you by any chance heard of these Druids, as they call themselves? The young people camped 'ere?'

'I have. They come visiting.'

'Visiting you?'

'The emporium.'

'Your shop.'

'Emporium. Shall I tell you what the *Oxford Dictionary* says an emporium is?'

'What?'

' "A pompous name for a shop." ' Annie chuckled. 'They've visited twice, some of them.'

'What did they want?'

'They rummaged through the historic garments. One bought

162

the woolly Balaclava worn by the Duke of Balaclava himself at the charge of the Light Brigade. Ye'll know the poem? "Cannon to right of them, cannon to left of them." '

Peckover said, 'There wasn't a Duke of Balaclava, was there?' The lad might know but he was pretty much out of it. 'You're thinking of Lord Raglan and raglan overcoats.'

'I'll thank ye not to tell me what I'm thinking.'

She was on her feet at the table, transferring buttery rowies to a cake tin. She popped two into a paper bag.

'Speaking of 'istory, ma'am. Sir Wilfred Cuff-Bingley. You'll recall him?'

'He lost himself in the mist on the braeside and the sheep did eat him up, clothings and all.'

Her eyes gleamed. Peckover could not be certain if she were testing him, mocking him, or loopy.

He said, 'Thank you. That's it, then. Except you and the late laird, Fergus, and little Jamie. I've not quite grasped why, after all these years, and nobody who knows but yourself, you're telling me and my colleague 'ere.'

The colleague, sable-swaddled, on his feet and listing, bowed precariously. He accepted the bag of buttery rowies from Annie Menzies.

Annie tightened her shawl about her shoulders and said, 'You don't need to know. It'll be of no assistance.'

'Per'aps you'll allow me to judge that.'

'I'd not want to mislead the police.'

'I'm glad.'

'Then, 'tis your socks.'

'Socks?'

'I'm head over heels for your socks.'

Merriment welled in Annie Menzies, spilled chortlingly from her lips, and as quickly subsided.

'Ye'll let yourselves out,' she said, and started to shuffle from the kitchen. 'I'm thinking I'll lie down a wee while.'

TWENTY-ONE

Anyone who isn't confused doesn't really understand the situation

Edward R. Murrow

On the road to the Ram a car behind them closed fast, flashing its lights, overtaking, and spraying the Toyota's windshield with smutch.

'Thash the Sarsh,' Twitty said.

'Thought you were asleep. It was?'

'The bastard.'

'Steady, mate. What's 'e done to you?'

'Nothing persh'n'l. Statement of fact. Solid citizen, Jamie Menzies. Wrong shide the blanket.'

'Wrong side the bleedin' road. Damn nearly ran us into the 'eather. What's 'is 'urry?'

Peckover turned on the short-wave. Murder room, Sergeant Wilson, buzz-free reception. A courting couple had come upon the laird's Jeep in a copse near the old kilt mill, a half mile from the Druids' camp. Superintendent Geddes and most of the murder team in attendance. No laird.

The tail-lights of Sergeant Menzies's Escort had vanished. Peckover judged the car would be already at the mill. Alternatively, it had slewed off the road, down a brae, and into a bog.

Slewed would do to describe the lad. Slewed, stewed, and legless, close enough. Young Jason would need to be kept from public view. That ruled out visiting the mill. With everybody else traipsing in and out of Dougal Duncan's Jeep, Scotland Yard wouldn't be missed.

*

They had to queue up to enter the Ram. First in line were four new guests: male, elderly, wind-ravaged, and encumbered with luggage that included suitcases on wheels, golf bags, and golf carts. Gordon Smith, night manager, pretended to be of assistance, holding back the electrically-operated glass doors that needed no holding back, but neglecting to offer to hold golf paraphernalia or take charge of the suitcases.

Next in line, Constables Colquhoun and Forsyth, relieved from bog man watch by two similarly subordinate wretches.

In reception one of the sportsmen said, 'That was the mother of all chip shots at the fourteenth.'

Another said, 'Rain or shine the greens have to be an improvement on Strathaber.'

Americans. Gordon Smith informed Peckover with relish that each had a room to himself reserved months ago and they were the last rooms. Nae room for the blackie.

'Too bad,' Peckover said. 'People play golf in winter?'

'Aye, fanatics.' The youth's eyes widened. 'Are they under suspicion? They weren't ever here until this minute. I know nothing. I know only they're retired. They plan to play on every links in Scotland.'

Peckover did not wish to know how many links Scotland had. The golfers toiled up the stairs with their baggage and room keys. Twitty, armed with boombox and books from his car, gave critical attention to a fish in a glass case on the wall. The fish gazed directly ahead, ignoring him.

'Your lucky day, lad,' Peckover said. 'You can 'ave Miriam's bed.'

'Wha' about supper?'

'You want to eat?'

'Dunno.'

'You've got the buttery rowies.'

'Not shupper, buttery rowsh.'

'You're not eating down 'ere. I'll bring you up something.'

Peckover asked for the second key to the room.

Gordon Smith said, 'Ah canna do that. 'Twould be against regulations. The room's registered—'

'Just give me the key, twirp, or I'll breathe on you.'

Twitty went pyjamaless to bed with *Ivanhoe* and no way of knowing if he were in the spare bed or the Guv's. He left the bathroom

165

light on and its door open because he had a queasy feeling he might be spending some time there. Not wanting to fall over anything he dazzled the bedroom with light from every fixture he could find: ceiling, bedside table, dressing table, the square metre of entranceway. He should probably have been watching television news – what was her name, Gina, at Laird Castle – but he was having trouble focusing and didn't feel up to it or her.

Felled by a cultural phenomeon!

He doubted he would advance far into *Ivanhoe*. The paperback was abominably printed. Blurry. The print expanded and contracted as he lay looking at it. He would skip the Preface. Each chapter seemed to kick off with a quotation, some quite lengthy. Why and to what purpose? He would skip the quotations too.

DC Twitty felt poorly.

Annie Menzies should have seen the goblet at Château Laird. Would have been shown it, wouldn't she? Prize possession? Ten happy years, the late laird's doxy? She hadn't sounded to have heard of it.

He was horizontal but was that good or bad? He lifted his head and peered. Where was the bathroom? Someone had moved it.

Stones of Skelloch, they were a creepy horrible place. The dig too. If he'd been a local bobby he might have been there now, the dig, guarding Inverballoch Man.

What was the Guv up to?

Twitty fell asleep with the lights on. His posture was that of a gallant knight on a tomb, holding a paperback instead of a sword.

Peckover looked into the murder room. Sergeant Wilson at the encoding radio; someone collating printouts from somewhere; the lads recalled from bog man watch drinking tea; the hoyden in the blouse with the epaulettes filing her nails. Everyone else was off scouring the wilderness for the laird or investigating his Jeep at the mill.

Not quite everyone. Two or three youthful faces he recalled from the murder room had adjourned to the Rob Roy Bar. From the press conference and round and about Peckover also recognized several scribes, happier to be here than at home or back in the office. Bar centre, high on a padded stool, beset and flirted with by the coppers, who could not believe their luck, and by two or three of the younger Grub Street hacks, sat flushed mini-celebrity Gina Patel, late of Dundrummy Castle's doorstep. Her newsroom had presumably recalled her, grudgingly, to prevent her perishing from exposure. She had shed her ski jacket and woolly helmet, revealing glossy black hair and a jersey with broad blue and white bands, like a Chelsea supporter. Peckover would not have sworn blue and white was Chelsea. He did his best to avoid soccer. She appeared to be enjoying herself, protected from horseplay as she was by a knot of TV technicians, overseeing events from a distance of a few inches.

It was not for him to order the policemen back to work, especially when the barman was pulling for him a pint of bitter against the dehydration brought on by however many wee drammies there had been.

He didn't see Mavis. He didn't want to see Mavis but not seeing her he found slightly unnerving. Such, he supposed, was the power of her reputation. Had she solved the Potter murder from her barstool at the end of the counter, from where she deployed her spies, was motherly and sexy with stray green coppers, and dispensed modest cheques as necessary? The Miss Marple of the Cocktail Lounge might even now be on the blower dictating a Potter narrative with correct questions and answers that would leave the police looking like hobbledehoys.

Heading for the Gents, Peckover spotted Mavis at a table with Posy Cork. Mavis had her ciggie and a G and T, Posy had a coffee cup.

He pushed open the door to the Gents and with his first breath smelled pot. Two of them: a bloke in steel-rimmed glasses pretending to be washing his hands, and one who looked like a recruiting officer for the National Front, pretending to be waiting for his mate to finish washing his hands, and holding one of his own hands out of sight. Smoke from the joint drifted up behind his shorn head.

'Evenin',' Peckover said, stepping up to the porcelain. 'A damp one but there you go. Roll on spring.'

They had their dreamy eyes on him, probably trying to work out if he were fuzz, press, management, or nobody. He had enough on his plate without announcing himself, confiscating the grass, taking their names, searching them, bringing in Twitty for corroboration – no, not Twitty, not tonight – and hauling them off to Sergeant Menzies, love child, at the police station, if it was open. Bloody daft law anyway. First thing these two would probably do would be to claim they didn't inhale. Powerful precedent the other side of the pond.

The steel-rimmed one, drying his hands, said, 'How's the investigation coming along, officer?'

'Excuse me?'

'The laird, he's still missing?'

'Who're you then?' Peckover rinsed his fingers. 'Funny aroma in 'ere. Chancing your arm, aren't you?'

' "Luck be a lady-y-y tonight",' sang the steel rims.

'What's your name?'

'You have it written down somewhere by an ethnic gentleman. Very courteous.'

'Wee Willie Wankie,' said the National Front, and grinned.

The steel rims said, 'Truth is, my humble opinion, you are fundamentally not interested.'

'In what?' Peckover said.

'Us. Pot.'

'Not Potter?'

'We know nothing about that.'

'Remains to be seen. Just don't leave the area.'

'We're under suspicion?'

'Top of the list. You're right about the pot, I'm not interested, but we're not all as sloppy as me. There are striplings the other side of the door can't wait to add to their score card. I'll send 'em in.'

'We were just leaving, with your permission.'

'Yer, you wouldn't do that,' said the shorn yob, and he ground his foot on his reefer.

Peckover leaned forward and peered into the lenses of the less unsavoury one.

He said, 'You play the clarinet?'

Steel Rims smiled as sweetly as an angel on high or a high angel. 'You'll be the other one from Scotland Yard. Heard about you, Inspector.'

'Chief Inspector.'

National Front held the door open for the chief inspector. The display of correct manners disconcerted Peckover. Lounge bar clamour and legal smoke smote him.

He asked, ''Ow's the treasure 'unting? Don't say "What treasure 'unting?" '

'What treasure hunting?' the clarinettist said, and giggled. He became as grave as was compatible with being stoned. 'Since you mention it, what have you heard? I mean officially. The horse's mouth. It's not the money—'

'My eye it isn't,' said the National Front.

'—it's the magic, the music. Can you imagine? It'd be like infinity and epiphany and the thirtieth of February. The amulets, medallions, gold torques, cups, plate—'

'Like Snettisham,' Peckover said.

'Yeah!'

Stoned and weird, Peckover decided. The one who had sung commercials would be likely in the bar. Hadn't the lad said something about a colossal dog?

He said, 'Wouldn't belong to you anyway, mate. Treasure trove. You 'and it over. No exceptions for Druids, far as I know.'

National Front belched.

'You must have heard something.' Steel Rims licked his clarinettist's lips. 'What're the chances?'

'For magic or the money?'

'Did you talk to Potter? Or those women, the archaeologists? Are we wasting our time?'

'Not if you find treasure.'

Peckover aimed himself past Gina and her thrilled entourage and towards his beer. Posy Cork had left. Mavis hadn't. She sat on her perch at the bar, a sozzled pro. He didn't know the *Herald*'s deadlines but at least until midnight she could probably phone in an inch of stop-press to excite Glaswegians over their salty breakfast porridge and kippers.

What he would have liked to have known, but at the time hadn't thought to ask, was if commotion and war were the same thing or separate. Fergus Duncan had changed since the commotion and the war, Annie Menzies had said. The commotion might have been the war, but if not, what commotion was it?

Peckover carried his beer from the bar to the telephone in reception to call Miriam, tell her he adored her in spite of the haggis, and to check on Sam and the tooth fairy, and Mary's problem in kindergarten with her best friend, Christabel, whom she said she hated but kept asking home, and being asked to Christabel's home, for dressing-up games and hair-pulling.

DC Twitty, awaking to darkness as black as a bog, knew straight away that this was wakefulness of the sort that was not going to go away. The only solution would be to get up, find juice and cornflakes, and press on with life.

'Och,' said somebody.

Twitty lay very still.

'Hoots,' said the voice, close by.

Twitty had no inkling where he was but he believed he recognized the voice. He dimly remembered taking notes in a kitchen somewhere, but after that, what?

Annie Menzies, hers had been the kitchen. Before that, the old gent with the pipe and cowboy books. Rain. Alice McSporran and the lawyer fellow. At some point the Stones of Skelloch where activity had been thought to have been noticed but none found. Posy Cork had said some stone or other was the recumbent stone but you could believe dawn sacrifice and chanting Druids if you wanted to.

In his skull three billiard balls, perpetually in motion, cannoned off each other.

'Wi' a hundred pipers an' a' an' a',' sighed the voice.

Question was, where were his clothes? He preferred not to risk waking up the Guv by turning on lights, wherever they were. He sat up gingerly, probed his legs out of the bed, floorward, and trod in something that squelched.

'Smoutie blasties,' chuckled the Guv.

Twitty groped through the dark more or less one-leggedly, holding for support to the bed, then to whatever came his way, such as a wall. The first door he found was locked so presumably it led to the corridor. His knee bumped against something that might be a bed, though not the one he had slept in. A second door was ajar. He went into the bathroom, closed the door, and found the light. All he wore was his watch. 5.05 a.m.

In spite of his hoppings most of whatever he had trodden in must have come off on the carpet, but between the toes remained a pale, lumpy substance that he had no wish to identify. He stepped into the shower and soaped and steamed. He stole three inches of Peckover's toothpaste and chewed. Opening the door a chink, he sighted in an armchair his clothes, haphazardly shed. He tiptoed for them. On the carpet by the bed where he had slept was a tray with a plate of glop indented with his footprint. Macaroni cheese, *specialité de la Maison* Ram. Also a fork, napkin, and can of Coke.

Dressed, noiseless as a burglar, his loot a boombox, a paper bag containing two scone-type edibles for breakfast, and a can of warm Coke, Twitty unlocked the door to the corridor.

'Campbells are comin', O-ho, O-ho,' mumbled Peckover.

A regional station that Twitty had not come across before quietly pounded out on the boombox Bob Marley's 'I Shot the Sheriff' from back in the Bronze Age. Seventies anyway. He kept the volume down so that the pounding would not overexcite the billiard balls. His head seemed to have calmed somewhat.

He cruised south on the Glasgow road. He had no intention of stopping to investigate the Stones of Skelloch. They had been investigated and found wanting. He had been there. But he had to go somewhere because he was not about to sit in the murder room, or discuss football with the night manager, or jog in the dark. The only other places he roughly knew the way to were the dig, Dundrummy Castle, possibly the mill, not that he had been there, and all those had police in attendance. As a gatecrasher from London he couldn't be sure what sort of welcome he would have. He could probably find the homes of Alice McSporran and Angus MacGregor, certainly of Annie Menzies, but he doubted they'd be charmed to see him at this hour.

So, by elimination, the Skelloch Stones.

You never knew. Might be Druids howling, dogs chanting, King Dave leading a dawn rave-up on his clarinet. Posy Cork had dismissed dawn sacrifice as boys' comic book stuff. Probably because gore was melodramatic, unlike scholarly recumbent stones and the position of the sun. She couldn't have it both ways. At the dig, yesterday, she'd said there had been human sacrifice. The priestly Druids shut up their victim in a wicker cage and set it on fire, which was all right because his soul was immortal. She had also said that some of the loonier nineteen-nineties Druids might consider themselves reincarnated from the Druids of two and three thousand years ago.

5.35 a.m. Hours to go until dawn. Twitty looked through the window for a sky lit with the glow of burning wicker cages.

No glow other than from a wedge of furry moon, but hereabouts were the Skelloch Stones. He U-turned, stopped the Fiesta at the roadside, and switched off the engine, lights, and boombox. He wound down the window. The cold air invigorated. However many hours until dawn, the bedroom at the Ram had been far darker than here. He was able to make out the Stones, black lumps high up on the grey moor. No cavorting Druids. One thing he wouldn't be telling the Guv or anyone was that he had sat here, nowhere, at half-past five in the morning. They'd call in the shrink.

Then, though he saw no Druids, he heard one. From the Stones came a cry, a truncated bleat, a yawp no sooner begun than cut off.

Twitty stared and listened.

Whatever the sound had been it was unmusical and it was not repeated, or not yet. Might have been a sheep, except he would have been able to see white woolly sheep, and there weren't any.

Dave's clarinet tuning up? A Highland goblin? Ghoulies, ghosties, long-leggity beasties, things that go bump in the night?

Posy Cork, repository of legend and lore, had said that the Stones screeched at the full moon and when the head of an Inverballoch family died. He'd have described what he had heard as more a yelp than a screech. Then again, could have been a screech. Could have been wholly in his hungover head, a side-effect of sottishness.

The moon wasn't full either, it was a whiskery nail-clipping. Whether or not an Inverballoch patriarch had just surrendered his spirit, how was he to know?

Another side-effect of sottishness was manifestly softening of the brain. Time to be on his way before he beheld a phantom bagpiper striding among the Stones playing 'Scotland the Brave'.

One of the distant blobs of Stones moved.

As it could not have done so, reasoned Twitty, either he had caught a shocking dose of delirium tremens – so young and so, on the whole, abstemious! – or something else, not a Stone, had moved. Impossible to tell in this subfusc wasteland. At least it wasn't moving any more.

Yes it was.

Twitty climbed from the car, locked it, and started up the moor.

He broke into a run, which was foolhardy. His foot had only to skid on a megalithic boulder or enter a vole pit and he could languish here with a broken ankle pretty much for ever, eyed by surprised voles. Meanwhile he bounded goat-like uphill, trying simultaneously to watch where his jogging-booted feet would land, to pay attention to the Stones ahead in case one should budge again, and to be alert for screeches. The Stones grew larger and better defined, a hugger-mugger of black lumps, most of them recumbent, two or three leaning. At least there was no rain, he realized, fatuously pleased. Better yet, when he reached the Stones and there was nothing, not rain or anything except the Stones and himself, sweating and irrelevant, it wouldn't matter that there was nothing, he wouldn't need to be embarrassed. He was alone and nobody would ever know that he had stormed the Stones of Skelloch as boldly as Wolfe had stormed the heights to the Plains of Abraham to capture Quebec.

So here they were and here he was, panting, standing on a long-toppled Skelloch Stone, and wondering if he were committing a sacrilege by standing on it. He trod across the spongy turf and between and over the indestructible blocks of granite.

Nobody.

'Hello?' he said.

A thin wind ruffled his expensive hairdo. He looked back down the moor to the shoebox-sized Fiesta, conspicuously white. Nothing else was on the road.

5.52 a.m.

No point returning yet to the sleeping Ram, but nothing to stay here for. The Stones neither moved nor screeched. He placed his palm on the cold flank of one of the erect Stones much as a visitor in an art gallery molests a sculpture until spotted by a guard and whistled at. The Stone sighed with pleasure, unless the sound was one of the voles, roused from hibernation and shaking itself. Twitty ducked and lurched sideways as somebody came from the other side of the Stone and jumped on him from behind. The assailant missed for the most part his moving target, but he thudded into Twitty's hip and caught hold of a leg and a segment of the Dr Zhivago sable.

Ambush-artist and policeman went to the ground in an unnatural embrace, kicking and punching with whatever limb was free and able. Twitty was so enraged with himself for his inattention that he went berserk, throwing to the wind all the finesse and niceties of self-defence learned at police college, or at any rate touched on, and in any event largely forgotten. He became a flailing street-fighter, butting, kneeing, and gouging. He frightened himself. He would have bitten the bloke's nose off had it come in range. Whoever had jumped him tried to retaliate in kind, and he was big, but only a sumo wrestler falling on him and flattening him could have put Twitty out of action, and the lout from behind the Stone evidently realized it. He succeeded in hitting Twitty in the face, but then, finding himself momentarily at liberty, he struggled up and began to run.

After him like a sprinter from the starting-blocks, Twitty, with his first step, trod on the absurd tongue of his jogging boot, tripped, and fell headlong upon the tufty sod.

He picked himself up and hobbled a few paces in pursuit. The failed mugger was a hundred yards distant and careering along well. Where to, Twitty had no idea. Perhaps the mugger hadn't either. Simply away might be enough. Pines fringed a sombre skyline. He was going in the opposite direction from the Glasgow road but there was usually another road going somewhere.

He attended to the tongues and laces. The famine-relief sable would be in need of ministration from a dry-cleaner, a superior one, By Appointment to Her Majesty. On or near his right eye seemed to be a puffy, watery area. Other yet unidentified regions of his rippling anatomy – the wonder of the age, the glory of mankind – throbbed.

He had no clue as to who had attacked him. Big enough for Our 'Enry but not, gorblimey, Our 'Enry. Nobody he had met, he was sure. Not King Dave or Sergeant Menzies or any of the coppers or the lawyer cove, Dick Haig. Not a woman, not Angus the Pipe, Uncle Tom Cobbleigh, and decidely not the laird, because here was the laird on a slab of granite, dead, or at any rate not moving. Sir Dougal Duncan, supine, lay bound, gagged, and glistening. On his temple was a lump like a Victoria plum, as if he had fallen from a tall building onto his head.

Twitty knelt, gently lifted the laird's head, thereby, for all he knew, administering the *coup de grâce*, and unknotted the gag, which he guessed was one of the laird's socks. Like Diddle Diddle Dumpling My Son John the laird had one shoe off and one shoe on, and one sock off too. The bruise on the temple was quite nasty. In the red hair above one ear was further damage. The glistening was from foul grease on the scarf and the laird's face. The grease was up his nostrils, in his ears, and plugging the open mouth. Twitty scooped the substance from the mouth with first one finger, then two, and wiped the muck off on the slab. He kept scooping because it was solid stuff and went far back, perhaps down whatever the tube or pipe was called as far as the stomach. When he had the worst of it out he would see about finding the pulse, if any, but this sludge was the priority. Not that he was a doctor. The laird began to vomit.

6.02 a.m.

Twitty untied the laird's hands and feet. A small tub or barrel stood near by on the grass, and beside it its lid.

By 6.15 a.m. the laird still wasn't saying much. In fact he hadn't said anything yet, though he was trying to sit up. Twitty had not decided whether he should discourage the laird from sitting up, cover him with his sable, and risk leaving him so that he could return to the car and find a telephone, or stay put until the laird was able to walk and they could totter down the hill together like John Anderson, my jo, John, and his wife, which was one of the rare poems by Burns that he had understood at first reading.

He found the headpiece that had flopped off the fled mugger's head during the tussle, one of the practically peakless huntin', shootin', and fishin' jobs worn by the county set to point-to-points. He put it in his pocket. To Twitty the cap meant nothing, other than being evidence. He wasn't to know but it would mean something to others, such as Posy Cork.

TWENTY-TWO

Oh little did my mither ken,
    That day she cradled me,
What lands I was to tread in
    Or what death I should dee.

Scottish Ballad

Around the time that the eleventh laird of Dundrummy and DC Twitty, the bruiser's cap in his pocket and a tub of historic butter under his arm, tottered down the moor, supporting each other like old pals after a college reunion, police discovered a rust-rimmed Saab in the piney woods off the road to Dundrummy Castle.

The computer came up with the car's ownership in less than a minute. Playing it safe, Superintendent Geddes roused Posy Cork on her room telephone. Posy roused Leah. Constables Colquhoun and Forsyth, who were beginning to get on each other's nerves, were detailed to escort the ladies to the Saab for corroboration.

The tub of diminished butter was back in the Ram's kitchen fridge, beside which, as butter guardian, sat the doxy with the epaulettes, painting her filed nails. To forestall her complaints of sexual discrimination in being allotted a duty so humiliatingly otiose, Geddes had had to convince her that the butter was the most vital single item of evidence in Scottish criminal history.

The cap was in the murder room, on Peckover's head. Posy would be shown it when she returned.

'If the cap fits, wear it,' Peckover said, and he took the cap off and put it on the table beside the AA *Illustrated Road Book of Scotland*. 'He's got a big 'ead. Burly bugger. Played rugby for Penarth, right? Class side. Loads of oomph and zest and grinding the other team's faces into the ground, I wouldn't wonder. Who'd you play rugby for, lad?'

'Played soccer. Harrow Second Eleven.'

'Second? Not the First?'

'They already had someone from Trinidad. The prime minister's son.' Twitty cupped his hand over his eye. He stank of disinfectant. 'They had a Chinese, fantastic violinist, the German ambassador's son, the heir to the Emir of Qatar – four bodyguards he had – and a nephew of the Sultan of Brunei. There had to be a correct political balance. We had two girls in the Second Eleven.'

'You should 'ave that eye attended to.'

'It's nothing. So when are we going to find him? He was running east from the Stones.'

'We'll find 'im. Pity you didn't 'ang on to 'im.'

Geddes glanced up from perusal of the Ordnance Survey map, South-West Highlands. 'You did well, sonny.'

'Don't say that,' Peckover said. 'He's already got a swollen eye. You'll give him a swollen 'ead. Something you should know, lad. Annie Menzies died.'

Twitty took his hand from his eye. The eye was still an eye but empurpled and in need of a pirate's patch or a steak.

He said, 'What time?'

Peckover looked puzzled. 'Sometime in the night.'

Geddes said, 'She was ninety-one according to Sergeant Menzies. Might have been more. The children don't always know. He's bereaved. Be nice to him.'

'Half-past five?' Twitty said.

'Possibly.'

'Died of a presentiment, that's possible too,' Peckover said. 'Not that a presentiment is allowed on a death certificate any more than old age is. I shouldn't say this but Annie Menzies told us Laird Fergus was Jamie's father because she 'ad this presentiment she was about to go, perhaps she wanted to go, but first she needed to tell somebody and there we were. My opinion. If she did 'ave a glimpse of the hereafter she wasn't wrong. What do you say, lad?'

'What about?'

'Presentiments.'

'Dunno. Maybe.'

Twitty was not about to worry about it. He had begun to believe that if the supernatural lurked anywhere, the Scottish Highlands could be the place. The yowl he had heard at half-past five had surely been the laird's protest at being stuffed with butter. Then again, might have been the Stones screeching at the death of Annie Menzies. She had been head of a family of two, herself and

Jamie. If the yelp had been from the laird, the Stones still might have screeched for Annie, silently.

Inspector Gillespie, equipped with tape-recorder, notebook, and back-up sergeant, had driven the buttered laird to the closest establishment with nurses, St Ann's, a hospice at Spittal of Kegbeg. His absence allowed sunshine to seep into the hearts and minds of the few police left in the murder room.

The search had switched from the laird to a burly, capless, carless, Princeton–bound – a trip now looking to be on indefinite hold – Junior Research Fellow in Primitive Religions, presumed dangerous, and believed to be footing over the banks and braes, possibly in the direction of the woods near Dundrummy where he had abandoned his Saab, though that would be a fair slog.

Peckover retreated with his notebook to a vacant table and put on his spectacles. He pretended to note down particulars on the Potter murder, or what looked to be an attempted murder of Dougal Duncan, or similarly pertinent police matters.

> She has gone clothed in white
> To Fergus her knight,
> On her finger a gold wedding ring is;
> A presentiment came
> And carried her hame,
> The fairest of fair – Annie Menzies.

'Sir!' called bleary Sergeant Wilson, in headphones at the encoder. 'We have a sighting!'

A patrol car had sighted a lone figure emerge from a bosky patch of evergreens not two miles from the Ram, then dodge back into the trees.

Geddes, Peckover, and Twitty in their respective cars drove from the Ram to the sighting. They would have done better to have stayed put.

In the next two hours came two further sightings of Mike Trelawny, if indeed it were he. Each time he slipped away, either lying low or faster on his feet than the police had given him credit for. His feet had access to topographical features inaccessible to wheeled transport.

The problem for the police was that the terrain was not featureless, a blank if undulous sheet that would expose the least speck.

For cover were wooded areas, extensive gorse and broom, streams that corrugated the mountain slopes, and derelict crofts. By nine thirty most such features, the crofts anyway, were under surveillance. A police helicopter roamed the slate sky.

Sergeant Menzies made one of the sightings entirely by accident. He had never met Mike Trelawny and had barely heard of him before the name came over his car radio. Orphaned, grieving, the sergeant had driven off in his Escort to be away from the Ram and all the Potter cafuffle, and when he was enough away, to bellow his anguish. West of the golf course he had taken the Kirkbuckie Road. By the stone footbridge over the burn stood a man in a military-type coat. Hefty, thirtyish, bare-headed, he answered the description from the murder room. When Sergeant Menzies stopped the car and opened the door, the man by the bridge started away at a canter.

'Halt, i' the name o' the law!' Sergeant Menzies shouted.

De'il tak him, the scoundrel was nae haltin', he was runnin'! Failure to halt, 'twould be anither charge against him!

There was no chasing the rogue up the mountain. The fellow had unco prodigious legs. He was as good as out of sight already.

Sergeant Menzies stood in the road, weeping. He looked around to be sure he was alone, lifted his face and his arms, and bellowed his bereavement.

'Oh, Mam!'

When the sighting by Sergeant Menzies came through, Messrs Geddes, Peckover, Twitty, and sundry uniformed policemen were back in the murder room with tea following a false alarm that had taken them halfway to Garrymuck of Cud.

The painted lady with epaulettes put her head round the door, saw the brass, and retreated back to butter watch in the kitchen.

Peckover said, 'Where are the women? Posy Cork and Leah?'

'Waiting for the forensics team from Glasgow University,' said Geddes. 'Due any time.'

'I 'ope they're not going to be disappointed.'

'I hope they are. There'll be other bog bodies. There's only one Cuff-Bingley.'

'Long time ago, Bob.'

'Not as long ago as bog bodies.'

'Cuff-Bingley isn't part of the national 'eritage and there's no money to be made out of 'im, unless you're aiming to write a book. Some people are going to feel 'orribly betrayed if it's not a bog man. They'll be sick as dogs.'

'Not me. I never liked unfinished business.'

'Well, we'll know soon.' Peckover gulped tea. 'Has to be one or the other.'

'Why?' said Twitty. 'Might be neither. Might be somebody else, a nobody, then everyone will be miserable.'

'Don't confuse matters, lad.'

At this point Sergeant Wilson at the radio received the call from Sergeant Menzies at the bridge at Kirkbuckie.

'Kirkbuckie?' Geddes put his coat back on. 'Never mind bog bodies. Where's Kirkbuckie?'

Deathshead Gillespie found his chief, the meddlers from Scotland Yard – the blackie had a black eye, at least that – Sergeant Menzies, and assorted lesser ranks, standing in the morning mist at the Kirkbuckie crossroads. At a radio in a police van a constable wearing a black mackintosh stayed tuned to the murder room.

Gillespie's mood was not merry. Inverballoch had had no *Financial Times*, which was to be expected, but neither had Spittal of Kegbeg nor newsagents on his brisk diversions to benighted Benlochry, Bridge of Grill, and Aberauchter. They hadn't even a *Glasgow Herald*, though they would have it about noon. 'We have little call for the London papers here,' the helpful madam at Aberauchter had advised, 'ye'd best try Edinburgh.'

Superintendent Geddes asked, 'How's our laird?'

'Excitable,' said Gillespie. 'Ye'll no make a lot o' sense o' his ravings on the tape but I hae the drift.' He opened his notebook. 'We'd been two minutes at St Ann's when he started on about discharging himself, as if he were a gun. Ready?'

'Shoot.'

'Sir Dougal Duncan ejects Posy Cork and Leah Howgego from his Jeep because suddenly he decides he must be alone for his first view of his bog man not distracted by women. He stresses 'tis his bog man. Communing with it on his ancestral acres will be a mystical experience. When I suggest that a coroner might judge this an inadequate reason for bouncing two women on to the roadside and would he explain further, he becomes angry. The rest o' his tale I happen to find credible.'

'Let's have it, then,' Geddes said.

'Half a mile further on the laird stops for a hitch-hiker who'd been in the trees but comes rushing into the middle o' the road with his thumb out. The laird knows him, 'tis Miss Cork's boy-friend, thought to have returned to London. Mr Trelawny hits him with a rock and Sir Dougal wakes up in the night at the Stones of Skelloch, alone and tied and wi' one of his socks in his mouth. His account has gaps. I'd say he could plead loss of memory, though he doesn't. Mr Trelawny shows up and says it had been a narrow squeak, old boy. The fuzz had come tramping in, so he'd hit the laird again to keep him from uttering, and he wasn't light as a feather, but Trelawny had carried him off until the all-clear. He tells the laird he nicked Andrew Dinwiddie's knife off the haggis plate. He dropped it under the table until the interval before the speeches when everybody got up and milled about, and he killed Potter to put an end to the dig.' Gillespie flipped a page in his notebook. 'Mr Trelawny's words, according to the laird, were, "I want this dig finished with. Posy's coming with me to the States. She can teach Freshman English. I'm marrying her and I'm not spending my life as number two to an archaeologist who'll fetch up as Dame Posy of Inverballoch and God knows what else while I'll be nobody. The slogan is, No Dig – No Dame." ' He looked up from the notebook. 'Except that murdering Potter doesn't end the dig, and Miss Cork as good as tells Trelawny at the dig itself, yesterday, that if it's a choice between him and the dig she'll carry on digging. Trelawny tells the laird, sorry, old boy, but now you go to your ancestors because if anything will seal the doom of this dig, that will. First Sir Gilbert, then Sir Dougal – and who next?'

'Trelawny told the laird a terrible lot,' Geddes said.

'He could afford to,' said Gillespie. 'He was going to kill him.'

'With butter?'

'Butter and relish, the way the laird tells it. Relish meaning pleasure. Trelawny tells him he's never liked him – his easy access to Posy, every day, his familiarity with her.'

'A dawn sacrifice at the Skelloch Stones,' Peckover said.

'Asphyxiation by butter,' said Twitty.

'If that doesn't work, or if the dying looks like taking for ever,' Gillespie said, 'he could hit him again with a rock. And again and again. The laird admits he took the butter from the Ram's fridge. He says it's his, he's entitled to it, and he intends to sell it. Trelawny found it in the Jeep.'

Sergeant Menzies, red-eyed, said, 'We'll track the blackguard down and encircle him.'

Gillespie flipped to the next page. 'After depositing the laird at the Stones, Trelawny had driven the Jeep to the kilt mill and come back to the Stones on foot. The mill's a hop and a skip from the Druids, and he hoped the Jeep there would implicate them. At the Stones he boasts of his accomplishments to the laird while waiting until dawn or thereabouts to murder him. If he's throwing suspicion on the Druids he needs the time of death to be fixed around dawn – sacrifice time. His mistake, I'd say, was being too scholarly and hanging on to the right time – dawn. If he'd settled for a three o'clock sacrifice he'd have had it over and done with before Sunny Jim here happened by.'

Gillespie gave Twitty a quizzical look. Twitty didn't care for the 'Sunny Jim' but he had been called worse. He hadn't one hundred per cent simply 'happened by' either. Posy Cork had pooh-poohed dawn sacrifice and chanting Druids but she'd not denied such rites had happened in Druid days. Something, if only a hangover, had drawn him to the Stones of Skelloch.

Geddes said, 'Mr Trelawny had a busy night.'

'He's having a busy morning, sir,' said the constable in the van. 'He's on the golf course.'

TWENTY-THREE

So goodbye dear, and Amen.
   Cole Porter, *Just One of Those Things*

Blue skies ought to have been ordered for the television cameras energetically assembling to film the pursuit of Mike Trelawny on foot and at large on or near Aberauchter golf links, not that he was anywhere to be seen.

The views were sensational. A grey-green tundra of winter moorland and mountains reached endlessly away, majestic and empty, though increasingly peopled. Cameras that had zoomed in only on sheep and icy brooks were now able to focus on footslogging coppers wielding the new-issue American twenty-four-inch truncheon. They were spread wide and moving methodically over the braes as if beating the heather for unseasonal grouse. Chilled candidates for rheumatism, the foot-soldiers no sooner obeyed instructions to change course, wheel, and converge on unseen Mike Trelawny, than they would be ordered to about-turn,target believed sighted south-south-east, steady as you go, men.

Rain drizzled down. The cameras made a brave fist of it. Rain or shine, the scenery was stunning, and the event less dull, most news editors were convinced, than a golf championship. The nation, those not deprived by having to earn a living, watched. The thrill was on a par with a war being brought live into the sitting-room, courtesy of the tube, but with nature instead of smart bombs. At home in Leith Street, Edinburgh, Willie Munroe, retired grocer, his breakfast finished, gazed at the screen.

''Tis a sight! Och, what it'll be when the sun comes out! Lassie, we'll awa' tae Inverballoch for June!'

Lizzie Munroe, shocked, said, 'After nineteen years we'll nae gang back tae Torremolinos?'

*

Advised by Sergeant Menzies, the brass and their assistants gathered on Brae Balloch, the rainswept highest point for five miles round. Here were some wrecked benches, beer cans, and a World War One memorial defaced with a spray-painted warning: Scottish Watch – English Out.

Twitty observed the graffito and asked, 'What's that then, Guv? What have we done?'

'Ye're here is what,' said Gillespie, unasked. 'We hae rural communities taken over entirely by Sassenach immigrants. Scottish Watch is for haltin' the Englishing of Scotland.'

'You're a founder-member?' said Twitty.

'Lad,' warned Peckover.

The views from Brae Balloch were over most of the golf links, the Ram, the roofs of Inverballoch, and if you turned and walked past the memorial, a panorama of glens and braes disfigured only by the laundry, jalopies, and rusty bangers at the Druids' camp. The High Command with their adjutants and batmen supervised operations as if they were Field Marshal Montgomery. Superintendent Geddes had his Ordnance Survey map. Inspector Gillespie had binoculars. Chief Inspector Peckover had put on his spectacles and was writing in a notebook. His aide-de-camp wiped drizzle from his good eye.

'Guv?'

'Yer?'

'Has anyone told Sergeant Menzies and the laird they're related?'

'Not that I know.'

'Who's going to?'

'You're volunteering? Clear it with Mr Geddes. You never know, they might be enchanted.'

'I wasn't volunteering. Job for an older man, wouldn't you say?'

Constable Colquhoun in headphones reported, 'Unidentified person sighted south-east trees east rim golf course, sir!'

'Who's that from?' Geddes said.

'The chopper, sir.'

Geddes peered eastward into the murk. 'Anyone see anything?'

Peckover took off his glasses and closed his notebook.

'Golfers,' Gillespie said.

'Gimme those,' said Geddes, and snatched the binoculars.

Nobody needed binoculars to see the golfers. At this distance they were four scattered gnomes towing golf carts, but they were in dazzlingly panchromatic slacks, hats and windcheaters.

'Amazing,' Geddes said. 'I have never understood how a nation as enlightened as the Scots could have given the world golf.' Annoyed by the sight of golfers, he moved the binoculars through an arc and lighted on a convoy of three vehicles. 'Who's the rabble on the road? Where do they think they're going? Not us, is it? Undercover?'

'Druids, sir,' Twitty said.

'Dammit, what're they doing here?'

'Free entertainment,' said Gillespie.

'Get them out of it!' Geddes was on police push-button automatic. 'Wait! They've stopped, they're alighting,' he announced like a commentator at a coronation. 'My God! What do they have with them?'

'Grendel,' Twitty said.

'What's a grendel?'

'Force of nature, sir.'

Peckover flicked a lump of moorland humus from the sleeve of Twitty's besmirched sable. 'Old son, this raiment has suffered,' he said. 'You have now a perfect excuse for putting it out for the dustmen.'

'I'll be sending the cleaning bill to Accounts.'

'Meanwhile, don't look round. One of your admirers.'

Twitty looked round. Mavis, in a tweed trilby and Inverness cape, clasping her handbag and a newspaper, was winding out of her brown Honda. Ignoring the inferior ranks, she strode directly to the top.

'Bob, congratulations from the *Glasgow Herald*. Can't be long now. He confessed to the laird, that correct? You've done a splendid job. How many men do you have out there?'

Geddes did not order Mavis thrown from the top of Balloch Brae. If he blew this, lost Trelawny, goodbye promotion, hello ignominy. Premature in her congratulations, astute Mavis had none the less read him correctly in his hour of need. She had given encouragement, offered a boost. She leaned against him, using him as a windbreak as she lit a fag.

'There he goes!' Constable Colquhoun said.

A figure in a long khaki coat had arrived out of sheltering trees and was sprinting toward the fairway that reached away to the second hole. The sweep of the police cordon, whether misdirected or unable to keep up, was a half-mile distant, beyond the golf course, combing a moorland slope.

'Get those men down here!' Geddes ordered.

'Sir!' cried Colquhoun.

'He'll go for the Druids' cars if he sees them,' Mavis said. 'I would. Not a lot of choice.'

Whether or not Mike Trelawny was aware of the Druids' clapped-out bangers on the road, his immediate challenge was the broad, sandy bunker in front of him. To skirt it or to charge through it, up to his ankles in sand? In the bunker a golfer from Teaneck, New Jersey, wearing magenta slacks and an egg-yellow jacket, was trying to get out. Eyes on the ball, shoulders square, he lifted his niblick for a third attempt. Mike Trelawny, taking the direct route, ran past and within a whisker of the golfer, slamming the ball deep into the sand with his foot as he went.

'Hey!' cried the outraged golfer.

An error. Barely aware of him until now, Mike Trelawny skidded to a stop, grabbed the number eight iron with one hand, punched the golfer with the other, and scrambled out of the bunker.

'Now he's armed,' growled Geddes.

'Bob, you have him outnumbered,' Mavis said. 'Forty to one? Fifty? Tell me, how many have had their leave cancelled?'

'Yon mannie's no wimp. If he flails that club, heads could be broken.'

'Bob, dear, relax. You can do nothing you're not doing. I've seen this sort of thing before. He has no chance.'

'Tain't necessarily so, Peckover thought.

On the golf course below Brae Balloch freckled Mike ran through the rough carrying a four-feet-long number eight iron. Having presumably spotted the police car that had ventured on to the fairway to the north, he had changed direction. He looked now to be heading for the Druids spectating from the road. A pair of ragamuffin children chased each other through the gorse. Peckover estimated two minutes maximum for Mike Trelawny to reach the Druids. He was hardly going to make an offer for the least unreliable of the bangers and start haggling. It would be give me the keys, and if they didn't appear he would swing the number eight. He might take hostages. He would take the two children if he could. What had he to lose? No wimp, as Bob Geddes had observed.

This is the way the world ends, not with a wimp but a banger.

The helicopter puttered about the sky. The legs of the khaki-coated figure, visibly tiring, bicycled through golf-links rough infested with errant golfballs. Peckover could not but feel a pang of pity. That was not to say he wished Trelawny anywhere but put away for a long time. But the bloke had won Posy Cork, no bad catch if you could accept her lectures, and he had lost her. He had lost Princeton and a career in academe. If he succeeded in commandeering one of the Druids' wrecks his life as a free man was still and surely at an end. How far would he get in one of these heaps, or, come to that, in a Lamborghini? Bob Geddes had ordered road blocks. Would Trelawny give himself up with a shrug, or crack skulls with the club in a frenzy of desperation, or snatch a car from the Druids and accelerate into a loch to kill himself?

Or none of these, as suddenly seemed on the cards?

'What the hell?' Geddes exclaimed, speaking for everybody.

Mike Trelawny was fifty yards from the Druids and their transport, closing on them, when galloping towards him came a canine mountain of muscle, bone, fur, and spewing drool.

'It's a game,' Twitty said. 'Watch.'

'Golf for dogs?' sneered Gillespie.

'It's called Fetch.' Twitty stepped forward, blinking his good eye, adjusting it to the murk and the imminent joust between man and beast. 'It's the golf club, see? Grendel's seen the golf club. If Trelawny throws it, Grendel will fetch it.' He spoke in the measured tone of a teacher imparting information to dimwits. 'Mavis knows.'

Mavis said, 'This one's a fetcher.'

Mavis knew, Twitty knew, but Mike Trelawny did not know. He stood his ground in the path of the charging behemoth, having no choice, and lifted high the eight iron. What he believed was that his escape, perhaps his life, hinged on braining this yellow beast. Nothing of this was fair, it was outside the rules and every possibility and combination of possibilities for error or success that he had weighed. Braining the brute would call for flawless aim and timing.

From Dave and Ramona came shouts. 'Grendel, heel! Whoa, Grendel!'

An ambulance pulled up behind the Druid community, probably not a moment too soon. The police car far away on the fairway executed a churning turn, flashed its rooflight, and injected a banshee wail into the Highlands quiet. The helicopter added to the din, arriving in the gloom above Mike Trelawny and bounding Grendel. Trelawny held the club raised and poised to strike. He swung it far too late. Grendel crashed into him. The golf club whisked away into space. Man and beast went down, the beast on top.

Grendel stayed on top, barking with ardour. Even had Mike Trelawny, underdog, been in the peak condition of his rugby football days he would have been no match for the thrashing, smothering hound. Its fangs clashed, its tongue lashed. Chest, belly, and splayed hind legs pinned him in the gorse. In these moments Mike Trelawny almost lost the will to live, though not quite. He opened his mouth to howl and received a helping of scalding, evil-tasting tongue that reached to his epiglottis.

'Grendel loves him,' Twitty said.

'It's an affectionate beast,' agreed Peckover.

'Grendel, heel!' Dave shouted.

Forlorn hope. The wailing police car performed the rescue. Constable Ross, a dog expert, owner of a poodle named Muffin, decanted from the driver's seat and grabbed the golf club. Shouting 'Ho, Grendel, ho!' he twirled the golf club like a drum-major until he had Grendel's attention. Then he flung it.

'Go fetch!' Constable Ross shouted.

Grendel thundered in pursuit. The ground shuddered. A Constable MacIntyre clicked handcuffs on Mike Trelawny.

Now the sun should have burst forth and a piper launched into 'The Bluebells of Scotland'. The rain came down with new vigour. Geddes and the adjutants ran to their cars, and Mavis would have reached hers had not Inspector Gillespie waylaid her. He smiled for the first time that year. It was the smile of a terrorist on his day off. He asked if he might borrow her *Glasgow Herald*. Mavis presented it and hurried to her Honda. Ignoring the failed front-page scoop and its Mavis Murray byline – Local Laird Missing in Burns Night Celebrity Murder – Gillespie sought the financial pages.

On the road below Brae Balloch, police helped Mike Trelawny with a jacket over his head into a squad car. A television crew tried to film the event and the police tried to shoo the crew away.

Constable Ross discovered that he must either keep flinging the golf club or be loved nigh unto death by Grendel.

TWENTY-FOUR

Here's tae us; wha's like us?
Gey few, and they're a' deid.

Anon.

Superintendent Geddes, Sergeant Menzies, and three cars brought Mike Trelawny to the police station on Argyll Street pending his transfer to Glasgow. The prisoner was uncommunicative, spent. He nursed his Grendel wounds, a mottling of embossed, reddened hickeys and congealed drool. The wounds would heal, the freckles resurface. Meanwhile his face resembled a colour plate of stricken corpuscles in *Aetiology of Tropical Diseases*. Sergeant Menzies, suppressing an urge to climb to the attic and once more howl his grief, informed the prisoner that he had the right to telephone a solicitor. Trelawny said he didn't want a solicitor, he wanted a doctor.

'Did ye hear that?' whispered Constable Farquhar. 'The feller's a hypochondriac.'

After fifteen minutes of unanswered questions Geddes drove to the Ram.

Mavis breezed in and said, 'Well done, Sergeant. Exemplary. What are the precise charges?'

'Who let ye in? Nae smokin' i' the polis station, madam. Outside wi' ye, if ye please.'

Outside, a rosy-cheeked constable denied entry to a half-dozen clamouring reporters. 'Ah hae strictest exclusionary orders,' he proclaimed, then felt a rush of sympathy. 'Likely ye'll be granted a press conference.' Had he overstepped the line? 'Next week.'

At the adjacent Annie Menzies Antiques Emporium the curtains were drawn shut.

*

189

In the murder room Superintendent Geddes telephoned Glasgow CID. Gillespie telephoned his broker. Peckover telephoned first Chief Superintendent Veal at the Yard to say he hoped to be back in London that evening. Then Miriam.

Miriam said, 'Stay on if you're enjoying yourself. Really. We're fine.'

'The bairns?'

'The who?'

'You know who. Them.'

'Sam's loose tooth, the other one? It's out. Mary kicked him. She says it was an accident.'

Twitty telephoned a name in his notebook, Claudia, in London. He left a message saying he would not be able to make Paul's Wine Bar this evening, terribly sorry, he was in Scotland, important duties helping out the Scotties, he'd ring later in the week.

A lone copper kept at bay the scribes and cameras in the corridor. They were not many. Those not laying siege to the police station had zipped off to the dig.

Geddes clapped his hands and strode to the door. 'Let's be going, then.'

A Land-Rover had navigated up the moor to the dig. The rutted track at the foot of the moor was choc-a-bloc with the cars and vans of police, press, television crews, two women archaeologists, and an undetermined number of Druids agog to see if treasure had been buried with the bog man, votive offerings of gold and silver. To those just arrived from the murder room the distant dig looked already congested. Impatient too, no doubt. On orders from Superintendent Geddes the police on bog man duty for the past four hours were allowing no digging until he was present.

'Listen,' Peckover said, listening.

Twitty listened and said, 'What?'

'That thudding. It's Miss Cork stamping 'er foot. She wants to get on with it. She'll 'ave steam coming out of 'er ears. Your job, lad, is to keep 'er away from me.'

'Won't be easy once she has her bog man, Guv. She'll have hugs and kisses for everyone.'

Peckover and Twitty trudged up the moor. Geddes marched ahead. Gillespie lagged, concerned about forecasts of a cut in interest rates. The rain had dwindled to a drizzle. Or had it stopped? Peckover wondered if after a while in the Highlands people became inattentive to differences in rain, aware only of wet and dry.

Twitty pondered on the possibilities of an almighty squabble for the butter, not only between the city museums of Glasgow and Edinburgh, but with the police museums putting in a claim. This was the butter with which the murderer, alleged, of Sir Gilbert Potter, archaeologist, had come close to despatching local laird Sir Dougal Duncan, and might have succeeded but for the heroism of a supremely alert, handsome detective constable on loan from Scotland Yard.

'What're you laughing at, lad?'

'Sorry.'

On the high ground beyond the dig a committee of sheep nibbled.

'You in love with Miss Cork?'

'Guv! How can you even think it?'

'Usually in love with somebody, aren't you?' Peckover took off his hat and wiped damp from its inner rim. 'Meanwhile, prepare to meet your first bog man.'

'You're sure that's who?'

'It's the only happy ending. Everyone wants a bog man.'

'Not the Super.'

'He'll survive. Cuff-Bingley's never bothered Bob Geddes before and 'e's done nicely enough. From today he's slap on track to becoming Chief Super with or without Cuff-Bingley. The bugger is, none of this makes sense unless it is Cuff-Bingley.'

'I know.'

'What d'you know?'

'No, I don't know. But that goblet that's supposed to have been in the laird's family for ever, on the shelf over the fireplace, or that's where we're told it was until this laird switched it to a safe. Annie Menzies knew nothing about it. She'd never seen it or heard of it and she was a regular visitor. So perhaps it didn't exist in her time with Laird Fergus.'

'Ten 'appy years,' Peckover said, trudging. 'Until the commotion and the war, and Fergus changed, married a Lowlander, et cetera. The war was the war, the commotion was Cuff-Bingley. Cuff-Bingley, what happened to 'im, was what changed Fergus.'

'We don't know that.'

'You're right, we don't.'

'We'll not be finding out either, not here and now.'

'Why not?'

'Because they're not going to dig up the body and brush it off and let us all have a look. They cut out the whole block of peat, put it in a box, and take it to a mortuary or somewhere where they work on it with dentist's vacuums, toothpicks, dry ice, Clingfilm—'

'Somebody's been 'aving instruction from Posy Cork.'

They reached the dig. Had they looked back they would have seen the present laird of Dundrummy with bandaged head, self-discharged from St Ann's, starting up the moor with a constable at each side ready to gather him up if he stumbled. If the constables hoped for a lairdly tip in return for their readiness they were in for a disappointment.

An Escort foraged for space among the parked vehicles. A police van from Glasgow Central had arrived in Argyll Street for Mike Trelawny, and Sergeant Menzies, having passed on, as it were, the baton, had postponed further grieving in order to stay at the hub of things, which was now the dig. He would be needed. Was he not Inverballoch's first and true representative of the law?

Everybody wanted to be in on the televising of a historic disinterment.

The constables on bog man duty, rootling through boxes, had found string and stakes of the sort useful for supporting tomato plants. Their makeshift cordon held at bay, ten paces back from the excavation, everyone except the archaeology and forensics teams and senior police officers, or it would if properly respected and patrolled. With the arrival of Superintendent Geddes and those from the murder room, the VIP viewing area within the cordon filled to capacity.

Posy Cork, Leah Howgego, two unsmiling young men in sneakers and winter coats, and a bustling, matronly woman with a commanding voice made short work of removing and folding the canvas. But where to put it?

'Please,' appealed Posy Cork. 'Could everyone get back or out and give us some space?'

Part of the problem was that shovels, cartons, and an outsize wooden coffin, or at any rate, box, brought from the Land-Rover, property of the Department of Anthropology, Glasgow University, occupied much of the dig's perimeter.

Geddes called out, 'A little co-operation, please,' and waved his supernumerary forces back.

A cameraman came over the string and slithered towards the dug rectangle, filming. The policeman who stepped in front of him and stood there had his folded arms filmed in close-up. When the cameraman sidestepped, the policeman sidestepped. The cameraman withdrew, grumbling.

Posy, Leah, and the forensics woman with the loud voice etched with trowels, then defined with pegs and twine, an oblong round the lumpy shape in the pit. After they had finished they climbed from the pit. The anthropologists in sneakers stepped in with shovels.

All this took time. The media were bored, the majority of policemen were bored. Accustomed to being bored, they coped. Much of their day-to-day routine involved standing about, waiting. Superintendent Geddes and Scotland Yard were not bored but they were not excited, conscious that the identity of the thing in the peat would not be revealed here but elsewhere in some manner of chilly operating theatre with refrigerators and X-ray machines. The clot of ragtag Druids enjoyed themselves, anything being an improvement on the fruitless scouring of the wilds with a metal detector and sitting around twiddling their thumbs until the next solstice. They had shut Grendel up somewhere and they behaved well, staying behind the cordon. To have ventured into the VIP sector would have been to risk manacles and a police wagon. They were Druids, which meant, in the eyes of some police, scumbag lowlifes.

The excavating of the body began to look as if it might take for ever because the men with the shovels were no longer digging but in a huddle with the women on the rim of the dig. A disagreement seemed to have arisen.

Peckover watched the laird, his head copiously bandaged, climb over the string and join the archaeologists and forensics team. If anyone was entitled to a front-row seat, Sir Dougal presumably was. This was his land. Many metres of bandage covered his head from eyebrows to nape of neck. He looked like an Afghan tribesman.

Twitty watched Mavis ignore the string and approach Gillespie. He recognized the pebble lenses of the *Dundee Advertiser* attempting to befriend a BBC television crew. When King Dave and Queen Ramona noticed him looking their way, they waved. Twitty thought it better not to return their wave. In spite of Grendel's success they were still Druids, or whatever they were, and the Guv and the super might be watching. The super had joined the debate between the archaeologists, the exhumers from Glasgow University, and the turbaned laird.

Posy, Leah, and the commanding woman stepped into the trench with hand brushes. They kneeled and began their scrupulous brushing.

Twitty had seen this before. He hadn't found it a riveting spectacle, except for Leah's bejeaned bum. After ten minutes with nothing to behold except the bum and, by now, the bog body's exposed okra fingers that he had seen before, and the foot with lace-up shoes, he walked to where the Guv and the Super observed the brushing in silence. The media behind the string were restless, looking at their watches and buttonholing policemen in futile attempts to discover exactly what was going on. The rain had more or less stopped.

'Enlighten me, Guv.'

'I gather it's not 'ighly professional but they're seeing if they can expose just enough to determine if it's three thousand years old or fifty. Five-o. If it's three thousand they'll dig out the whole block as planned.'

'If it's fifty?'

'They've saved themselves a load of time and trouble. It's somebody contemporary and they can go 'ome.'

The archaeologists and the older woman continued their delicate brushing. Posy and Leah brushed at the feet, the older woman brushed where the head would be if there were a head. Leah straightened and knuckled her back.

'Bob, if it's Cuff-Bingley your CID are going to be drinking your 'ealth in pints,' Peckover said.

'Hm,' grunted Geddes.

A milky sun emerged. Posy and Leah had interrupted their brushing to watch the older woman. She was brushing with her brush and scraping and delving with her fingertips. Her kneeling posture was that of a squashed Z, her eyes following her progress from a matter of inches. As she brushed and probed she uttered helpful comments in a carrying voice. 'Yes, indeed.' 'Quite so.' 'What have we here?' Posy chewed her lower lip. Leah inserted two or three of her fingernails between her incisors. Teeth-time in Inverballoch. Out of the peat the older woman drew a pair of spectacles. With small regard for the rigours of archaeological preservation or the rules of legal evidence she wiped them on her sleeve. She carried on brushing.

'Here's the nose,' she said.

She kneeled upright and held out the spectacles to Posy.

'So sorry, my dear. We have no evidence of eyeglasses prior to the thirteenth century, and I strongly suspect hornrims are a twentieth-century invention. We mustn't delude ourselves any further. See, the trousers you've exposed, those are surely turn-ups. And really, such shoes.'

Gribley and Smutch, Twitty was eager to inform her. Piccadilly. Purveyors of fine footwear since 1809.

The older woman stood up. 'We can leave this to the police, don't you think, my dears?'

Peckover told Geddes, 'Congratulations, Bob.'

TWENTY-FIVE

All shall be well and
All manner of thing shall be well
                              T.S. Eliot, *Little Gidding*

The anthropologists in sneakers wasted no further time. They had wasted the best part of a day already. Not that they were sour about it. Excavations were a lottery. They lifted the wooden box and carried it empty to the Land-Rover.

Word spread among the mob at the dig. To be precise, two words, hyphenated. Cuff-Bingley. To most the name was meaningless and a frustration. The media breached the cordon like the hordes of Gideon and bore down on Superintendent Geddes demanding meanings and calling out questions. Gina Patel brandished her arm as if desperate for permission to be excused. Geddes could dream up nothing better than a delaying tactic.

'Press conference at the Ram, four o'clock,' he announced. 'Wait. Five o'clock. Make that six. Thank you for your support.'

Sergeant Menzies loomed. Peckover trusted he was on his way for instructions from Geddes or to offer him advice. The hope was dashed.

'Mr Peckover, sor.'

'Afternoon, Sergeant.'

Sergeant Menzies took off his cap, revealing his frosty poll, white as confectioner's sugar. He held the cap respectfully over his heart and sighed.

'Sor. Am Ah correct in my understandin' that ye were the last tae hae converse wi' my mither, Mrs Menzies, in our kitchen behind the Antiques Emporium? Ye an' the blackie?'

'You may well be. A lovely lady and in fine fettle. We enjoyed 'er company. It's a shock. She talked about you, Sergeant. Most

196

admiring and affectionate she was. A sad loss. She was chatting and reminiscing to the end.'

Someone, meaning probably himself or Twitty, was going to have to tell Jamie Menzies about his half-brotherdom with the laird, not a duty to be relished. On the other hand, both Jamie and the laird might be enchanted by the news.

Alternatively, why couldn't the sergeant continue in ignorance? His mother had kept him in ignorance. The laird could be kept ignorant too.

Peckover said, 'She was baking buttery rowies. She gave us samples. Ambrosial.'

'Sor?'

'They were good.'

'Aye, she baked braw bonnie buttery rowies.' The sergeant's eyes brimmed. 'Ah'm beholden tae ye an' tae the blackie too.'

Twitty chafed but waited. He counted silently to five.

'Guv?'

'What?'

'There, heading off. Shouldn't we have a word with him? Get it over?'

'Who? Where?'

'The turban.'

For somebody who had spent the night being hit with a rock, once or twice anyway, and plugged with butter, the laird was making brisk, unaccompanied progress down the moor.

Sergeant Menzies said, 'Will Ah recover the laird for ye, Mr Peckover, sor?'

'Please, Sergeant. Thank you.'

'Too bad, Miss,' Geddes said. 'It'll be a disappointment.'

'A bog man was a needless distraction.' A disappointment too, bitterly so, but Posy was not about to admit it. 'At least now we can get back to the meat.'

'Meat?'

'A Roman settlement.'

Leah, nodding, said, 'A Roman settlement.'

'Ah, the Romans,' Geddes said. 'The real McCoy, eh?'

'The real McCoyski,' said Leah, and put her fingers to her lips.

By the time Sergeant Menzies and Constable Colquhoun were returning up the moor with a reluctant laird, Mavis and Gina Patel had become fast friends, pretending to each other to be pooling all they knew.

Constables Forsyth and Ross had been assigned to dig up Cuff-Bingley, or whoever it should turn out to be, and to ask Ms Cork's permission to borrow spades.

Druids Dave and Ramona kept warm with a kiss so protracted and public that Gillespie tapped Dave on the shoulder with the *Glasgow Herald*.

'Stop that,' Gillespie said. 'This isn't Hollywood.'

Leah climbed from the trench carrying brushes and cardboard.

'You'll be glad to see us gone,' Twitty said.

'Why?' said Leah.

Twitty could not think of an answer to that.

He said, 'Perhaps, this evening, that's to say, if you've nothing else. Like, of course, Miss Cork, you might want to be together. I mean.' What was the matter with him? 'Perhaps we might, er, eat? Um, dine?'

'Where?'

'Where?'

'There isn't anywhere except the Claymore. In the Ram.'

'What's wrong with the Claymore?'

'It isn't Glasgow.'

She was suggesting they drive to Glasgow?

'Or London,' Leah said.

'You know London?'

'I live there.'

'You do? Where?'

'Golders Green.'

'Hey! The far north. I'm south. I'm not sure I've ever been to Golders Green. Perhaps we could meet there.'

'Instead of tonight?'

'As well as tonight.'

'It wouldn't have to be Golders Green, would it?'

'Himself, the laird in person, sor!'

Sergeant Menzies saluted Peckover.

'Thank you, Sergeant. Stay with us. Sir Dougal? Sorry I can't offer you a chair. All we were saying' – nobody had been saying anything but it was time to chance his arm – 'was that after your father, Sir Fergus, murdered and buried Wilfred Cuff-Bingley—'

198

'What? What? Outrageous!'

'—he, your father, appropriated as his own the Celtic goblet that Cuff-Bingley had dug up—'

'Bloody well was his own! Wasn't that snooping, thieving Cuff-Bingley's! It so happens we're standing on the Duncan ancestral estates—'

The laird's mouth hung open.

'Yes?' Peckover said.

Sergeant Menzies, uncomprehending, wore his solemn face. Twitty kept quiet. This was the Guv's little triumph.

'I'm guessing here,' said Peckover, 'but Cuff-Bingley had just or recently unearthed the goblet, perhaps a few coins, bits of pots, got them in 'is knapsack, when your father showed up, very irate. He didn't kill Cuff-Bingley for the treasure, he killed 'im because he was sick to death of treasure-hunters rooting about on his land. Lost 'is temper. Might 'ave been self-defence.'

'Doubtful,' said the laird.

'Excuse me?'

'Otherwise you're pretty much spot on.' Sir Dougal sounded more surprised than anything. 'My word, d'you know this is quite a relief?'

'Sergeant, p'raps you'd ask Mr Geddes to join us?'

'I will, sor! On the double!'

They gravitated to the edge of the dig. Constables Forsyth and Ross, master diggers, had exposed the peaty limbs, torso, and head of a recognizably human cadaver. They burrowed their noses as best they could in the upturned collars of their greatcoats.

'How long have you known?' Geddes asked the laird.

'At my father's deathbed. Sorry if that sounds melodramatic but it was rather. I was only a boy.' The laird lifted his hand and molested the turban as if to make sure it were properly in place. 'He was still obsessed with treasure-hunters, in fact more than ever. He told me he'd killed and buried Cuff-Bingley, he couldn't remember exactly where, but to keep him buried, and the Duncan name free from taint, I must be sure to send all treasure-hunters packing.'

'His dying wish?'

'You could say that.'

'You allowed Potter and the women in.'

'Couldn't afford not to. What if they came upon more treasure?

Or Roman remains? One way or another there'd be money in it, and the chances of happening on Cuff-Bingley were so slim I hardly gave it a thought. In fact not until yesterday when Posy and Leah said they'd found a bog body.'

'So off you went to see for yourself. What if Mike Trelawny hadn't intercepted you?'

'If it were Cuff-Bingley I'd have destroyed it. Him.'

'How?'

'How do I know? Buried him somewhere else. Sunk him in Loch Lomond.'

'Too bad if you'd destroyed a bog man. You'd have known the difference?'

'Wouldn't anyone?' Sir Dougal stared into the trench. 'Men's wear by Moss Bros, what's left of it.'

Geddes had to agree. Considerable wet, smelly decomposition had set in but the corpse was clad and shod. The constables had dug to a point where all that was required was for the body to be lifted out of the trench. They rested on their shovels, looking optimistically up and about for whoever might be taking over.

Gillespie told them, 'Dinna stand there. Seek i' the pockets.'

Reyn-Bardt, Peckover reflected. Similar but not the same. Reyn-Bardt had confessed to a murder. The evidence, the skull he had confessed to, had turned out to be early Dark Ages. But he had confessed. If the rotting remains in the trench turned out not to be Cuff-Bingley, the laird had still confessed.

Confessed was not quite the word. Confessed on behalf of his father was what he had done. Dougal Duncan had killed nobody. He had come close to being killed. His offence lay in not having spoken up twenty-five years ago, or since. Fairly minor stuff, given an adequate lawyer.

Peckover said, 'Sir Dougal, did your father say – sorry about this – how 'e did it?'

'Cuff-Bingley's spade.'

'He say what became of it?'

'No.'

'Hm. Perhaps we should keep digging.'

'The spade of St Patrick!' said Twitty.

A rusted blade and four inches of shattered shaft in the Annie Menzies Antiques Emporium. What neater for disposing of a murder weapon than to sell it? Not that anyone had bought it.

'What?' Peckover said.

'Sorry, sir. Nothing.'

'Pull yourself together, lad.'

'Mr Geddes, sir?' said nose-holding Forsyth, reaching up with a wallet from a Moss Bros pocket.

Geddes found in the wallet a driving licence and a folded white card, both with the name Cuff-Bingley, Wilfred. He passed them to Peckover.

'Wartime identity card,' Peckover said. 'I wasn't around but everybody 'ad one. See the initials and stroke four? That's' e's fourth in the family after 'is parents and an older brother or sister.'

'Henry, it's Cuff-Bingley. Spare me the family.'

Having got from the dig all they were going to get, the media had begun drifting off down the moor. The Druids hung on in case. They didn't know what in case of but they had nowhere more exciting to go. Peckover put a hand on Sergeant Menzies's shoulder and manoeuvred him towards the laird.

He said, 'I've news to delight you both.'

Why would they not be delighted, marooned in these Scottish Highlands year round, sheep and whisky and nothing much else, but now with a blood bond to bring them together? They would discover relatives in common. They would chuckle over family foibles. They could pay a reasonable fee to the College of Heralds or whoever helped with this sort of thing and trace their family tree. One side of the family, the Duncan side, would be cut-throats, and the Menzies side perhaps simple, inbred, farming stock. The shared knowledge of half-brotherdom would warm the bleak Highlands nights for them both. And we'll tak a cup o' kindness yet, for auld lang syne.

Peckover told them.

They smiled uncertainly, though only for a moment.

'You're no a Duncan ever!' the laird of Dundrummy cried at Sergeant Menzies. 'You're after my land and a title, you leeching, white-wigged slouter!'

'Protestant criminal!' shouted the sergeant.

'Gentlemen, please!' Geddes said.

Sergeant Menzies reached out and pushed the laird. 'Ye're nae brither o' mine! Nae a half-brither, a quarter-brither – what's next? – nae an eighth-brither, nae ony brither, ye beardy croot!'

'Croot? Croot, is it?' The laird pushed the sergeant with both hands. 'Out of my sight, you superannuated apology for a policeman!'

'Aaagh! Clishmaclavers!'

From the sergeant's mouth the word sounded like a war cry. He exploited his advantage by punching the laird on the arm.

'Ho!' cried the laird, and he punched the sergeant's shoulder. 'Assault on a bandaged man!'

'Ye'll want bandages after Ah'm done wi' ye, ye blellum!'

'Blellum yourself! I'll blellum you!'

The laird punched the sergeant on the chest. The sergeant grabbed the laird by the arm and swung him in an arc. To keep from falling the laird held on to the sergeant's sleeve. They toppled into the trench and on to the Moss Bros legs of Cuff-Bingley.

A cameraman who had not yet joined the drift down the moor scurried to the trench with camera poised. Geddes foresaw an embarrassing situation.

'Sergeant! Laird! Please, gentlemen! Forsyth, do something, man!'

The laird and Sergeant Menzies grappled in the peaty pit. Constable Forsyth strove to separate them but too tentatively to be effective. How could he risk the stranglehold he visited on ruffians at the Celtic–Rangers match when one of the contestants here was a sergeant, the other a laird? Geddes jumped into the trench, joined the tussle, and was by accident jabbed in the neck by the elbow of Sergeant Menzies. The cameraman filmed.

Peckover and Twitty backed away.

'We've a right lot of smoutie blasties 'ere,' Peckover said. 'Dunno about you, lad, but I'm off 'ome.'

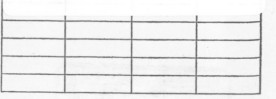